To the memory of my late parents
Eugene ('Bill') and Norah Granger

Chapter One

When I was very small, not more than three years old at a guess, some grown-up figure took me to the children's playground in a nearby park. I wish I knew who it was. Even now, nearly twenty years later, I'd go and find her and give her a piece of my mind. I know it was female, so wasn't my dad, but it wasn't my grandma. It ought to have been my mother because this was before she walked out on us all when I was seven years old. But to my knowledge my mother never took me to the park or anywhere else. In my one clear mental image of her before that time she is sitting in front of the mirror of her dressing table, carefully applying lipstick. She is wearing a dress in shiny green material. She smells nice. I think she is beautiful.

On that day in the park, however, I think I must have been with some older child in whose charge I'd unwisely been put. There were other people around but they were, I suppose, totally occupied with their own small children and unaware of me. My memory serves up a background of shouts and laughter, dusty trees and trampled green grass with many bare worn patches defiled by dog dirt. Against this urban idea of an open space my temporary guardian hauled me up some steep, slippery metal rungs and we found ourselves at the top of a long slide. Not the little slide for tots but the big slide for older children. It gleamed in the sunshine, polished and silvery, a torture machine of the first order.

Arms wrestled me into a seated position at the top and a voice commanded, 'Go on, down you go.'

I was petrified. I clung to the raised metal edges. I was sure I was so high up I must be near the treetops and the birds but I was too scared to raise my eyes from the ground far, far below. It looked very hard, unwelcoming and unstable at the same time. It lurched about in my vision, rising up and sinking, waltzing from side to side. The rims of the slide didn't look high enough to prevent me toppling out sideways. As well as dizzy I felt horribly, painfully sick. I've disliked heights ever since.

'No!' I screeched.

'Oh, stop making a fuss!' commanded my kindly carer and gave me a hearty shove.

My clinging hands were ripped from their desperate grip. I hurtled down, wind whistling past my ears, at a speed I'd never experienced before. At least, my outer shell did. My inner organs, heart and stomach, seemed to have remained back there at the top. I was powerless to do anything about it. I wasn't old enough to know what death was but I was sure I was rocketing towards a final end of some sort. I'd never come out of this alive. I'd never go back home and see my family again. It lasted seconds and seemed to take hours. Then I reached the bottom and was caught in someone's arms.

I was lifted from the slide and stood up on my wobbling legs. Belatedly my heart and stomach caught up with me and I was sick, really sick, as only a small child can be.

My carer was furious. 'What did you do that for, Francesca?'

Above my head a battle soon raged. 'Well, I'm not going to clean her up.'

'You've got to. We can't take her home like that.'

The park keeper arrived, stout, angry and red-faced, and joined in, probably furious at the possibility of the park being sued. I howled.

I was taken home, still howling, and there was another argument. The air filled with yelling voices while I stood in the midst of it all, snivelling in my vomit-stained clothes. Then Grandma gathered me up, took me away to be bathed and made everything right again. It would be nice, in the adult world, to have someone there who'd walk in when everything was going wrong and make it come right. Pity it never happens except in detective stories, I suppose, when the detective does the sorting out. My experiences of detection have not been like that at all. There are always loose ends or ends which are tied up in unexpected or not altogether satisfactory fashion. Life takes a hand and plays odd tricks. I sometimes think the most unwelcome gift a genie could grant anyone would be that of being able to see into the future. Looking back is difficult enough.

My childhood is full of memories like the slide one. I must have had some fun times but they didn't imprint themselves in the same way. It makes me wonder whether some imp of ill fortune has always hopped along behind me, waiting his chance. Perhaps bad memories just squeeze out the good ones, like the evil that lives on after someone's death and the good that's interred with their bones. I know my Shakespeare. I mean to be a proper actor one day. I did most of a drama course in my teens until circumstances forced me to quit. I've only done amateur stuff since. But I'll make it to the real stage one day, you'll see.

In the meantime I take any job offered that's legal and lets me keep my independence. I even do a little confidential work for people. I like to call it that. Calling yourself a private detective is dodgy. Clients expect an office. The tax people expect proper records. Most of the work is stuff I wouldn't want to touch. A friend of mine, Susie Duke, runs a detective agency and I know most of what she does is pretty seedy. I'm unofficial and take the jobs I want to do. Or that had been the idea until that Monday morning in August.

It was holiday time. The tourists had moved into London and those office workers who could, had taken themselves off to foreign sunspots. This year, as it happened, they needn't have bothered. We had a splendid sun-drenched summer at home. Even in Camden, where I was living, walking along the heat-baked pavements one could imagine oneself in a distant exotic city where life at midday retreated behind shutters and all unnecessary activity was suspended. Along the length of Camden High Street the racks of fantastically hued clothing outside the shops and packed on rails in its crowded markets no longer appeared garish and out of place. They looked quite natural with the sequins sparkling in the sunlight and the bright colours giving the impression parakeets had escaped from nearby Regent's Park zoo and nestled among the coat-hangers. The shopkeepers had dragged wooden chairs into the shade and watched passers-by with lazy indifference. Even the pushers selling marijuana down on the bridge over the canal couldn't be bothered to tout for trade. They leaned against the brickwork watching the sluggish water down below, the occasional slow progress of a pleasure craft, walkers on the towpath and the pale-faced group of youngsters sitting in a circle at the foot of the steps, like so many nomads round a camp fire, to snort coke.

Bonnie, my dog, didn't like the heat at all, so that morning I set out to take her for a walk right after breakfast, before the sun got up. My intention was to take her as far as the newsagent's where my friend Ganesh works for his Uncle Hari and I work on a part-time basis, when needed. There I hoped to cadge a cup of coffee and a look at the tabloids for free before strolling home. Bonnie was happy, pattering along, stopping to sniff occasionally. I felt pretty happy myself. But I'd only just turned out of the road where I lived when a large sleek car purred to a halt beside me. The driver got out and hailed me across its roof.

'Oi, Fran!'

I'd taken little notice of the car but a greeting like that can't be ignored. This wasn't just someone who knew my name. It was someone who felt free to be familiar. I squinted at him. The sun was shining into my face but I could make out his burly form easily enough. He raised an arm and wiped perspiration from his brow.

'I was on my way to your place,' he said.

'Hello, Harry,' I said unenthusiastically. I made to walk on, even though I knew it was a vain attempt to escape destiny. If Harry was here looking for me it was because his boss, Mickey Allerton, had sent him. The happiness in me evaporated. Here we go again, a voice said in my brain. What is it with you, Francesca Varady? It was as if a booming voice, like the old lottery commercial, informed me *it could be me*. It nearly always was me, not winning lotteries but drawing the short straw. Hey! I said crossly to the invisible imp, just go and play in someone else's backyard for a bit, will you?

'Don't be in a hurry,' Harry was saying in a friendly voice. He was a friendly man for a bouncer. He was a professional, he told me once. He prided himself on that. 'Didn't you hear me? I come looking for you. He wants to see you.'

A kind of discretion prevented him naming his employer

aloud, as if listening ears might be all around and some inkling of Mickey's private business leak out. Mickey Allerton is a very private man. I don't know if much of what he does is illegal. Probably it's mostly legal on the very edge of the meaning of the word. He's the sort of person who doesn't take unnecessary risks. In Mickey's world all the risks are borne by others. This is why a summons from him would make anyone wary. The horrible thought struck me that Allerton himself might be in the car. I stooped and peered inside. It was empty. I probably looked my relief.

'Nah,' said Harry, watching me with amused tolerance. 'He's at the club. Go on, get in.'

I wondered if it was any use pleading a pressing engagement and admitted to myself that it wasn't. I opened the rear door of the car and slid on to the seat. Bonnie hopped in with me, puzzled at this curtailing of our walk but loyally assuming we were going somewhere interesting. She scrabbled up beside me and settled down; ears pricked and paws neatly together like a dog who spent her life travelling in fancy motors.

Harry retook his place behind the wheel and slammed the door. He turned to stare at me over the back of the seat. 'Oi,' he said again. 'Don't let that dog get up on the cushions. It's all real leather. She'll scratch it.'

I pushed Bonnie down into the well by my feet and asked boldly, 'What does Mickey want?' I didn't expect to be told but there was no harm in asking.

' 'Ow do I know?' he returned.

We rolled away from the kerb. I sat studying the back of Harry's brick-red neck where it bulged uncomfortably over his collar. Pearls of sweat trickled down it. His close-cropped greying dark hair studded the roll of flesh with damp battered bristles. It looked like a past-its-best nailbrush.

I supposed we were heading towards the Silver Circle, one of Mickey's adult entertainment clubs. He had an office there. I'd originally met Allerton in the course of one of my previous investigations. I'd managed by pure chance to do something which had pleased him but that didn't mean I was anxious to see him again. He, on the other hand, was apparently keen to see me. I ought to be feeling surprise instead of just dread. The surprise was missing because something had always told me that I would see him again, that it was a question of 'when' not 'if' Allerton would send for me. Once you're drawn into the orbit of someone like Mickey, your name goes down in his little book.

But what could he want from me, of all people? I sat bolt upright, not because I was worried about the 'real leather' seat but because my stomach muscles were clenched so tightly I couldn't lean back and relax. I might as well have been an aristocrat on the way to the guillotine, although as a tumbrel the car was comfortable enough. One or two pedestrians looked curiously at us as Harry drove smoothly around one-way systems: big Merc, chauffeur, me seated rigidly to attention in the back like a royal personage. I resisted the temptation to raise my hand in a listless wave as we glided past.

At my feet Bonnie whined. She had picked up my sense of unease and now didn't like this any more than I did. She pushed her little black nose into my knee and I put down a hand to stroke her head reassuringly. Her ears drooped and her brown eyes were anxious. She's a small animal of terrier type, mostly white with some black patches, curiously placed. If you look at her from one side, she's white with a black patch over her eye and a larger one on her flank. If you look at her from the other side she has no patches at all except a tiny one on her back leg. The result is that, depending on which side you see her from, she is like two different dogs. It's the sort of detail which might usefully confuse a witness if the occasion arose. It hasn't yet. Give it time.

We had reached a narrow street beside the block which housed the club. Harry got out and, ever the gent, came round to the pavement side and opened the rear passenger door for me. I scrambled out, impeded by Bonnie who was so keen to get out of the car she squeezed between my feet and nearly brought me down flat on my face.

'Steady does it,' said Harry, putting out a meaty hand and gripping my shoulder.

We set off towards the corner. I walked in front and Harry followed. That was so I couldn't double back and run away. When Harry wasn't driving Mickey's car he was guarding the club door. It wasn't like Mickey to leave the entrance unattended and it wasn't today. As Harry and I reached it, another male figure emerged from the gloom within and briefly intercepted us before he saw who was there.

I didn't know the new man but he was of a sort once seen, never forgotten. He was tall with an exaggerated muscular build. I guessed it resulted from excessive weight-training. I can't stand that kind of physique myself. Mostly those guys are all bulging biceps and triceps, with necks the same width as their heads. They have a funny way of standing with their arms hanging by their sides and their feet turned out. This one was blond-haired, thin-lipped and had the round bright blue eyes you see on dolls. As is generally the case with bodybuilders, he clearly thought himself the bee's knees.

' 'Ello, Ivo,' said Harry and something in his voice suggested to me that he shared my opinion of muscleman. 'Boss there?'

'You are late,' said Ivo. He had a distinct accent I couldn't quite place. 'Mr Allerton is waiting.' He emphasised the last word and accompanied it with a disdainful glance at me.

I met the glance with a steady look. I knew he meant Mr Allerton wasn't to be kept waiting at any time and certainly not by nonentities like me. He didn't like me staring back at him showing neither awe (which he expected) nor admiration (which he'd have preferred). He blinked and into the china-blue eyes came a very nasty look indeed. Harry gave me a little push in the small of the back. I sensed a message. Harry didn't want me making an enemy of Ivo. He knew Ivo better than I did and the warning push was to be taken seriously.

Bonnie made a decision at this moment. She wasn't going into the club. She trusted my judgement up to a point but that point had been passed. She didn't like the look of the place and that was that. She flattened herself on the pavement and I couldn't drag her forward. It was then Ivo made a mistake.

'Mr Allerton is a busy man,' he said. 'Get rid of that animal.' And he stooped to grab her collar.

The next moment he jumped back, swearing in an unknown language, nursing the bitten fingers of his right hand. The blue eyes blazed with rage.

'Pick her up!' snapped Harry to me. At the same time he moved to place his own considerable bulk between me and the doorman.

I scooped up Bonnie, tucked her under my arm wriggling protestingly, and hurried past Ivo inside. He said something to me in his own language as I entered. I didn't know what it meant exactly but I could guess the general drift.

'It wasn't her fault; he was stupid to do that!' I hissed to Harry.

'Yeah,' said Harry quietly. 'But old Ivo there is a head case. You stay clear of 'im.'

As it was still early, the club wasn't open for business but getting ready for action later. The foyer smelled of cigarettes, alcohol and sweat mixed with that of commercial disinfectant and lavender air freshener wafting from the toilets. It was decorated with large glossy pictures of the entertainment on offer, every kind of female body beautiful available thanks to plastic surgery and bottled hair colour. In stark contrast, an elderly woman pushed a vacuum cleaner back and forth across the carpet. She had a wrinkled darkly tanned skin and in her broad flat expressionless face all hope had long since died. She didn't look up as we passed by her, but worked on bringing a note of mundane reality to that world of lip-gloss and hairspray.

The curtains over the arched entrance to the main part of the club had been looped back. Through them I could see the stage and, standing on it, a black-haired girl in a shocking pink leotard with her hands on her hips. She was glaring down at a small bald man who was yelling up at her.

'Try and make it look sexy, can't you? You look like you're in a perishing aerobics class!'

Before I could hear the girl's reply we'd turned into a side corridor. I lost sight of the stage but I heard a piano strike up, followed by the clumping of feet on the wooden boards and wails of despair from the bald *répétiteur*.

Mickey Allerton was waiting for me in his office at the end of the corridor. He was a well-built, well-groomed man in his fifties with the softest-looking skin I'd even seen on an adult, male or female, like a baby's. His back was to me and he was watching one of the three CCTV screens behind his desk. It was the one showing the stage on which the girl was dancing. She had energy if not grace.

'She'll have to go,' said Allerton as we came in.

'Fine,' I said in relief, turning back to the door.

I cannoned into Harry who gently but firmly turned me back again to face the desk.

Allerton swivelled in his chair to face me. His eyes were silvery grey, like fish scales. 'Not you,' he said. 'Her.' He jerked a thumb at the screen behind him. 'No talent, that one.' He nodded at a chair. 'Sit down, Fran. Why are you holding that dog?'

'She bit your doorman,' I said. 'Look, I haven't got that kind of talent, either.'

I put Bonnie on the ground but imprisoned her between my legs. I wasn't risking her snapping at Mickey if he came out from behind that desk. She was still in combative mode with the ruff of hair at the scruff of her neck standing up stiffly.

Allerton ignored the information about Bonnie biting the doorman. That was Ivo's lookout. 'Is it likely,' he asked in a weary voice, 'that I had Harry bring you here because I wanted to hire you as an artiste?'

'No,' I admitted. I'm on the short side and have the kind of figure my grandma described as 'gamine'. Other people have been less tactful. The girl out there on the

13

stage might not be 'talented' but at least she looked right.

'Then don't talk stupid. Harry, go and get us some coffee.'

I was sorry to see Harry go. He was Allerton's heavy but I still felt safer with him there.

'Well, Fran,' said Allerton, leaning back in his chair and placing his well-manicured hands palms down on the desktop. He wore a large ring with some kind of gold coin set in it. 'Long time, no see.'

It wasn't that long a time but, as far as I was concerned, it couldn't be long enough. I gave him a sickly smile.

He didn't return it. Allerton didn't waste smiles. But he extended opening courtesies with a vague gesture of his beringed right hand. 'How are things? Got a job?'

'Not at the moment,' I confessed. 'I was working as a waitress but the place was closed down.'

He nodded. 'I heard about that. They were working some kind of wine scam, weren't they?' He tapped his fingers on the desk. 'I'm very careful where I buy wine for my establishments. I've got a reputation.'

Yes, he had. I bet no one would dare to try and sell him plonk bottled up under an expensive label.

'I'm glad you're free at the moment,' he went on. 'I've got a little job for you. You're still in the private detection business, aren't you? Part-time, as I understand.' Now he grinned briefly. 'I heard about the play, too.'

There seemed to be nothing about my recent activities Mickey Allerton didn't know. 'I'm sort of still in the private investigation business,' I said. 'But I haven't got the facilities to help you, Mr Allerton. I'm on my own.'

'Facilities?' He mimicked my voice and looked amused. 'You don't half come out with some winners, Fran. I don't need any facilities, whatever they are. I just need you to do a little job for me.'

'Susie Duke is still running her detective agency,' I said desperately. 'Perhaps she'd be better—'

'You don't know what I want, do you? So shut up and listen,' he invited me. 'Susie Duke isn't suitable for this one. You are. Just the ticket, in fact.'

Harry brought in the coffee at that point. Allerton opened a drawer in his desk and took out a small dispenser of sugar substitute tablets. He tapped two into his cup.

'Got to watch my weight,' he said. 'Doctor's orders.'

'Give up the sugar altogether,' I suggested.

He shook his head. 'I can't drink coffee without a sweetener. Tea, just possibly. But coffee? No way.' He contemplated the steam spiralling from his cup.

Harry handed me my cup and retreated to the back of the room. Bonnie, at my feet, had relaxed her guard and settled down. I waited for Mickey to tell me in what way I was just the ticket. He seemed to be taking pleasure in making me wait or perhaps I was just so wound up it seemed as though he was. He picked up a spoon, stirred his coffee, put the spoon gently back in the saucer. At long last he looked up. He opened his mouth. This was it. He was going to announce some awful shattering news. I held my breath.

'I tried that Atkins Diet,' he said.

'Oh, yes?' This was hardly what I'd expected and it threw me completely. Probably this was Mickey's intention. I tried to sound normal but my voice was like something issuing from a computer. 'How did you get on?' I croaked tinnily.

He shook his head in sorrow. 'I like roast potatoes with my Sunday lunch and chips with my steak. I found it difficult to give them up. Besides, my doctor said it wasn't right for me.'

An Achilles heel! Was Mickey Allerton, whom I'd been inclined to view as omnipotent, in thrall to his medical adviser? I wondered if he might be a hypochondriac. The most unlikely people are. Still, any sign of weakness in him was to be stored up in memory. You never knew, it might be useful one day.

'It's not so much a job I've got for you,' he said. 'It's more an errand. I want you to take a message to someone for me.'

I didn't ask him what was wrong with the phone, e-mail or snail mail. But I was reminded of that poor Greek bloke who ran miles with the news of some victory and once he'd delivered it, dropped dead – and he'd brought good news. I had a funny feeling Allerton's message would bring the recipient bad news. The ancient custom, as I'd heard it, was to kill the bearer of such tidings. Either way, being a messenger isn't a job with good long-term prospects.

Allerton had resorted to the desk drawer again and now drew out a glossy photograph. He passed it to me across the desk. I took it gingerly.

It was of one of his artistes, a promotional picture like all the others tacked up on a display board in the foyer. This one was a pretty girl of about my age. She wore an outfit which tipped the nod towards the cowgirl style, more rhinestones than it seemed possible to attach to so little material, dinky boots with high heels and completed by a little white Stetson atop her mass of blond curly hair. Her face was plastered with too much make-up, a lot of pearlised mauve eyeshadow and glitter stuff on her eyelashes. She was giving the camera a come-hither look while clinging to an upright pole.

'Lisa Stallard. Dancer,' Mickey passed out his information in laconic, bite-sized snippets. 'Good one.' He leaned back. 'She walked out,' he said.

There was a hint of surprise in his voice. Artistes didn't walk out on him. This was probably a first. He still couldn't quite accept it.

'I want her back. Customers liked her.'

I had every sympathy with the girl who'd walked out of this seedy dump. She had courage. If Mickey wanted her back, I decided, he could go and find her himself. I wasn't going to do it for him.

'Look,' I said. 'If she doesn't want to work here, well, I expect she's got a reason.'

The fish-silver eyes fixed me unpleasantly. Behind me Harry gave a faint warning cough.

'It could be anything,' I ploughed on in an effort to retrieve my social gaffe. 'I mean, a sudden departure doesn't suggest she didn't like it here. Perhaps she's got a family emergency at home.'

Allerton leaned forward slightly. 'She went without a word. I paid her good money. She's not gone working for anyone else. I asked around the other clubs. But you're right about her going home. That's what she's probably done. One of the other girls told me.'

He jerked a thumb at the CCTV camera behind him. On it the girl in the pink leotard was sitting on the edge of the stage, drinking a bottle of water.

'That one,' said Allerton. 'The stupid talentless bitch,' he added ungratefully.

The pink leotard girl was a snitch and the runaway had been foolish to confide in her. If you're going to do something Mickey Allerton won't like, at least don't tell anyone else working for him what you intend.

He could see what I was thinking and shook his head. 'I don't want you to get the wrong idea, Fran. I could send Harry here after her. But she'd misunderstand. I don't want to put the frighteners on her. That's why I want you to go. I want you to ask her why she left. So that we can sort things out and she can come back. She's not in any trouble as far as I'm concerned. I'm on the level with this. All I want is for her to come back. I told you, I was paying her good money, but I'll increase it. You're about her age. You'd know how to talk to her. She knows you don't normally work for me. You don't look frightening.'

'I don't like it!' I burst out. 'It's up to her what she does. It's supposed to be a free country!'

'That girl,' said Allerton, 'could go far. I had plans for her.'

I was afraid of that.

Again, prompted by the misgivings in my expression, he leaned forward. 'No, not those kind of plans! I'm opening a new club on the Costa del Sol. I was intending to send her out there and put her in charge of the acts. Make her a sort of artistic director, if you like. She wouldn't have to get out there on the stage if she didn't want to. Of course, it'd suit me if she did. I told you, she's talented. But really I want her to scout for other girls. Make sure that the club puts on a really classy show. I'm going upmarket. She's the right sort of girl for that, nice spoken, like you. Probably went to a proper school for young ladies, like you.'

I'd never told Mickey about my schooldays but clearly someone had. I ran quickly through a list of my close acquaintances in my head, wondering which one had passed out private information on me. But it could be anyone, really. In the past, when I'd shared squats with people, we'd often sat round of an evening chatting about this and that. Perhaps it hadn't been so hard for Mickey to run a background check on me, after all. In future I'd keep my mouth shut about my past. Like the runaway pole dancer, I was finding that a little innocent detail could turn out a weapon in the wrong hands.

My dad and my grandma Varady scraped together the money to send me to a private school. I think they were compensating for the fact that my mother had left us. I was a messed-up kid and I messed up being at the school. Eventually I was expelled. When I remember the struggle Dad and Grandma had to keep me there I'm not proud of this. Grandma did home sewing, making wedding dresses and so on. She sat up late into the night at her old treadle machine; her swollen feet pushing the plate monotonously back and forth with a faint squeak at every move, working away for me to have a better future. I think I must have been a particularly odious brat. They loved me and I took their love and tossed it aside like it was nothing. If life has sometimes treated me harshly since then, I look on it as a sort of penance. (That's what comes of being educated at primary school level by nuns.) But one thing I did learn from them, there's right and there's wrong. If you believe that, sooner or later you have to make a stand.

I swallowed. 'Mr Allerton, believe me, I'd like to oblige you. But I honestly don't think I could persuade this girl to come back. Why should she listen to me? Suppose I found her and she refused? What would you say when I got back? You'd blame me.'

Allerton was shaking his head. 'No, no, Fran. You've got it wrong. All I want you to do is go and find Lisa and explain to her about the job I've got lined up for her in Spain, right? Tell her I'm not angry. I'm disappointed that she didn't confide in me and tell me what was wrong. I really don't know why she took off like that and I'd like to. It's good business to have the staff happy. If she had a problem, we could probably have fixed it. I just want her to come back to London, sit down here and talk it through with me – just like you and me are doing now. Friendly.'

'Do you know where her home is?' I asked, hoping it might be some out-of-the-way place I couldn't possibly be expected to find.

'Sure. Oxford. I've got the address.' His tone was brisk. He thought he'd talked me round.

Not yet, he hadn't. 'I can't just go to Oxford for an unknown length of time,' I said. 'What about my dog?'

Now Allerton smiled. It was a wide slow smile which showed such excellent teeth he must have had them fixed. I was reminded of a shark. I realised too late that I'd handed some sort of advantage to him. I shouldn't have mentioned Bonnie.

'No problem,' he said easily. 'Harry will look after her. Harry's good with dogs, aren't you, Harry?' He looked past me to his sidekick, invisible behind my back.

'Yeah,' said Harry. 'We always have a dog at home.'

'What, a pit bull terrier?' I snapped. My grip on Bonnie tightened and she squeaked protestingly.

'No,' said Harry regretfully. 'My missus don't like them. We got a couple of them hairy little buggers, Yorkies.'

The thought of Harry walking a pair of animated hairbrushes silenced me for a moment. But while I floundered, seeking some argument against Mickey's proposal, Allerton moved on.

'See?' he said smoothly. 'All laid on. Of course, if you're not satisfied that Harry could look after the little tyke, I could ask Ivo. She bit him, you said?' The shark's teeth flashed at me again.

I felt sick. The message was clear. I went to Oxford and carried Allerton's message to Lisa, or Bonnie was handed over to Ivo, the muscular psychopath with the grudge. I didn't like to think what he'd do to her.

'All right,' I said. 'But promise me, Ivo doesn't get near her. Promise! I want your word.'

Allerton's word probably wasn't worth much but I could ask.

'Don't you worry,' he soothed me. 'We understand one another. Now then, here's her address.' He fished a piece of paper from that desk drawer and then a fat envelope. 'And here's some cash for expenses. We'll settle your fee when you get back. I'm a generous man. You'll be all right.'

'And if I don't bring her back with me? How will you know I've even seen her?'

He frowned. 'Get her to give me a call. I'd call her but she'd hang up on me. She's gotta call me.'

I understood his reasoning. Lisa had had the courage to walk out and probably had the courage to put the phone down at the sound of his voice. Reckless courage. Allerton couldn't afford to let people show him that kind of disrespect. Any sign of weakness in a man in his position gets known. He'd be obliged to do something about it. Just now he seemed anxious to avoid the rough stuff and had called me in. But all that could change. It was up to me.

'No e-mails or text messages! I want to hear her voice. Understood?' The silvery eyes glittered at me.

'I wouldn't try that kind of trick!' I said, irritated.

'No, love, of course you wouldn't. Because I'd find out, wouldn't I? I'll give you my mobile number so she can find me, any time. So can you. Keep me up to date. Give me a progress report. Of course, I'd prefer it if she comes back with you. But I'll settle for a personal call from her.' The fish-silver eyes were cold. 'But you don't get paid any more than is in this envelope.' He tapped it. 'Not unless she gets in contact, right? I pay for results. I don't pay for failure. If you were to persuade her to come back to London with you, well, then you'd be in line for a nice little bonus. Remember that.'

'All I want,' I said, 'is my dog.'

'Better be quick and get it done, then, hadn't you? They pine, dogs, as I've heard. Right, Harry?'

'Yes, boss,' said Harry expressionlessly.

Allerton held out another slip of paper. 'It's all arranged. This is the address of a bed-and-breakfast place where you can stay. The woman who runs it used to work for me. She's expecting you.'

So even when I got to Oxford I wouldn't be out of Mickey's orbit. There would be someone there, checking on me, making sure I was doing what I'd been sent there for.

I've read of people gnashing their teeth in rage and it's what I felt I wanted to do. It wouldn't have helped and I didn't. At least I could prevent Mickey seeing just how upset I was. Not that he didn't know it, but a refusal to let him see it was the only way I had just at that moment of depriving him of complete satisfaction.

Harry moved forward and held out his hand. I bent to stroke Bonnie's head and then I handed the lead to him, meeting his gaze.

'I like dawgs,' he said again. I knew he was trying to reassure me.

'Now scram!' ordered Allerton. 'I'm a busy man.'

Harry escorted me out. Ivo was still in the foyer. He was in deep discussion with the girl who'd been up there on the stage. She wasn't in her leotard now, but skintight pants and sleeveless shell-pink satin top. Pink was obviously her colour.

I write 'discussion' but she was doing the talking, haranguing him in that language I didn't recognise. However, the fluency the two shared suggested the girl and Ivo were compatriots. In a foreign country, that can count for quite a bit. Even if you've nothing else in common, exiles stand together.

When I was young, various elderly Hungarian visitors

would appear at the house and be given coffee and chocolate cake by Grandma. They weren't friends in any deep sense. They were part of the community, the Hungarian Diaspora which had followed the revolution of 1956. They'd known my grandfather, by then deceased. They saw it as a social obligation to call on his widow. I've flunked any opportunity I've ever had to learn another language. At home we spoke English. Occasionally I'd hear Grandma and Dad out in the kitchen exchanging a few words of Hungarian. I suspect now they were discussing something they didn't want me to know about, like where my mother had gone and why. I could have asked either of them to teach me but I never did. At school they tried to teach me French; but all I remember is someone called Pierre going somewhere on his bicycle. I was busy at the back of the room fooling around, as usual.

Under the onslaught of words from the girl Ivo stood looking almost sheepish. Big tough guy that he was, he put me in mind of a small boy caught being naughty. I wondered briefly what was going on.

The girl was aware of my curious stare; she was a sharp one, I reckoned. She turned a look on me which was definitely hostile. I'm used to dealing with unfriendly scowls and returned hers with interest. At this, real anger flashed in her eyes. I had intended to avoid eye contact with Ivo, mindful of Harry's warning. But he gave me a quick sullen glance which made the hair on the nape of my neck tingle. They both fell silent and unsuccessfully attempted to look uninterested. I knew immediately that the two of them had been talking about me. But what was I to them?

I hadn't time to puzzle it out. Bonnie, by Harry's feet, had recognised Ivo and growled softly. Harry gave a warning tug on her collar.

'You'll manage it all right,' he said to me. It was less an expression of comfort than an instruction. 'Be a doddle,' he added.

The moment of parting had come. I patted Bonnie's warm little body which was quivering with anxiety and walked out of the club, leaving her behind. She didn't understand and yelped protestingly. I turned to call back to her reassuringly and saw her straining at the leash, almost choking in an effort to follow me. Tears of rage and frustration started to my eyes as I hurried round the corner. I've never cried over bad luck. But this filled me with such anger I felt I would burst and the tears popped out propelled by the power of fury. I was angry with Mickey, who'd done this to me. I was angry because of the look in Bonnie's eyes. It wasn't my fault this was happening but she couldn't know that. As far as she was concerned, I'd walked away from her. Bonnie would never have forsaken me but I'd left her, to make things worse in the hands of people I didn't trust not to harm her. If I got her back again, she'd forgive me, but I'd find it less easy to forgive myself. As for Allerton, I'd never, ever forgive him. Not that my grudge mattered a jot to him. He probably had more serious enemies than me.

I cursed the fact I'd been walking Bonnie when Harry found me. But although that had made things easier for Allerton, it hadn't materially affected the outcome. If I'd been alone, Harry would still have taken me to Mickey's office. While I was there, someone would have gone to my flat (visitors of that kind always know how to let themselves in), collected Bonnie and brought her to the Silver Circle. And now, to get her back, I had to carry out Mickey's wretched errand. I dashed away the tears and scowled murderously at innocent passers-by who naturally assumed I was another case of Care in the Community and gave me a wide berth. I felt physically sick. I felt just as I'd done that day long ago when I'd been forced to the top of the slide and shoved on my way by hands more powerful than mine. I was hurtling down, unable to control events, towards an unknown and unpleasant destination and there was no Grandma Varady any more to make it better.

Chapter Two

When I've got a problem I generally make straight for my friend Ganesh to ask his advice. I don't necessarily follow it, which annoys him. I should, because he thinks clearly and is generally right. (I don't tell him this, naturally.) But I like his opinion because it helps me form my own opposite one. I'd been on my way to the newsagent's where he works, anyway, before I'd been hijacked and taken off to the Silver Circle, so the newsagent's was where I made a beeline for now.

The shop usually presents an innocuous standard appearance for such undertakings. There is a board in the window carrying personal ads. For fifty pence you can hope to sell your old fridge, gain customers for your home hairdressing service (but not for other home services; Hari is a very moral man) or swap something you don't want for something someone else doesn't want. That way you probably end up with something no one wants. A would-be-cute placard showing a row of depressed dogs bears the legend 'Please leave us outside!' I hadn't thought anything could make me feel worse, but that did. Bonnie is the one and only dog to whom the restriction does not apply. Hari makes an exception for Bonnie because he's convinced she's a good watchdog. There is a stand outside the door with today's headlines scrawled on it and a dented waste-paper basket which no one uses, preferring to scatter sweet and ice lolly wrappings on the pavement for Ganesh to sweep up later, grumbling. These things are fixtures. But today was different. Even in my distraught state I couldn't ignore the addition.

Outside the door, the sun's rays sparkling on its pristine new surface, was a garish yellow and pink space rocket. It bore the legend '50p a ride' and a small child had already found it and clambered inside. From there he was loudly demanding that his mother put fifty pence in the slot and she was equally loudly declaring, 'I ain't got it, right? So get out of there!' I edged past them.

Ganesh's Uncle Hari was at the counter. He beamed at me from between stacks of chewing gum, chocolate bars and disposable cigarette lighters.

'Ah, Francesca, my dear. How are you?' He leaned closer and whispered, 'You have seen it?' He waited, glee and hope on his face, for my reply.

'Yes,' I confessed. 'You can't miss it, Hari.'

'No!' he crowed. 'All the children want a ride. It will be very successful.'

It isn't like Hari to see success on the horizon. Hari

believes that unless you keep a sharp lookout, disaster will creep up and tap you on the shoulder at every stage of life. The way I felt that morning, I was inclined to agree with him. It was disconcerting to find him rubbing his hands over his new project.

A shrill wail was heard from outside. The mother had hauled her toddler from the rocket and was dragging him down the road.

Hari's optimism shrivelled and died. 'So little money,' he said disapprovingly. 'To make your child happy, so little money. I can't understand it. What is the matter with people that they can't see a bargain?'

'It's new,' I said. 'Once they get used to the idea that it's there, it will get plenty of use.'

Hari considered that and accepted it. He nodded. Then he peered down at my feet. 'Where is the little dog today?'

'A friend's looking after her,' I said dully.

Ganesh came out of the stockroom at that moment and said, 'Hi!' He then looked at me more closely and dumped the boxes he was carrying on the counter. 'OK if Fran and I nip off for a coffee break?'

This was addressed to Hari whose eyes immediately searched the shop for some urgent job that Ganesh had to do at once. But he wasn't quick enough to trap Ganesh, who'd already opened the door leading to the flat above the shop and was halfway up the stairs.

I mumbled at Hari and followed.

'All right!' said Ganesh who was waiting for me, arms folded, in the middle of the sitting room. 'What now?'

'How do you mean, what now?' I asked defensively.

'Something's wrong. You've got a long face and that shifty look that always means you're in trouble. Out with it. What have you done now?'

When Ganesh lectures me I get annoyed as anyone would. And why should he assume I had done anything? But, as I was saying, I have to admit he's the voice of wisdom in my life. If I listened to him, as he's fond of telling me, I wouldn't have half the problems I wrestle with almost daily. On the other hand, if I listened to Gan, I'd be working behind the counter of a dry-cleaning business. This is Ganesh's obsession: that the area needs another dry-cleaner's and he and I could run it. I've told him, I don't like the chemical smell of those places. I don't like the idea of handling other people's dirty clothing. I particularly don't like the idea of running a small business because it's just so much hard work and you never get any time off.

'Look at Hari,' I say to Ganesh. 'Look what running this shop has done for him. He's a nervous wreck. He works all hours and never ever relaxes. Even when the place is closed for trade, he's sitting over the accounts and scratching his head over the VAT returns.'

But Ganesh always replies that's just Hari. He and I would do things differently. I don't believe it.

'I'll make the coffee,' I said now to gain time, and made for the kitchenette.

Ganesh followed and hovered impatiently in the doorway as I boiled the kettle and spooned out coffee granules.

'What's with the space rocket?' I enquired.

'Don't ask!' growled Ganesh. 'Does he ever listen to me? No, never! Does he listen to some wise guy who turns up persuading him that he'll make a fortune from a plastic rocket? Oh yes, he'll listen to him. I've had dozens of good ideas for improving business. He's turned them all down. Then he goes and sticks that – that eyesore right outside.'

'It might turn out popular with the kids,' I offered.

'It's downmarket,' said Ganesh loftily.

I told him he was a snob. But the rocket was obviously a touchy subject and best avoided.

'Well?' he demanded when we'd got our drinks and retreated to the worn red plush sofa.

I would have to tell him all of it eventually, but I jumped in with both feet and gave him the situation in a nutshell.

'Mickey Allerton has kidnapped Bonnie and is holding her hostage.'

'Do I look like I've got time to listen to your rotten sense of humour?' retorted Ganesh crossly. 'Hari will be yelling up the stairs at any moment, wanting me to go back down to work. Get on with it.'

'That is it, honest, Gan.' I explained what had happened that morning.

Ganesh listened, sipping coffee, and then observed, 'It stinks.'

'Yes, it does. I suppose I can trust Harry to look after Bonnie but I don't trust that Ivo. You should see him, Gan. He's like an android. And why should Mickey do that to me? It's a mean, despicable trick.'

'I don't mean the dog,' Ganesh interrupted.

Ganesh doesn't share his uncle's enthusiasm for Bonnie. This is not because he has anything in particular against her but because he mistrusts all dogs. They do tend to bark at him. I tell him it's because they sense his fear. He says he isn't afraid of them; he just doesn't like them, all right?

'I mean, the whole story Allerton told you stinks. Don't have anything to do with it, Fran.'

'I've got no choice, have I?' I retorted bitterly.

There was a long silence. I finished my coffee. 'What in particular strikes you as not being right?' I asked at last.

'None of it's right,' said Ganesh firmly. 'But if you want to take just one point, how did this girl come to work for Mickey Allerton in the first place and how long had she been there before she ran off? He tells you she's not a native Londoner but comes from Oxford. She talks posh and he thinks went to a good school. What's she doing performing for the sad old gits and grubby little pervs who frequent that club? What brought her down to London in the first place? I know he says he never employs runaways, but this sounds to me suspiciously like just that.'

'He says she's my age, twenty-two,' I countered.

'He's not going to tell you she's sixteen, is he?' snapped Ganesh.

'Mickey's not a fool. If she was sixteen he wouldn't go chasing after her – or send me. Too tricky. I've got a photo.' I extricated the glossy Mickey had given me and handed it to Ganesh.

Ganesh studied it, cowboy hat, rhinestones, mauve eyeshadow and all. 'She looks about twenty-two,' he admitted grudgingly. 'Not that you can tell underneath all that muck on her face. But why does he want her back? Yes, I know he's setting up in Europe and he wants her to work in Spain for him, or so he says. That sounds like a story he thought up on the spur of the moment to me. If it's the truth, why didn't he tell her when she was there in London, working for him? Did he offer her the job and did she turn it down? Why did she turn it down? Why did she run off back to Oxford without a word to Mickey? If she'd been working there for a while, what was it suddenly made her think she couldn't stand it any longer? Was there a row? As a story it's got more holes than a sieve.'

He drained his coffee mug. 'And how does he have her home address? Even if she told a fellow dancer she was going home, she'd be crazy to let the other girl know her parents' address. She'd be crazy to tell the other girl what she meant to do, anyway. I don't believe it. I don't believe she did tell this other girl she meant to go home. If she was running away without telling Mickey, she wouldn't tell anyone who worked for him, either. Would you? Think about it.'

He was right, of course. 'Perhaps he has her parents' address because he needed to have the name of next of kin? You know, something to do with insurance?' It was a feeble attempt at explanation but I couldn't think of anything better.

'Oh?' said Ganesh sarcastically. 'What insurance would this be? In case she fell off the stage and broke her neck?'

The carpet beneath our feet quivered from a series of hefty blows from below. Hari was banging on the shop ceiling with a broom handle, a signal that he needed Ganesh downstairs.

'I've got to go,' said Ganesh, getting to his feet. 'I suppose you'll go to Oxford because you're worried about Bonnie. But the girl might not be there. The only explanation I can think of as to why she told someone she was going home, if she did, is that she was laying a false trail. That does make sense to me. Even if she is in Oxford, you might not find her straight away.'

'Mickey's fixed up a B and B for me,' I said gloomily. 'It's run by some former employee of his.'

'Thinks of everything, Mickey Allerton, doesn't he?' growled Ganesh. 'He hasn't given you a street plan of Oxford, I suppose? How are you going to find your way about?'

'I'll get one at the station when I arrive.'

He frowned. 'Hari might have one. Hang on, I'll look.'

I followed him to the battered roll-top desk in the corner of the room. 'Why would Hari have a street plan of Oxford? Has he ever been to Oxford?'

'I don't know,' said Ganesh. 'But you know Hari. He keeps everything, just in case it turns out to be useful one day. We've loads of junk around the place with zero chance of any of it being useful. He's like a perishing squirrel. He's got dozens of street plans. I don't know where they all came from.'

He burrowed in the desk and from a pigeon-hole dragged a pack of tattered town street maps. 'Here we go. Coventry, Bath, East Grinstead . . .' He shuffled the stack. 'Here we are, Oxford, see?' He held up a mangled bunch of papers held together by yellowing sticky tape.

I took it from him in disbelief and carefully opened it out. It looked like something Bonnie had been chewing. The cover price was fifteen pence and inside the cover a hotel in a central city position was advertising bed and breakfast for the price a sandwich costs today. The map had to be over thirty years old. But it was Oxford all right. Ganesh and I spread it on the table and looked for the street in which the B and B was located into which I was booked by Mickey.

'Here,' said Ganesh, pointing. 'This little street here off the Iffley Road.'

'Thanks,' I said. 'I'll have to mend this. Will Hari mind if I borrow it?'

'He'll be delighted. It will prove he was right to keep it

and all the others in the first place. Hang on, I've got something else you ought to take with you.'

He vanished into another room and came back holding out a small oblong object, a mobile phone. Now, I know everyone these days has a mobile, but I don't, right? I haven't got anyone to call on it and if I ever do, there's a payphone in the hallway of the house where I live. I wasn't aware Ganesh owned one, either.

'Since when?' I asked, pointing at it.

He had the grace to look mildly embarrassed. 'They're cheap enough. It's the pre-pay sort, so there's about ten quid's worth of call time already on it. It won't cost you a thing. It will mean you can get in touch with me if you need to. Look, this is how you switch it on. Press this button here when someone calls and press it again when the call is finished.'

'Does Hari know you've got it?' I asked innocently, taking the little phone from him.

'Well, no.' Ganesh was beginning to sound cross at my questions. 'You know how he is about anything new – except that ruddy rocket. He always grumbles about cost but it's my money, isn't it?'

'Yes, it is!' I agreed. 'Thanks, Ganesh, just the thing.' I pocketed it.

Ganesh looked pleased. I understood why he had bought it. Ganesh feels that living here with Hari, and working all day every day in the shop, the modern world is leaving him behind. Things are made worse by the fact that his brother-in-law, Jay, is an accountant and has what's called a career. The answer, I always tell him, is to walk out of the shop and make his own life. He always replies that I don't understand. (That's when he isn't replying, all right, what about the dry-cleaning business?) The truth is, it's always easier to solve other people's problems than your own. Ganesh knows the answer to mine, and I know the answer to his. I don't listen to him. He doesn't listen to me. But we talk about things, and that's what matters.

Beneath our feet the floor quivered as Hari assaulted it again with the broom handle. The look of pleasure was wiped from Ganesh's face. 'Listen to that,' he muttered. 'Nobody knows what I've got to put up with!' He reached back into the desk and took out a roll of sticky tape which he handed to me. 'Help yourself.' He stomped out.

I mended the street plan as best I could and then went to the kitchenette and washed the mugs. On my way out through the shop, Ganesh stopped me. 'When are you leaving?'

'Now, I suppose. Mickey's given me the money to buy a train ticket. I can't waste time. I want Bonnie back before Ivo gets his hands on her.'

'Wait until tonight,' he begged. 'Then I can come with you and at least satisfy myself about the place you're staying in.'

I shook my head. 'I can manage, honestly. I'll just go to the address, spend a bit of time trying to find her and, if I do, give her Mickey's message. If she won't come back I'll try and get her to phone him, at least. Then I'll return here and try and persuade him to give back Bonnie. My big worry is that Lisa won't be at her parents' house. Then what do I do? I can't go to Mickey completely empty-handed.'

Hari popped out from behind a rack of greetings cards. 'Oxford!' he chirruped. 'Dreaming spires, isn't it? You won't lose my excellent street plan?'

'I'll look after it, I promise.'

'I have always thought,' continued Hari, 'that those flat boats look very unsafe. Punts, they are called. Do not go in such a punt. You can fall out.' This was more the old Hari I knew, never looking on the bright side. Much more in his nature than a sudden addiction to plastic rockets.

'I promise that, too, Hari,' I told him. 'I won't go in any punts.'

'You falling out of a punt is the least of my worries,' growled Ganesh. 'At least leave me the address of this B and B.'

I scribbled it down for him and he stuck it in his pocket. He walked out of the shop with me and stood on the sunny doorstep gloomily contemplating the space rocket which waited in solitary splendour for custom. I left him to it and wondered how long it would continue to dominate the pavement before either Hari decided it wasn't making money or Ganesh blew a fuse and insisted on its removal. You see why I don't want to go into business? You spend your life worrying about a flying ice lolly.

At home again, the flat seemed horribly empty without Bonnie scampering to meet me as I opened the door. In the kitchen her brown pottery water bowl, helpfully printed with the word DOG, stood filled. Near it lay what was left of a rubber bone scored by her sharp little teeth. I averted my eyes from both and hurried to put my toothbrush and a change of underwear, clean jeans and a shirt in a bag. Then, although the weather was a little warm for it, for good measure I added my best blazer bought in a charity shop, just in case I needed to look respectable. The sooner I got going, delivered my message and, with luck, persuaded the runaway at least to phone Mickey, then the sooner I'd be back here and Harry could bring Bonnie home.

Harry *would* bring her home. I must never allow myself to doubt that. As for Allerton, I shook my fist in a useless threat and addressed the empty air. 'Just you wait, Mickey Allerton, I'll get you for this, you'll see!'

Call it childish bravado or just my dramatic training expressing itself, it made me feel better. Buoyed up by unrealistic visions of future vengeance, and armed with Hari's museum piece of a street plan, I made my way to Paddington Station.

I came up from the Tube into the sprawling cavern of the normally busy mainline station. Now it was between the morning and evening peak travel times and relatively deserted. I found the computerised timetable display and discovered I'd just missed a train.

'Shit,' I said aloud. 'Nothing's going right.'

I was dimly aware that a small dark-haired young woman in a short skirt and cherry-red jacket was standing next to me, staring up at the same screen. As I spoke, she glanced at me curiously and a touch sharply. I'm accustomed to smartly dressed people looking at me in a critical way and it doesn't worry me. As it happened, that day I didn't look too scruffy in my opinion. I wore clean jeans and shirt and with my last pay packet from my defunct job had even invested in new trainers. Still, she probably thought I was one of those lost souls who wander about London holding endless conversations with unseen companions. What did she know about it? I thought rebelliously. I bet she didn't have my worries. I was allowed to talk to myself.

However, I retreated to the semi-privacy of the screened off Heathrow Check-In area where I bought myself a coffee and, suddenly realising it was early afternoon and I'd missed my lunch, a tuna sandwich to go with it. I took them to a table and sat down to study Hari's street plan.

Oxford's mainline station where I'd arrive was to the west of the city centre. The B and B where I'd be lodging was situated off the Iffley Road to the south-east, well out of the city centre. With some difficulty I located the road where the Stallards lived and that, wouldn't you know it, was in a large residential area to the north of the centre. Without transport, I was going to have to rely on the buses or do an awful lot of walking. In the present heatwave, that didn't sound like a good idea.

It was time to go for the train. I folded the map away and got up. At a nearby table, the dark girl in the cherry-red jacket got up too. I suspected she meant to catch the same train and while that could be no more than a coincidence, and probably was, I didn't like it. My nerves were pretty jumpy. I didn't need strangers taking an unhealthy interest in my plans.

I resisted the urge to turn my head and check whether Cherry Jacket was walking behind me as I strode purposefully to the platform where the train stood waiting. Look confident, Fran, and you'll feel confident! I told myself. People don't mess with you if you look on top of things. I stepped into a coach through the open doors and now risked a glance outside. It was nearing the time of departure and the hurrying crowd of would-be passengers scurried past with expressions of pale-faced intensity. You could see the indecision on some: jump on now and walk through the coaches to find a seat or carry on down the platform and risk the doors closing and shutting them out. They were like a mass of disturbed beetles. Among them I caught a fleeting impression of tight black leggings and a pink top which plucked a chord in my memory. Before I could focus on that, Cherry Jacket walked past the open doors without a glance. But I sensed she'd seen me.

She must have got in the same coach at the further end. I wasn't surprised to encounter her walking towards me as I was making my way up the central aisle looking for a seat. We met halfway and exchanged glances of recognition. She smiled. I scowled and pushed my bag up on to the luggage rack. She wasn't put off, however, shoved her briefcase in alongside my bag and took the seat opposite me.

Although the train was filling up fast there were still plenty of free places and I felt vaguely annoyed that she'd chosen to put herself right in my line of sight. Fortunately someone had left a copy of a tabloid paper on the seat next to me so I picked it up and buried my nose in it.

It only takes so long to read a tabloid. Even after I'd done the crossword we still had some time to go before reaching Oxford. I got out the street plan again. My travelling companion spoke.

'Visiting Oxford for the first time?' she asked pleasantly.

I debated whether to ignore her but I had no call to be rude to her, after all. 'Yes,' I said shortly, hoping she'd leave it at that.

'Will you be going up to the university in the new term?'

That took me aback. 'No,' I faltered. 'I'm just visiting a friend.'

She smiled kindly at me with exceptionally regular white teeth, like a toothpaste commercial. 'It's a lovely city,' she said. 'You'll like it.'

'Yeah,' I muttered, 'I'm sure I will.'

She wasn't put off by lack of encouragement. 'I mean,' she went on, 'it's got its boring areas and slightly dodgy ones, the parts you wouldn't put on a tourist schedule, but you'll find it's got so much to see, the colleges and churches and the parks. I hope you'll have the time to do it all.'

Now, I'm not stupid and this was a way of asking me how long I planned to stay in the city. 'Yes,' I said in a manner I hoped finished off the conversation.

She seemed to take the hint and didn't speak again, not until we'd arrived and both stood up to take our luggage from the overhead rack.

'Good luck,' she said.

It was a casual remark, meaning little. But in my circumstances, which she couldn't know, it struck an ironic note and I must have shown something of this in my face because before she moved out into the central aisle, she gave me another of those curious sharp looks.

The area outside the station was busy. It had been a hot day here too; the sun still shone brightly and the air shimmered with heat radiating from the buildings behind me. I looked round for a bus stop and debated whether to splurge some of the spending money Mickey had given me on a taxi.

A car rolled to a stop beside me, the window whirred down and a by-now-familiar smile was turned on me again. 'Waiting for your friend?'

'Yes!' I snapped.

'Not shown up? I can offer you a lift.'

'I don't need a lift,' I snarled. I was beginning to put the pieces of the jigsaw together. 'I told you, I'm waiting for somebody.'

'No,' she said in that kindly way, 'I don't think you are.'

I stooped so that I could meet her glance at even level. 'Why don't you just show me your warrant card?' I invited.

She looked a little startled but rallied quickly. 'All right.' She delved in the pocket of the cherry jacket and held up a rectangle of plastic showing her mugshot and identifying her as Detective Sergeant Hayley Pereira. The driver of the taxi behind us, who had been tooting to let us know we were in his way, now decided to pull out round us and drive off with his foot down.

'How did you guess?' DS Pereira asked, genuinely wanting to know. Plainclothes coppers never like to find they've been rumbled. They honestly believe they blend in with the crowd. Not in any crowd I've ever been part of.

'I know,' I said, 'when someone's trying to pick me up, whether it's a man or a woman. You could be talent-scouting for a vice ring, but I'm not the type you'd want to recruit as a hooker. You might be representing some do-gooding charity. But you haven't got that pious look. So, you're a copper.'

'Sounds logical,' she agreed, putting the warrant card away.

'Tell me,' I asked her. 'Do I bear a striking resemblance to some wanted person?'

She raised neatly plucked eyebrows. 'No, I don't think so.'

'So, Sergeant,' I went on, 'I'm a bona fide traveller with a valid ticket. You don't have any reason to suppose I've committed an offence. I haven't even dropped a crisp packet or stuck my chewing gum in the slot at the turnstile. I don't have to give you my details. You don't need to know my business. You don't have any cause to pull me in.'

She sighed. 'I'm not pulling you in, believe me. You don't have to get in the car. But I'd like it if you'd let me give you a lift to wherever you want to go.'

'Why?' I demanded. I was well aware the cops don't offer taxi service. She wanted something.

'Because I'd like to be sure you have somewhere to stay tonight.'

'I won't be sleeping in a doorway.'

We had reached stand-off. I sighed. The police have a way of making you an offer you can't refuse.

'OK,' I said. 'And then that's the end of it, right?'

'Sure,' she said, reaching back to open the rear door. 'Sling your bag in there.'

I put my bag on the back seat and shut the door. Then I walked round and got into the passenger seat beside her.

'Where to?' The car rolled smoothly forward.

I gave her the address of the guest house and she nodded. But I hadn't expected this journey to be made in silence.

'What's your name?' she asked in a friendly way.

'Fran,' I said.

Before she could press for my surname I decided to head off any further questions by asking a few of my own.

'Just why have you picked on me?'

'I haven't "picked" on you, Fran,' she returned reproachfully. 'It's as I told you on the train. Oxford's a really nice city. Everyone thinks there's just the university but there's lots more besides. Naturally, because even without the students we have a big permanent population, we have all the troubles that brings anywhere. We have our homeless, our beggars, our winos, our druggies—'

'Thanks!' I interrupted. 'I look like I fall into one of those categories, do I?'

'No, you don't. Look, I'm standing at the timetable display at Paddington Station and next to me, studying the same Oxford timetable, is a young woman who's clearly worried. She's upset because she's missed the train and she's talking aloud to herself.'

'Doesn't everyone from time to time?' I countered.

'Sure. I do it myself. But then, when I go for a coffee, I see that same young woman again. She's studying a street plan that I recognise as Oxford. It's my manor, if you like. I know the layout of those streets like the back of my hand. She's heading for a strange place and trying to orient herself before she gets there. If it's Oxford then it's the wrong time of year for her to be a student, long vacation. She might be a prospective student going to have a look round.'

'So you checked to find out if I was,' I said. 'That was almost the first thing you asked me.'

'And you weren't. You seemed to be streetwise and able to look out for yourself. I was right about that, wasn't I? Your reaction just now, demanding to see ID and telling me why I had no right to pull you in, all suggests you've dealt with the police before! There's no reason that should bother me. But you seem to me to be unhappy about something, worried. You said vaguely you were going to see a friend. You didn't want to talk in the train and you don't now. I'm beginning to wonder if you might be in trouble of some sort.'

'I'm not,' I lied.

She smiled at me. 'I used to work in the probation service,' she told me, 'before I decided to join the police. I worry about young people with problems.'

'I do not have a problem,' I repeated slowly and forcefully. 'I am not on probation and I'm twenty-two years old, not a kid.'

'You look younger,' she said.

'Yeah, it's because I'm pint-sized and don't do the make-up and fashion thing.'

She flushed. Perhaps she thought I was getting at her. But too bad, I was the one getting the unwelcome attention.

We were driving down a long street and to either side, from time to time, appeared the imposing frontages of what I supposed to be the colleges. I couldn't help rubbernecking. Pereira obliged by telling me that this was the High Street and naming the buildings we passed.

Our route opened out. 'We're coming up to Magdalen College and Magdalen Bridge. That's the Botanic Gardens on the right. If you're interested in boating you can hire a punt just under the bridge.'

'I've been warned to stay out of punts,' I said.

We rolled over the bridge and came to an area where several roads met, with a patch of dusty vegetation in the middle.

'This is called the Plain,' Pereira continued her tour guide commentary. 'It used to be a cemetery.'

'Nice,' I said.

'And this is the beginning of the Iffley Road.'

That meant we were nearly at our destination. Thank goodness, I'd be rid of my guardian angel soon. She turned the car into a side street and pulled up before a red-brick villa with bow windows and an illuminated sign in the ground floor window reading 'Bed and Breakfast. No Vacancies.'

'Oh dear,' said Pereira. 'You're out of luck, Fran.'

'No, I'm booked in. They're expecting me.' I opened the door and scrambled out. As I retrieved my bag from the rear seat she made one last try.

'I have to go to London for an early-morning meeting,' she said.

I just smiled at her. 'Thanks for the lift.'

I ran up the steps to the front door and rang the bell.

My police escort hadn't moved off but sat waiting in her car to see what happened.

There was a pause, longer than I would have wished. I refused to turn my head and meet Pereira's eye. At last I heard sounds of movement and then the yap of a small dog. I was already unsettled and that sound nearly finished me off. For one wild stupid moment I wondered if Bonnie had been spirited to Oxford to meet me, but it couldn't be so and it wasn't.

The door opened. A woman with hair an unlikely shade of red, wearing black trousers and a striped blue and grey shirt, stood before me. Tucked under her arm was a wriggling miniature poodle. It fixed me expectantly with its shiny little eyes, its pink tongue waggled and it gave another friendly yap of greeting.

'Hi . . .' I said, my voice choking.

'Sorry, dear,' said the redhead. 'I've got no rooms free.'

'I'm Fran Varady . . .' I began.

Her face brightened and she interrupted me. 'Oh, you're Mickey's girl. Come on in, then. I was wondering when you'd get here.'

I wasn't Mickey's girl and I would have to disabuse her of that quickly. But right now I had other things on my mind. I snatched up my bag and stepped into her hallway.

She looked past me. 'Who's that, then?'

'Plainclothes,' I said.

'Blimey, dear,' she returned. 'You didn't take long to get yourself noticed, did you? What did you do?'

Chapter Three

'I haven't done anything!' I told her. 'Look, can I come inside? She'll drive off as soon as the door's shut. She's just checking I'm staying here.'

The landlady didn't argue with that. Let's face it: she didn't want a copper parked outside her front door keeping observation. No one would. It's the sort of thing the neighbours notice and it makes them nervous. She moved aside in a way which struck me as clumsy, and let me walk past her and drop my bag on the floor. Then she pushed the door closed and set the poodle down. He ran to sniff my jeans and then stood on his hind legs to put his narrow paws against my knee and panted at me happily. I scratched his woolly ears. He wore a pale blue leather collar with rhinestones on it.

'This is Spencer. He likes people,' said the landlady. 'I have to pick him up when I open the door in case he runs out. Do you want to take a look out of the window in there and see if your friend has gone?'

She indicated the room which originally would have been the house's front parlour. I went inside and looked through the bay window, knowing that most of me was hidden by the B and B sign which hung there. Pereira's car was nowhere to be seen. I'd finally shaken her off. I turned away in relief. With the police you can never be absolutely certain. Although I'd assured the landlady my unwanted guardian angel would leave once she saw I was accepted in the house, there had been the possibility she'd sit out there for a while to make sure I hadn't just talked my way in on a temporary basis. It was sod's law that I'd run into a nosy copper at Paddington and I hoped she wasn't going to complicate matters. They were complicated enough already. Not, of course, that I'd come to Oxford to involve myself in anything criminal. I told myself this forcefully, subduing the awkward persistent twinge of doubt. But I guessed Pereira's interest in me was less because I might be in trouble than that I might turn out to *be* trouble, for her.

I was now free to study the contents of the room in which I found myself. It was decorated with flowered wallpaper of the sort I hadn't seen in years and still had an old-fashioned fireplace although these days a gas fire was installed in it. Otherwise, it was furnished with small tables each neatly laid with two place settings and salt and pepper pots. There was a lingering background odour of bacon.

'It's the breakfast room,' said the landlady from the door. 'Breakfast is from eight to nine thirty, or you can have it earlier if you let me know the night before. I don't do evening meals. There are lots of little places in the area where you can eat.'

She was either a very patient person or she wasn't overburdened with other tasks at the moment. She didn't appear to mind how long I lingered.

'That's OK,' I told her. 'I don't think I'll be staying long.' I realised I owed her an explanation as to why I'd arrived in the company of plainclothes. 'I just had the bad luck to meet up with that sergeant on the train. I didn't give her any encouragement but she kept asking me questions. I don't know why. She insisted on driving me here. She said she wanted to be sure I had somewhere to stay.'

'Ever been homeless?' the landlady asked unexpectedly but in a pleasant way.

'Yes, for a little while. It was quite a time ago. Does it show?' I was surprised.

'No, dear, of course it doesn't. My name's Beryl. Do you want me to show you your room?'

She turned and lurched towards the staircase. The poodle pattered after her. I picked up my bag and followed.

We climbed slowly to the first floor. It was clear now that Beryl had some kind of walking difficulty. She held on to the banister and hauled herself up. When we arrived, she opened the door to a room at the back and stood aside for me to enter.

'I hope you'll be comfortable. I don't offer a proper en

suite although you've got your own washbasin, see? But there's a bathroom right across the hall and toilets on each floor. There shouldn't be a problem because there are only three other people staying, two tourists and a travelling rep, I know the sign in the window says I'm full, but I just switched that on to stop people coming and asking for rooms. It's been a really busy summer and I wanted a bit of a rest.'

'I'm sorry Mickey asked you to take me,' I apologised. 'It's extra work for you.'

She waved that away with a hand tipped with scarlet nails. 'No, dear, not a bit! I'm always happy to do Mickey Allerton a favour. I used to work for him, years ago.'

I put her age at around fifty now, but she still had style, despite the lame leg. The bright red hair was tucked into a neat French plait and she was carefully made up and wore large pearl cluster earrings.

'I was a dancer,' she said with a note of sadness in her voice. 'Good days, they were. I had a lot of fun.'

'Look,' I said. 'I don't work for Mickey, not in his clubs. I don't sing or dance or strip. I'm an actor although I haven't got an acting job right now. Mickey just asked me to come to Oxford to do an errand for him.'

I glanced at the poodle. I could tell her about Bonnie being held as surety for my good behaviour but I decided against it. She obviously had a high opinion of Allerton and I didn't want to damage it. Theirs was an old acquaintance. I was a ship passing in the night – I hoped.

'All right, dear. It's your business. When you've unpacked, come down and have a cup of tea with me,' she invited.

I thanked her and she left me to it. I heard her awkward progress down the hall and then down the stairs. I wondered what had happened to her leg and remembered Ganesh's sarcastic remark about falling off the stage.

The room was furnished very comfortably in a similar old-fashioned way to the breakfast room, but benefited from the early evening sun which cast a warm apricot glow over everything. Through frilly net curtains I gazed from the window on to the long narrow garden at the rear of the property. For ease of maintenance most of it had been paved. There were a couple of wooden seats but some colourful plants in pots were the only growing things apart from a knobbly wisteria trained against the far brick wall and scrambling across the lintel of a wooden door in the middle of the wall.

People say evenings like this are peaceful but I find them unsettling. I understand why ancient peoples like the Aztecs worried so much about the sun setting. There is a kind of finality about it, an awareness of the long night ahead. There's a saying, however, about not letting the sun go down on your anger. Today it was going down on mine. I was still angry with Mickey Allerton and I would stay angry, even after all this was over, no matter how things turned out.

I turned back from the window and sat down on the

one upholstered chair and took a further look at my temporary home. It was odd to think that this was exactly what it would be for the next two or three days, my home, my space. Yet it had nothing of me in it. Everything was contrary to what I felt myself to be. I am not a frilly-curtain person, nor a lilac-bedlinen one. I averted my eyes from the awful picture on the wall depicting a child with unfeasibly large eyes and a tear rolling down his face. Why would anyone want such a picture? I wondered. How could anyone think it cute? I wasn't just in a strange city where I knew no one. I was in an altogether alien world. I had a mad impulse to search the room for listening devices, like James Bond in a new hotel room. Perhaps the bug was located behind that picture or the mirror on the dressing table . . .

I caught sight of myself in the mirror and stood still before it, trying to see myself as DS Pereira had. I still didn't think I looked like someone who might be on the wrong side of the law nor even someone who might once have been homeless. But Beryl's question had shaken me. There was something about me. I couldn't see it but others could. It wasn't anything to do with appearance, looks or dress. It had to be something else: body language, and a kind of wariness.

One of the people who had a flat in the converted house in which I lived kept a cat. My dog Bonnie and this cat lived on terms of mutual respect. They ignored one another. But whereas Bonnie was friendly with the other tenants, the cat avoided us all, everyone except its owner. Whenever I'd tried to make friends with it, it sat down at a distance and stared at me with unrelenting yellow eyes. If I moved towards it, it moved away. When I stopped, it sat down again. There was a distance between us and it was to be kept. The cat had been a stray and the tenant had taken it in. It had been a scraggy, half-wild moggy. Now it was plump and sleek but it hadn't lost its mistrust, its belief that you only survive if you keep your own space and others keep theirs. Was I like that? Did they read it in my eyes? I didn't like the idea.

It's not difficult to become homeless. There is a belief among people who don't know any better that those who lack a roof over their heads do so by choice. After all, they reason, there's always help somewhere. But there isn't. Or if there is, it comes with strings attached. Many people on the street are there because they want to lose themselves, blend in with the anonymity of pavements and shop doorways. There are those whose marriages, careers and lives have fallen apart. There are those who are mentally ill. There are those for whom drink or drugs have become the beginning and end of existence, a never-ceasing cycle. Their days pass in a blur of feverish desire, painful withdrawal symptoms, all-too-short rushes of relief and passages of oblivion. There are ex-cons who will end up back in gaol. There are youngsters running away from abusive homes, others from 'good' families against which they have rebelled and become lost, unable to go back to what they have left. Others have fallen out of the system, some have been in council care when children, but when no longer 'children' are in no one's care. Where should they go? Where turn?

I became homeless at sixteen because Grandma Varady died. My father had already died three years earlier. Grandma had been the tenant of the flat and the landlord wanted me out. He didn't care where I went. He advised me to 'go down the council'. I didn't want to share hostel space with drug addicts and the mentally ill. I slept in a local park. Later I shared the first of many squats. After a while I got a place to live with the help of someone I'd helped. That didn't last but I was offered my present place by a charity which, among other projects, had run the hospice in which my mother had died. I had a kind of security at last. But obviously my days of being 'of no fixed address' had stamped its mark on me.

'Snap out of it, Fran!' I told myself. 'Don't start brooding. The sooner you start, the sooner you'll be able to get back to London.' That was where I belonged. There no one cared what I looked like or what my past had been. That is the blessed anonymity of big cities, their magnet-like appeal.

It didn't take me long to unpack my bag. I pushed Hari's map in my pocket and made my way back downstairs.

Beryl hadn't told me exactly where to find her but logic took me to the rear of the building and the rattle of teacups guided me there into a large, bright kitchen. The landlady was putting the pot and milk jug on a round pine table which was already set with the cups and a plate of chocolate biscuits.

I sat down, accepted a cup of tea and tackled the situation head on. There really was no other way. 'I don't know how much Mickey told you . . .' I began.

She waved her scarlet-tipped nails at me. 'I don't worry about Mickey's business. You don't have to tell me anything. I said to Mickey I'd be happy to have you here and if you want to know anything about Oxford, just ask. I can't do any more than that because of my leg.' She reached down with a teaspoon and tapped her lower left leg. It made a dull hard sound. 'Lost it,' she said cheerfully. 'Below the knee.'

'Was that in an accident at the club?' I asked in horror. Perhaps Ganesh had been on the right track, after all.

She shook her head vigorously. 'Bless you, no. I fell off a bus at Marble Arch. It was Christmastime and you know how busy that area is at that time of year. The pavements were crowded. They had police out with loud hailers doing crowd control. I was on the bus and I thought I'd be clever and just jump off when it slowed down. But that's not as easy as you think. I stumbled and then a taxi hit me. It was my own fault. The leg wouldn't mend. In the end they chopped it off, just below the knee and gave me a false one. Of course, my dancing career was over. Things would have been bleak but, as it happened, an auntie died and left me this house here in Oxford. So I had the idea to set up a B and B. I was already over thirty and well, if you work the clubs, you need your looks and your figure. Mickey came up trumps. He gave me a bit of money to see me over while I got the business going. He's a good sort, Mickey, if you play fair by him.'

I didn't ask her what happened to people who didn't 'play fair'. It was even clearer that Beryl thought Allerton was the bee's knees. I'd have to be careful what I said. She was a nice woman, but she was a direct line back to the Silver Circle. I imagined that either Mickey would be on the phone daily to her to check on my progress or she'd received orders to bring him up to speed. I'd have to make it obvious that I was trying my best to carry out Mickey's errand. However, as someone who had not only known Mickey Allerton but had also worked for him, perhaps Beryl was uniquely able to give me some indication as to why Lisa Stallard might have bolted back to Oxford; if indeed that was what she had done. It would make my job so much easier if I knew why she'd left in the first place without warning her boss.

'You really enjoyed working in the club, then?' I asked nonchalantly. 'You didn't mind the smoky atmosphere or some of the dodgier punters?'

She frowned as she poured the tea. 'Mickey was always very careful to keep undesirables out of the club. He runs a very good class of place, Mickey. He picks all the acts with care, nothing tacky, if you know what I mean. Like, just yesterday, when he phoned me about you coming here, he told me a girl had turned up to audition a week or two ago and it turned out she did an exotic dance with a blooming big snake. He reckoned it was vulgar and he told her, no way could she work for him. All the other girls were pretty relieved, too. You don't fancy a snake loose in the dressing room, do you? Not one the size that thing was, apparently. A python, Mickey said. Even the doorman freaked out when she came in with it. Mickey didn't fancy the look of the thing himself!' Beryl chuckled. 'No, I reckoned the old Silver Circle was a nice place to work.'

'So nothing there a girl could object to, if she was in that line of work?'

'No, dear!' Beryl appeared shocked. 'I wouldn't say that about all the clubs. Some of them are real sleazy dives. But Mickey always wanted to go upmarket.'

I wondered just how upmarket Mickey thought he could take the business. But with an ambition like that, if Beryl was on the level about it and not just blinded by gratitude towards her old employer, there seemed little obvious reason why Lisa Stallard had suddenly decided to run for it. Unless, of course, she was involved in something else. The unwelcome feeling of unease returned, nestling in the pit of my stomach.

To drive it away, I took out Hari's map and unfolded it on the table.

'Where did you get that?' Beryl asked in wonder. 'That ought to be in a museum. I can let you have a better one than that. There's some tourist stuff up in your room, leaflets and the like. One or two of them have probably got a map of the city centre in them.'

'I'm interested in this area.' I pointed at the area where I believed the Stallards lived. 'What can you tell me about this part of town?'

'Very nice,' said Beryl. 'Expensive. It costs a lot of money to buy a house there. Otherwise I'd move my business up that way.'

'I want to find someone who lives there. I've got an address from Mickey. I thought I'd go up there this evening and look round, just to get my bearings. Is there a bus?'

She told me that would be no problem and explained where to catch a bus which would take me right across the city to my destination. She also asked if I thought I'd be back later than ten, because if so, she'd give me a front-door key.

'I go to bed early,' she explained. 'I have to get up early for the breakfasts.'

I said I hoped to be back long before ten but perhaps I ought to take a key, just in case. It would be a long bus ride from the Iffley Road across the city to the area marked Summertown, where the Stallards lived.

Beryl told me about the name. 'It was developed in the days when Oxford always had the fevers in the hot weather. Something to do with not having proper drains, probably. Everyone who could moved out to a healthier area until the cooler weather came back. It was the "summer town", see? It was a risky life in the old days, wasn't it?' she observed.

I could have pointed out to her that it was a pretty risky life now, even if we were spared the threat of being brought down with a low fever every time the bugs woke up from winter hibernation.

With both Pereira's and Beryl's efforts to interest me in the city's history and famous sights, I ought to have spent the bus ride taking more interest in passing scenery but my mind was on the job in hand. The bus set me down in a parade of shops, mostly closed now. It was the sort of area you could buy anything but not cheap as in Camden High Street. This was a classy area; even BBC Oxford had a place there.

The area also offered one immediate consolation. I had worried that wandering about a largely residential area, map in hand, obviously a stranger – and one who had already attracted the unwanted attention of authority – I'd attract more interest. But from the moment I jumped from the bus – taking care after hearing Beryl's tale – I saw that I could wander around here happily and no one would give me a second glance. There were quite a number of young people around and a broad assortment of others. All had in common that they were utterly absorbed in themselves. Some of the houses bore signs of multiple occupation. This area, this entire city I guessed, contained a shifting population of young people, drawn here either for the university or for other reasons. One thing I had noticed from the bus was the number of language schools here in North Oxford. I had passed several gaggles of foreign-looking youngsters. They, along with tourists, presumably moved in when the students went home for the long summer break. They made the population even motlier in content than it would have been anyway. It was all working to my advantage.

This changed when I turned off into the road where the Stallards lived. Here it was empty and quiet. The advantage I'd had of blending in with the crowd was lost. I was on my own. Time for a new strategy. I strolled down the street to the end, passing the number I sought, and then crossed over, strolled back again and took out Ganesh's mobile. Although my normal lifestyle didn't include walking round with a piece of plastic clamped to my ear, I was well aware that doing so could act as a cover for a multitude of activities. Pereira had noticed me at Paddington because I had spoken aloud to myself. If I'd had a mobile stuck to the side of my head, she'd have passed it off as normal. Another thing you can do with a mobile phone is stand still in the middle of the pavement. Pedestrians just part like the Red Sea and walk round you. They don't think it odd, because you are on your mobile. Half of them are doing the same, only they're walking along and carrying on a conversation across the airwaves. Ganesh has no one to ring, but walking along with the mobile clasped in his hand, he feels like everyone else.

So now I leaned nonchalantly on the wall of the house

opposite the Stallards', put the phone to my ear and, remembering to mutter into it from time to time and give it the occasional grin, I observed the house in detail. (You see what I mean? If you saw me leaning on your wall, muttering and grinning without a plastic ear appendage, you'd be on the phone to social services, wouldn't you?) The muttering and grinning were necessary. I had dramatic training and always did a thing properly. Besides, although there were no Neighbourhood Watch notices in any windows in this street, it didn't mean the neighbours weren't watching. It's what neighbours do. If my mouth didn't move and my face muscles twitch from time to time, they'd suss I was snooping and the phone was a cover. Then they wouldn't call social services, they'd call the police. The way my luck went, Pereira would probably roll up in her little car and haul me off again.

The Stallards' home, like others in the street, was a small terraced house with a bow front upstairs and down. It looked about the same age as Beryl's house. It had one peculiarity distinguishing it from its fellows. A shallow ramp had been built from the front door nearly across the narrow forecourt to the gap representing a gate. If there had ever been a gate it had long gone. The same was true of other houses in the road. Perhaps they'd all been taken in a wartime scrap metal collection. The ramp did away with the front doorstep and suggested one thing only. Somebody in this house moved around on wheels.

Even as I watched, the front door opened. It took me by

surprise and I let my hand drop from my ear for a moment before remembering I was in the middle of a telephone conversation and returned the mobile to its roost. Someone appeared in the open doorway. I had the rear view of a woman who was exiting the house backwards. This, it soon became obvious, was because she was pulling a wheelchair out with her. She backed carefully down the ramp out of the gate gap and only then turned the chair so that it faced up the road towards the shopping area I'd passed through earlier. The chair contained a man who, despite the balmy evening, was wearing a blue pullover and a little blue peaked cap. He looked considerably underweight and when she leaned over him to say something he raised a thin hand in acknowledgement. She went back to the house and pulled the front door shut. I noticed she didn't call out to anyone within. That didn't necessarily mean anything, but I was looking for signs that Lisa Stallard was there.

I was as certain as anyone could be that the couple were her parents. The ramp indicated they lived there and weren't just visitors. I put the mobile away with some relief – I was beginning to get cramp in my arm from having it stuck up in the air for so long – and followed discreetly after the Stallards as they set off down the street. I did not want them to be aware of me haunting their footsteps and I hoped they hadn't noticed me across the street when they'd come out of the house. If I was intending to call there the following day, it wouldn't help if they'd seen me hanging out the evening before. But the woman was completely taken up with her husband, talking to him in what seemed to be an encouraging tone as she pushed his chair along. I couldn't hear if he replied.

They reached the parade of shops and turned right along it. I crossed the road and followed them from there, keeping well back. From time to time they stopped before a shop front and looked in the window. When this happened I had to pretend to do the same. The Stallards then moved on at the same leisurely pace, not appearing to be in any hurry or to have a specific purpose. When they reached the end of the shopping parade they continued. Occasionally they would pass someone they knew and exchange a brief word. These passers-by didn't appear to be surprised to see them and I realised now what was happening. Mrs Stallard was taking Mr Stallard out for a regular evening outing, a breath of fresh air when the pavements were relatively empty, traffic lighter on the road and altogether fewer obstacles lay in their path.

I stopped short where I was, overcome with shame. What business had I, dogging them like this? These were people who had their own very real problems. Now they had the additional one of the sudden return of Lisa to the family home, supposing that Lisa had done that. How were they coping? Did Mickey Allerton know that Mr Stallard was in a wheelchair? I hated every part I was being obliged to play in this messy, embarrassing and underhand business. However, it was time to be professional about my task and not get caught up in personal emotions. The Stallards would be out for a while and I could go back to the house and check whether anyone else was there. I wanted, if possible, to talk to Lisa without contacting any other member of her family.

This time I walked down the road fairly briskly. I rang the front-door bell and waited. No one answered. I stepped back and considered the house frontage. I'd have to pay a return visit. That Lisa wasn't there now didn't mean she wasn't there at all.

Out of the corner of my eye I saw a curtain twitch at the upper front bay of the house next door. Time to move on. I turned and strolled away. I had passed about half a dozen doors when my ear caught the faint click of a door closing some distance behind me down the street. I didn't break my stride. Animals have the advantage over humans in being able to move their ears to catch sounds behind them. I couldn't do that, but even so, I was sure there was a soft footfall keeping time with my steps. I reached the shopping precinct again, and crossed the main road with the intention of stopping by the first bus stop I reached to wait for a bus to take me back. The person following me crossed over too. He or she was a novice at trailing someone. This was reassuring but also annoying. I didn't want this busybody, whoever he or she was, reporting back to the Stallards.

I passed a quaint old pub called the Dewdrop which

had survived intact between modern buildings with shops below and offices above. There was a bus stop here. I halted and turned round.

My tracker was a young man in jeans and a black T-shirt with trainer-shod feet. When he caught my eye he looked guilty and dithered between diving into the pub and putting a bold face on it and continuing. He decided in for a penny, in for a pound. He walked up to the bus stop and stood there with me.

The situation was bordering on the ridiculous. There we were, side by side, staring at the passing traffic, and painfully aware of one another. He'd been following me and he knew that I'd guessed it. No sensible person would have tried to bluff it out as he was doing. I ventured a glance sideways but he kept his eyes resolutely to the front and his spine ramrod straight in a way which would have done credit to a sentry at Buckingham Palace. Amateurs, huh!

Just then a bus did come along and I hopped on. Would you believe it? Sherlock Holmes hopped on behind me. I wondered, when we reached the city centre, if he'd get off there. But he stuck with me. The bus crossed the river over Magdalen Bridge and rounded the central shrub-planted area of the Plain, halting just at the beginning of the Iffley Road. I got off and yes, he got off too.

This was now just exasperating. Instead of walking towards my destination I stood still on the pavement. Holmes dithered again not knowing whether to walk past me and risk me doubling back behind him. I decided to put him out of his misery.

'You're following me,' I said to him, not unpleasantly. I even gave him a kindly smile, just to rattle him further.

He turned beetroot-red, right up into his tousled fair hair. 'No, I'm not.' His gaze was shifting all over the place now, unable to meet mine.

'Do me a favour. Do I look as if I arrived from the moon yesterday? You've followed me from Summertown. If you didn't want me to notice you, well, all I can say is, you're lousy at tailing someone. If you didn't care if I saw you, then perhaps you thought it would worry me. No chance. Where I come from, if you worried about the people you met on the street, you'd never go out. So don't mess me around. What do you want?'

With unexpected pugnacity he retorted, 'I ought to ask you that!'

'Why?' I countered.

'What do you want with the Stallards?' He was glaring at me now, trying to put the frighteners on me.

There was no way he was going to gain an advantage by blustering, not here on the open pavement, and certainly not now he'd tipped his hand by mentioning the Stallards. I wasn't alarmed by him but I was seriously annoyed. This was another unwished complication.

'Who are they?' I asked.

'I saw you!' He jutted his jaw at me. He was beginning to sweat now; I could see the pearls forming on his forehead. He was a good-looking guy in a sporty sort of way, the sleeves of the black T-shirt stretched over well-developed biceps. Probably he had more brawn than brain-power, judging by what I'd seen of him so far, but that didn't make him less of a problem. I wasn't only annoyed with him but with myself and abashed at my own conceit. I'd flattered myself I'd done a good job looking over the Stallards' house and trailing them. Obviously, I hadn't. My companion might be a bumbling amateur but I'd made it too easy for him. I also had a lot to learn about being inconspicuous.

He confirmed this. 'You came wandering down our road. You hung about on the other side talking on your mobile. Who were you talking to? Were you making some kind of report? Then you went after Jennifer when she pushed Paul out for their evening stroll. I thought that was odd and kept watching. Good job I did. You came back and rang their doorbell. You knew they were out. So either you're planning a burglary or you want to see Lisa. She's not in.'

The last words were spoken a little too defiantly. I interpreted this to mean she wasn't there that particular evening but she was staying at the house. This, in itself was useful knowledge. I had always had a small doubt that Mickey was right in saying she'd gone home. Now my companion had obligingly tipped me off. This guy was an interfering blunderer but evidently knew the family well. What was he? Just a neighbour? A friend? Lisa's boyfriend?

'That's it, is it?' I asked. 'A first-class snoop on your neighbours, aren't you?'

He reddened again, this time with anger not with embarrassment. 'You've got a bloody nerve! You were behaving in a suspicious manner. I ought to have called the police.'

'No,' I contradicted, 'I ought to call the police. You've admitted you've followed me. I call that harassment.'

A sarcastic grin spread briefly over his face. 'You won't call the police,' he said.

Well, he was right. 'Listen,' I told him. 'Just go home, will you? This has nothing to do with you.'

'Perhaps it does!' he returned, cocky now. He thought he had me on the run. 'Who are you, anyway?'

'Sod off, will you?' I repeated my request less politely. I turned and walked away. There was nothing else I could do. He walked boldly behind me now.

'Listen, chum,' I growled at him. 'You are seriously getting up my nose!'

'It's a free country,' he replied. 'I can walk along this pavement. If you think I'm harassing you, like you said, ring the cops. You've got a mobile phone on you. I won't try and grab it off you. I'm not daft.'

He was going to stick with me until he saw where I was headed. There wasn't anything I could do about it. He knew that, I did my best to ignore him and carried on until I reached Beryl's guest house. Here we stopped.

'This is it,' I said, turning to him. 'This is where I'm staying. Now you know you can toddle off back home.'

'I'll wait until you go inside,' he said obstinately.

Another one! Every time I set foot on the streets of this city, was some concerned citizen going to insist on escorting me to a safe haven? First Pereira, now this Neighbourhood Watch fanatic?

'Fine,' I said nonchalantly. I climbed the steps to the front door and put the key Beryl had given me into the lock. That convinced him.

'Wait!' he called urgently.

I should have ignored him but if he had something he wanted to say he was stupid enough to come knocking on the door. I didn't want Beryl – and ultimately Mickey – finding out about this pest. Mickey would be likely to arrange a small accident for the guy. I turned back. 'What?'

'If you're staying here, you're a visitor to Oxford.' He sounded smug.

Elementary, my dear Watson, I snarled mentally. The house was a ruddy B and B. 'So?' I said aloud casually. 'I'm a tourist.'

'Like hell you are!' he snapped. 'You've come from London. Have you come from that creep Allerton?'

Oh shit, this was getting more complicated by the minute. It was beginning to look as if others knew far more about what was going on than I did.

'Never heard of him!' I said and shut the door on him before he could argue.

I sneaked into the breakfast parlour and peeped from the window. He could still barge after me, hammering on the door and demanding to speak to me. I held my breath. He hung about outside undecidedly for a minute and then strode away. I heaved a sigh of relief but it was only temporary. He'd gone but he'd turn up again. Right now he'd hurry home either to warn the Stallards or Lisa herself about me. But Lisa wasn't there, he'd said, and certainly no one had answered the door. If I had to make a guess, and guess was all it could be, he wouldn't say anything about me to the Stallards before he spoke to Lisa. He wouldn't want to worry them unduly. He'd mentioned Mickey Allerton so he knew too much for my liking. But I didn't know how much the Stallard parents knew about Lisa's flight from the Silver Circle. I was ready to gamble they knew only some story she'd chosen to tell them and it wouldn't necessarily be correct in every detail.

It's called the Generation Gap. Basically it works like this. Young people don't tell older ones what they're doing because they don't want endless lectures and interference. They excuse their actions by saying they are anxious to prevent their parents worrying.

Parents and other adult relatives play their cards close to the chest out of an instinct born of fear. They don't know how their children will react to difficult news and how they, as adults, will deal with the reaction, when it comes. They hope that if they ignore the problem, it will go away. They persuade themselves they are protecting their children's innocence. They pretend to one another that what they are doing is 'for the best'.

When my mother left home no one told me she had gone for good. I mean, what did they think? That I wouldn't notice she wasn't there? I remember asking one evening as we sat down to supper, where was she? Dad looked glum and said nothing. Grandma ladled out goulash as if the survival of the Western world depended on it, and announced that my mother had gone on a little holiday and I should eat up quickly or my food would get cold.

The 'holiday' continued indefinitely and my mother didn't return. No one explained what was going on. I didn't ask about her again. I'd realised they didn't want to talk about it. Occasionally my grandmother, especially after sampling the home-made apricot brandy, would stroke my hair and call me a poor motherless child. I wanted to point out I wasn't motherless. I had a mother but she'd gone on this mysterious holiday. Later I wondered if she was dead but there had been no signs of the usual fuss around funerals. Dad hadn't got out his black tie. Grandma hadn't unearthed her rusty black velvet dress. No single flower in a vase stood before the portrait photograph of my mother which had perched on the mantelpiece. That picture disappeared altogether. What happened to it, I wonder. Did my father destroy it in anger or keep it hidden away in sorrow? It wasn't among his effects when Grandma and I parcelled them up after he died. Or perhaps it was, and

Grandma abstracted it before I saw it, still afraid of having to make explanations.

Neither during my childhood nor when I grew older did either of them come out and admit the truth that she'd bolted from the family home. I had to work that out for myself. I never knew why she'd done it and, in the early years, wondered why she hadn't taken me with her. Years later, when I did meet up with her again, I didn't ask her. You see, by then I was an adult and I, too, had learned to be wary of explanations. Nor did she offer any reason for having abandoned us, so the conspiracy of silence was complete.

They're all dead now, Dad, Grandma and my mother. There's a black hole left in my personal history.

Back to Lisa. Although I suspected, for the reasons given, she might not have told her parents everything, it would appear she'd been confiding in her dogged if incompetent neighbour. That was unsettling.

It was getting late now and I had eaten nothing all day except the tuna sandwich at Paddington and a couple of chocolate biscuits with Beryl. I decided to assume I wouldn't encounter the Stallards' self-appointed guardian and to go out to eat. He'd cleared off, thank goodness. I found a wine bar which did meals and ate a Greek salad with garlic bread. I felt better after that and as it was still light I went for a walk.

On Magdalen Bridge I leaned over the graceful parapet and stared down at the water below lapping against the moored punts. I thought of the bridge over the canal at

Camden Lock and felt homesick for the crowded London streets and skyline. I thought of Hari, who distrusted punts, and, looking at them, I was inclined to agree with him. Who in his right mind would take to the river on an extended tea tray? I thought of Ganesh, whose wise words I needed but couldn't have now. It was too late to ring the shop and what could I do if he told me, as he surely would, to get the first London train in the morning?

By now it was about ten p.m. but there were still plenty of people about in the area of the Plain when I crossed it on my way back to the guest house. It was dark and lights had come on in houses. There seemed to be a lot of bicycles propped against walls. At the guest house there were no lights except from the basement flat where Beryl had her private quarters. My key let me into a silent hallway. The poodle didn't show itself. I could hear the soft murmur of voices drifting up the narrow twisting staircase which led down to the basement flat. Perhaps Beryl was listening to the television. The voices broke off and someone, a man, laughed. A female voice joined in. It sounded a lot like Beryl. Not television but a gentleman visitor.

In the hall was a payphone and on a shelf beneath an Oxford area telephone book. I took the opportunity of being alone to look up the Stallards' number and make a note of it. Then I went quietly up to bed.

I couldn't sleep. I switched on the bedside light and read the tourist leaflets. After a while I heard someone else enter the house and footsteps on the stairs and in the upstairs hallway. There was a soft whisper of American voices. Some of my fellow guests had come back. Then it was quiet except for the distant noise of a car circling the Plain and gathering speed along the Iffley Road. Once I thought I heard the poodle yap and found myself thinking of Beryl and how she must have removed her false limb to go to bed. I wondered if she was sharing her couch with her male visitor and if the missing lower limb bothered him. Presumably not. Or perhaps, because there are some strange people out there, he even found the absence of the limb fascinating, a sexual turn-on. Then I wondered how Jennifer Stallard managed to get Paul to bed and if they had any kind of outside help. There is more than one kind of lameness. I was crippled in my actions, unable to decide for myself what I wanted to do, and obliged to take direction from others.

I swung my legs over the side of the bed and took a turn up and down the room, trying to work off my restlessness. My feet took me to the window where I drew back the curtain and peered out.

The weather was clear with no suggestion of rain at hand, despite one or two clouds scudding about, creating darker patches like ink splotches against the cobalt blue of the city night sky. I could see the whole length of the garden and just discern the little door in the wall at the far end. The moonlight bathed everything in silvery grey and stroked plant pots and flagstones with ghostly fingers. The shrubs appeared as bold shapes but I couldn't make them out in any detail. Above the rear wall was a lighter fluorescent glow which came from street lighting. As I watched I fancied a shadow moved against that wall, beneath its canopy of creeping wisteria. I pressed my eyes shut and then opened them to stare harder, trying to focus on the spot. But I didn't see a repeat of that tiny disturbance in the still garden scene.

Perhaps, I told myself, it was just a night breeze rustling the foliage of the wisteria or a marauding cat. It could even be a fox. They ventured into the cities these days. Often, returning home late at night in London, I had surprised some unidentified beastie and been fleetingly aware of small shining eyes before their owner fled. The night only ever appears to be empty. I remembered Grandma Varady persuading me that cats and shadows and night birds were nothing to be afraid of, as I lay in my infant bed spooked by the cry of an owl outside or an unexplained rustle and tap at the window pane, and believing myself besieged by monsters. It took only a little effort of the imagination to see them out there, prowling around. It suddenly occurred to me that I was probably more visible at my window to any creature outside than anything lurking out there would be visible to me. The light from my bedside lamp shone behind me, silhouetting me nicely and revealing details of my room. It made me uneasy although I told myself there was no one there to care. I let the curtain fall, padded back to bed and scrambled in, suddenly grateful for the lingering warmth from my own body on the sheets.

I switched out the light and lay back, listening and dozing in fitful spurts. My brief brush with nature had alerted my senses. At night sounds are magnified and this was quite an old house. Wood moves in changing temperatures, old floorboards creak, window and door frames settle, there are a hundred different kinds of rustle, rattle, crack and groan. When these houses were built each bedroom was given a fireplace. Up in that chimney, now blocked off, birds were probably roosting and as they shuffled about in their sleep they disturbed ancient soot which showered down in soft explosions of pattering grime.

I wasn't the only person who was awake at this late hour. Above my head must be an attic bedroom. Someone moved about up there. Among the other creaks I distinguished the regular pressure of footfalls. Now that I strained my ears, I made out the faint background noise of voices from a television set. Whoever it was, was a night bird of the human variety. It was oddly comforting to think I had companionship, of a sort, in the small hours of the night. Was I hearing the remaining guest, the travelling rep? I doubted it. That couldn't be much of a room up there. If the business rep wasn't the male visitor who might or might not be bedded down with Beryl, then I guessed he had been given the large bow-fronted bedroom at the front of the building.

I made an effort to put all these things from my mind. Perhaps, I told myself as I finally drifted into proper sleep, things will go better tomorrow. There's always a first time.

Chapter Four

It's odd waking up in a strange place. In the end I had slept like a log, despite all my worries and my brief midnight watch from the window. I opened my eyes, wondering briefly where I was. My eyes focused on the awful picture of the crying child and I remembered.

I got out of bed and cautiously stuck my head through the door. I had no dressing gown and the baggy old T-shirt which serves me as nightwear is only just about decent. But there was no one in view. Other guests, it seemed, were up and about before me. The bathroom door stood open. I nipped across.

When I made my way downstairs later the hall was empty, but from the foot of the stairs I could hear American voices drifting through the open breakfast-room door. More sound of activity came from the direction of the kitchen behind me and, before I could join the others, a small chunky girl with a mop of untidy dark hair shot out,

83

fixed me with a challenging eye, and asked in a heavy accent, 'Full English?'

'What?' I said, taken aback. I didn't know by what radar she'd known I was there.

'Do you want full English breakfast?' she repeated impatiently and in a louder voice. 'Or Continental?'

'Full English, please,' I told her.

'Be with you in a couple of ticks.' Having delivered herself of this unexpected colloquialism, she disappeared back into the kitchen.

I carried on into the breakfast room. The couple there stopped talking, looked up, smiled and bid me good morning.

I returned the greeting and they resumed their conversation. They were arguing about where to go that day. The girl was round-faced, curly-haired and had a kind of small-town respectability about her. She was for getting a bus to Woodstock to see Blenheim Palace. The boy, studious and bespectacled, hair brushed straight back like a budding White House spokesman, was for leaving that until later in the week. He wanted to take the Bodleian Library tour. He would.

The power-pack waitress erupted through the door and put a plate in front of me. It was laden with bacon, sausage, mushrooms, egg, tomato and, oh joy, fried bread.

'There is not the black pudding today, I am sorry,' she said.

'This will be fine!' I assured her.

'Toast? Brown or white?'

'Brown, please.'

She vanished in her disconcerting way.

The American girl looked across at me and said seriously, 'The full English breakfast is really good, you know? You can make it last all day and it comes with the room, no extra cost. Imagine that?'

The waitress was back with a rack of toast. 'Tea or coffee?'

This level of service was disconcerting me. I asked for coffee. By the time I'd eaten my way through all this food I felt like taking a rest, even though I'd just got up. The Americans had already left, armed with maps and backpacks. They gave me brief smiles as they passed my table, allowing me to observe their perfect teeth. I think they'd decided on Blenheim in the end. I wished I had their energy, but they were setting off for a day of fun. I was about to set off on an unwished task. No wonder I lacked enthusiasm. I pushed back my chair and was about to leave my table when the breakfast-room door opened and the remaining guest came in.

He was a tall, thin, balding man in a lightweight business suit. His whole appearance was nondescript to the extent that had the room not been empty now but for the two of us, I don't think I would have noticed him. The only thing remarkable about him was a rather snazzy brightly patterned tie. He turned a pale, oval face towards me, scrutinised me briefly from behind rimless spectacles, and nodded before taking a seat facing the door. He shook out his napkin and tucked it in his collar, presumably to protect the tie. The waitress bounced in and greeted him.

'Good morning, Mr Filigrew.'

'Good morning, Vera,' the pale man said. 'Scrambled eggs with my bacon, please.'

'Right-o!' said Vera, who had obviously committed to memory some outdated list of English idioms.

I was prepared to exchange greetings with my fellow-guest as I passed his table but he kept his head well down and made like he didn't know I was there. That was his privilege. I climbed the stairs heading for my room and encountered Beryl on the upstairs landing.

'Good morning, dear. Sleep all right?'

'Fine,' I said. 'The breakfast was great.'

She beamed at me. 'Glad you ate a proper breakfast. I'm all for that. You can't last all day on a piece of toast or a croissant.'

'I see you've got an assistant,' I said.

'That's Vera. She's a good little worker. She's here to learn English, just for a year. I was happy to give her the attic bedroom and pay her a bit. Good arrangement for us both, really.'

Her words explained who had walked about above my head during the early hours and listened to television. Perhaps, like me, Vera was a fan of old movies.

'Where are you off to today, then?' Beryl went on but before I could reply she held up her scarlet-tipped hand.

'You don't have to answer that. I don't want to know Mickey's business. I asked it automatically. Nearly everyone who stays here is a tourist.'

'One of the guests looks more like a businessman,' I said. 'That will be the travelling rep, I suppose?'

She appeared momentarily confused. 'Oh, that's Mr Filigrew. He's a regular. Yes, he's in business. Stationery supplies, I think it is.' She patted my hand. 'I hope you get on all right.'

I hesitated. I didn't particularly want to take Beryl into my confidence but, on the other hand, she knew why I was here in general terms and I ought to warn her about the guy who'd followed me the previous evening.

'Someone might turn up at the door while I'm out,' I said. 'He's about twenty-two or -three, a sportsman of some sort, perhaps—' Inspiration struck me. 'Perhaps he rows; you know boats, oars and things. He's got good muscles on the upper arms, fairish hair, and a short straight nose. He may ask questions. I don't want him to know what I'm doing. He may even mention Mickey Allerton but you needn't worry Mickey about him, he's not a serious problem. I ought to tell you, just in case he shows up.'

She was nodding. 'I'll keep an eye open. But don't worry. I'm just the landlady. If he comes asking questions, I don't know a thing.'

I passed the open breakfast-room door on my way out. Mr Filigrew had finished his scrambled eggs and was buttering his last piece of toast with fastidious white fingers.

He glanced up, aware of my presence in the hall, and looked down again without any sign of recognition.

I set out briskly towards the centre of the city and, when I reached the spot on Magdalen Bridge where I'd paused the previous evening, I stopped again and inspected the punts from above while I decided what to do. The water lapped against the moored craft and they made dull clunking noises as the current caused them to drift together and bump. A couple of ducks swam past. It looked very peaceful down there. Beyond the mooring, the river banks were lined with trees and beyond them appeared to be a really big stretch of open ground, which was odd for such a central position in a city. Perhaps it was a park or land belonging to one of the colleges, I didn't know, and this wasn't the time to puzzle over it.

I had a straight choice. I could go to the Stallard home, ring the bell and ask for Lisa. Or I could call her on Ganesh's mobile first and ask her to meet me in town. By now, if she'd returned home last night, the chap who'd followed me would have contacted her and warned her I was here. I didn't want to run into him again if it could be avoided and I didn't want to involve Paul and Jennifer Stallard unnecessarily. All of this would make for complications. I decided to phone.

A woman answered the telephone and I asked for Lisa. There was a pause and I held my breath. Had my unwished companion of yesterday evening warned the entire family?

But the woman, whom I assumed to be Jennifer Stallard, was calling Lisa's name.

'Lisa! There's someone on the phone for you.'

The receiver clattered as it was put down on a shelf or other hard surface. More silence then the sound of someone running down a staircase. Voices murmured in the background. I couldn't make out much but I heard Jennifer's voice say, 'No, it's a woman.' The receiver rattled again and a younger, suspicious female voice demanded, 'Yes, who is this?'

'Lisa?' I asked.

'Yes, it's me. Who are you?' The voice rose with a nervous shake in it.

I tried to sound reassuring. I hadn't come here to put the frighteners on anyone. 'My name is Fran Varady and I'd like to meet you to discuss—'

Clunk! The receiver was slammed down so hard it was a wonder it hadn't broken. My eardrum gave a sharp pain of protest. This was the reaction Mickey had anticipated if he'd tried to call her. I rang again, establishing that the phone at the other end was still in working order. The handset was lifted at once for a split second and then hung up. She'd guessed I'd try once more and I visualised her standing by the phone, hand outstretched, waiting to cut me off. Communication by phone was out. I would have to go back to the house and hope this time to find her at home.

Well, I reflected as the bus rolled towards Summertown

taking me with it, plan one had only been a gamble. Plan two, direct confrontation, was always going to have been the more likely one to pay off. It's too easy to put the phone down, more difficult to slam a door in someone's face. Not impossible, but more awkward. Someone passing by might see you do it. They remember and wonder about it. They discuss it with other neighbours. I was pretty certain Lisa wouldn't want that.

A snag was that now, thanks to my phone call, she would guess I was on my way and be waiting for me. Or not. She might have decided to go out for the day and avoid me. But that would leave me free to chat to her parents and I'd already decided she wouldn't want me doing that. No, Lisa would be at home now, pacing up and down, getting up a good head of steam and ready to blast me away when I showed my nose.

Knowing that I would probably have to call at the house I'd made an effort to dress respectably. I'd unpacked the blazer and hung it up in the bathroom that morning while I had my bath to encourage the creases to steam out. The day would probably turn out too warm for it but as yet it was still fairly early in the morning and the woollen cloth bearable although I had to push up the sleeves to three-quarter length.

I wondered, as I walked down the road towards the house, whether I'd run into the Stallards' self-appointed guardian again. But there was no sign of him. I took a good look at the upstairs window next door but no curtain moved. I heaved a sigh of relief. He could, of course, be inside the house with Lisa. She might have called up reinforcements in the shape of last night's tail. It remained to be seen. If he was there, I'd have to get rid of him. There was no way I could talk to Lisa with constant interruption from him and I didn't see why I should include him, anyway. I'd come on Mickey's business and Mickey's business didn't include Lisa's white knight. I rang the bell.

The door flew open almost at once and she stood there, breathing fury. I knew it was Lisa because it would hardly have been anyone else glaring at me like that. She must have been keeping a watch and seen me approach. She hadn't called up any help. She didn't need any. She could handle me all by herself, she reckoned.

Even though I'd been expecting to see her, it still came as a shock. She was nothing like her photograph. She had been a name until now, and a problem, but not a flesh-and-blood person. Without the rhinestones, the mauve eyeshadow, the cute little cowboy hat and curly hair, this appeared a different girl. She wore jeans and a loosely knitted white sweater with purple flowers embroidered on it. The sleeves of the sweater were too long and covered her hands to her knuckles, which made her look like a child who'd borrowed something of her mother's to dress up in. She was quite tall, taller than me. I'm on the short side, as I think I mentioned. Her fair hair was long and only a little wavy. Mine's reddish brown and very short. Her skin was good; late nights and stage make-up hadn't yet ruined it. She had regular features, a rounded chin and widely spaced grey eyes. All of this I had to take in within a few seconds of her opening the door and only that short space of time was available to adjust my thinking and approach. She looked the perfect English Rose, a Nice Girl. A nice girl who was about to bop me on the nose.

'Hi,' I began a little nervously, 'I'm—'

'I know who you bloody are!' she snapped. 'You rang earlier.'

'Yes,' I agreed. 'And I'd really appreciate it if you'd let me explain before you slam the door or yell for someone else to come and chuck me out. I'm not here because I want to be, right? That doesn't mean I can be sent packing. If you don't speak to me now, I'll try again. So help us both out and just listen, will you?'

'Mickey sent you!' She jutted her chin at me. 'How did he know I was here? You can tell him from me to—'

'You don't have to spell it out. I feel the same way about him.' It was my turn to interrupt.

She hesitated. 'So why are you here? I know you've been hanging about.'

'Your friend told you, I suppose,' I said. 'The well-built fair-haired bloke who tracked me last night?'

She shrugged. 'You mean Ned. He told me about his conversation with you. I already knew about you because I was with Ned, in his flat next door, the upstairs flat, yesterday evening when you came here. You hung around on the other side of the road pretending to speak into a mobile.'

'Oh, right,' I said, feeling foolish. My little charade hadn't fooled her. 'I should have thought about that when he came after me. It didn't occur to me you might have been together.'

'We were only talking!' she snapped as if I'd suggested anything else. 'Ned's a very old friend and I told him all about—'

She broke off and glanced furtively over her shoulder. 'I told him how I came to leave London and that I didn't want to go back.' She had lowered her voice now. 'It's been difficult. I haven't had anyone to talk to. I needed just to be able to tell someone.'

I thought of Ganesh and the number of times I'd poured my problems into his sympathetic ear. 'It's all right, I understand,' I assured her.

She heaved a deep breath. 'It scared me, seeing you out there, I don't mind telling you. I just felt in my bones you must be from Mickey and I said as much to Ned. I really didn't know Mickey knew where to find me. I remembered that perhaps I'd let slip once to him that I came from Oxford. But actually to have someone there, first across the road and then at the door, that's something else. It gave me the creeps, like Mickey's been watching me, ever since I left London. Ned told me to calm down, although he was pretty wild himself. He followed you when you left to see if you met anyone. We were afraid one of Mickey's heavyweights might be hanging about at the end of the road. I didn't know Ned meant to track you right across town, even getting on the bus with you. That was silly of him. You were bound to notice. But Ned wouldn't think about that,' she concluded fretfully.

'Ned's a complication I think neither of us need,' I said bluntly. 'Can we leave Ned out of things in future? I'm here alone. I haven't brought any muscle from the club with me.'

She bit her lower lip and stared at me. 'I don't think you and I need to have any future dealings. I don't want to talk to you again. You denied knowing Mickey when Ned mentioned him to you, but Ned wasn't fooled and neither was I. You had to be lying. You had to have come from him. You couldn't have come from anyone else. Ned advised me to leave at once. But I couldn't do that. I knew you'd try again. I shouldn't have hung up on you when you phoned. I should have made an arrangement to meet you somewhere private. But I panicked when I heard your voice. I thought, stupidly, that if I refused to talk to you, you might go away. Of course you didn't. I realised that when I calmed down. You would be on your way here. If I wasn't here, you'd talk to my parents. I had to be here and head you off. Just go back and tell Mickey I'm through with the club and I don't want to hear from him again, right?'

She had run out of words at last and now stood, arms akimbo, flushed but with some of the panic she'd mentioned now visible along with the anger in her eyes.

I tried again to sound non-threatening yet businesslike, despite my earlier lack of success. After all, this was just a scared kid. I knew she was my age but there's a scared child hidden in all of us and it takes over when we least need it to. Lisa wanted to sound and be tough. Somehow it wasn't quite working.

'Believe me,' I said, 'I'd like nothing better but it's not so simple.'

'Ned said I should go to the police if you turned up again.' She took one hand from her hip and began to twist her fingers in a lock of long fair hair.

'And tell them what?' I asked.

Again she hesitated. 'You were harassing me.'

'I didn't know you were with Ned when he saw me from the window next door. So I hadn't even set eyes on you when I talked to him. I didn't send you any message via him. I hadn't then phoned. Where's the harassment? Unless you count Ned tagging along with me all the way across town to the Iffley Road and insisting on finding out where I was staying!'

'He was trying to help. Mickey's harassing me.' Obstinacy was now displacing any fear.

'I'm not Mickey.'

'You're Mickey's stooge!' The anger was back, redoubled.

The accusation hurt. 'I am not Allerton's stooge!' I snapped back. 'I don't work for him, right? But he asked me to get you to agree to contact him and until I do, he's keeping something of mine and I don't get it back. I want it back. Understand?'

'Sounds like Mickey,' she said gloomily. Some of the aggression had faded. 'He'd twist your arm and make out he was doing you a favour.'

For a split second I thought I might be about to make a breakthrough and get her to talk to me, but as bad luck would have it a door at the far end of the hall opened and a woman appeared.

'Lisa? Who is it?'

'I'm a friend of Lisa's from London, Mrs Stallard!' I called out before Lisa could speak.

Jennifer came towards us, smiling in welcome. 'Then why hasn't Lisa asked you in?'

'It's early . . .' Lisa said lamely, glowering at me. 'Anyway, Fran has to—'

'No, I don't,' I interrupted brightly. 'Not for ages.'

'Oh, well, if you've got time, do come in. We were just about to have coffee.' Jennifer smiled at me before she turned and trotted back down the hall.

Lisa drew in a deep breath and stood aside for me to enter. The aggression was back, emanating from her in waves. As I walked past her into the house she muttered, 'If you say one word to them about Mickey Allerton or the Silver Circle, *one word*, right? You're dead! I mean D-E-A-D! Got that?'

'Sure,' I said. 'I get it.'

*   *   *

The small back room into which I was shown was on the dark side and stuffy. Sunlight bathed a garden and the conservatory which had been built on to the rear of the house. But neither the light nor fresh air permeated in here. In the conservatory a man in a wheelchair, Paul Stallard, was doing something with potted plants at a shelf constructed to be just the right height to enable him to carry out his indoor gardening. Jennifer was out there and telling him something, about my arrival I guessed. He stopped doing whatever it was, wiped his hands on a cloth, and turned his head to peer into the room. But because it was darker indoors than out there, he couldn't make out much and he turned the wheelchair towards the open double door into the room. There was no threshold and he was able to propel himself inside unaided. Everything here had been arranged for his convenience.

'Hello,' he said. 'You're Lisa's friend. How nice to meet you.'

He held out his hand. I went to shake it. The skin felt papery and I could feel all the bones. I didn't know how old he was; I guessed not very, not more than in his late forties, but his features bore the stamp of premature ageing, wrinkled skin and dark-circled eyes. His neck emerged scraggily from his pullover. He must once have been a tall man but now he'd shrunk into himself, a propped-up puppet, his useless legs skewed to an unnatural angle.

'I'm Fran,' I said.

'I'll go and get the coffee,' Jennifer said brightly. 'Make yourself at home, Fran.'

I sat down in a sagging armchair. Lisa took a chair right opposite where she could see every move I made. She pressed her knees together and chewed at her right thumb, her eyes fixed on me.

'Why don't you go and help your mum, love?' her father asked mildly. 'Fran and I will be all right here for five minutes.'

Reluctantly she got up and went out. As she passed me she met my gaze and in hers I saw not aggression now, but pleading. I smiled at her encouragingly.

One of the reasons the room was so dark, apart from lacking direct outside light, was that it was lined with bookshelves packed tightly with every kind of book from paperback thrillers to solid-looking hardback books of natural history and theatrical biography. This is what Paul Stallard did when he wasn't messing with the potted plants. He read, immersing himself in worlds he couldn't visit.

'It's very nice for us to meet one of Lisa's London friends,' he said.

'It's nice to meet you both, too,' I returned. I felt a heel. In this closed, claustrophobic world, the arrival of someone bringing news of an existence outside the house made this a red-letter day. The stuffy air held a papery smell like you get in libraries and in addition there was the odd background odour that you always get around illness.

'Did you come to Oxford especially to see Lisa?' he was asking. 'She didn't mention it.'

'She didn't know I was coming. I've got an aunt here.' I plunged into the story I'd made up during my cross-city bus journey, in case I was asked for an explanation of my presence in Oxford. 'She runs a bed and breakfast place on the other side of Magdalen Bridge. I'm staying with her. I had an idea Lisa was home and I thought I'd just call on the off chance she'd be here.'

'Are you a dancer, too?'

'No,' I said. 'I'm an actor. But right now I'm between parts. Resting, as the acting profession calls it.'

He smiled. 'Lisa's resting, too. Not because she didn't have work but because she was working so hard she got really tired and a doctor recommended her to take some time off. She's always wanted to be a dancer, right from a tiny tot. Sadly she wasn't good enough to make the Royal Ballet or any of the other ballet companies but she's found good regular work in the chorus line, as you'll know.'

'Yes,' I said. 'It's good work.' Chorus line? At the Silver Circle?

'She's been in the chorus of several of the big West End shows.' Paul went on to name a couple of the biggest musicals currently running in London. 'We've never been able to go to London and see a show, of course. But she's told us all about it.'

'Right,' I said. 'Yes, I dare say she has.'

'She has a good singing voice,' said Lisa's father proudly.

'Her mother and I are always telling her she ought to audition for one of the main roles.'

'There's a lot of competition,' I said. 'Acting is the same.'

'What was your last role?' he asked, genuinely interested.

'It was in an adaptation of *The Hound of the Baskervilles*,' I said. 'I played Miss Stapleton, the villain's sister.'

He nodded, pleased at recognising the reference. 'I'm a great admirer of the Sherlock Holmes stories. In that one Stapleton uses his wife to gain Sir Henry Baskerville's confidence, giving her a false identity as his sister.'

He didn't know how closely this paralleled what I was doing here. 'That's right,' I said uneasily.

'How did you manage for the hound?'

'Oh, we had a real one.'

'I'd like to have seen the production,' Paul said.

I was rather glad he hadn't. It had ended dramatically, but not quite in the way Conan Doyle envisaged. Our play had ended in a dogfight. 'You know what they say in the theatre about never working with children or animals?' I asked. 'Well, it's true.'

Thankfully the two women returned then trundling a wooden trolley with the coffee and some sponge cake. They'd brought napkins and bone china. I was the guest of honour.

'Fran's been telling me about her stage career,' Paul Stallard said.

I opened my mouth to say that, actually, the play had been staged in a pub, but closed it again. Why dispel the glamorous image this wheelchair-bound man had created of a world away from this stuffy book-lined prison? Lisa wasn't the only one prepared to let a false impression of her career take hold here. She had encouraged the Stallards in their vision of their daughter on the vast stage of one of London's bigger theatres. I'd seen the cramped stage of the Silver Circle where she'd gyrated round her pole. There was no way these two existences could be reconciled. But it wasn't for me to destroy their serene confidence in what Lisa had been doing in London.

Coffee was poured, real coffee. I appreciated that. Grandma Varady wouldn't have allowed a jar of instant coffee in the house but, since I'd been alone, my coffee making had been of the powder and hot water variety.

'Have you seen Lisa on stage?' asked Jennifer Stallard.

The cup shook in her daughter's hand and the coffee slopped. Lisa mumbled and patted the front of her white sweater with her napkin.

'I'm afraid I haven't,' I said. 'I mean to, one day.'

'Perhaps Lisa could arrange for you to sit in on a rehearsal?' Jennifer went on brightly.

'It's not usually allowed to bring friends to rehearsals,' Lisa said sharply.

'So,' said Paul to me. 'What do you do, Fran, when you're not acting?'

I could have replied, I was sitting there and acting out a role right then. I said, 'I take odd jobs. I was a waitress in a pizza parlour. I work mornings sometimes for a newsagent near my home. I go to auditions. It's tough. Everyone wants to be a star or, if they can't be that, to walk on and speak three words.'

Paul chuckled. 'I used to dream, when I was young, I might be an actor. But I realised I didn't have sufficient talent. But I've encouraged Lisa in her stage career. She does have the talent. I don't just say that because I'm her father.'

'It's all right, Dad,' Lisa said unhappily.

He chuckled again. 'I'm embarrassing her,' he said to me. He didn't know the half of it. Now he set down his cup. 'Come out into the garden, Fran, and meet a friend of mine.'

He turned his chair awkwardly. Lisa put down her cup and went to help. She pushed him out of the room, through the conservatory and into the back garden. I followed.

I'm not a gardener, but I thought I might have been able to keep a plot tidier than that one. Long grass grew everywhere; in it were embedded lumps of rock and what looked to me like discarded junk. Buddleia, familiar to me from the sides of London's railway tracks, had set itself wherever it fancied and trailed purple, heavy-scented cones of tiny flowers from its twisting arms.

'The butterfly tree,' said Paul, indicating it. 'The blooms attract them. Lisa, take Fran to see Arthur. He's at home today.'

Lisa said nothing. She left the chair and walked through the long grass to a corner where a sheet of corrugated iron sheeting had been left on the ground. I followed. Lisa stooped and lifted the sheet.

'There he is,' she said.

I'm afraid I reacted badly. I hadn't known what to expect and when I saw it, I squeaked and jumped back.

'It's a *snake*!'

'It's only a grass snake,' Lisa told me in a flat cold voice. 'They're harmless. You don't have to be scared of it.'

'Lisa's right,' said her father. 'Arthur there is *Natrix Natrix*, the grass snake. They like to be around water and several of my neighbours have garden ponds which mean a good supply of frogs. Arthur is partial to a frog lunch.' Paul smiled. 'As yet, none of my neighbours has reported missing any fish from their ponds. But Arthur would be quite capable of taking one of those. The Latin name, *Natrix*, means swimmer. Grass snakes are quite at home in water.'

'I haven't seen one before,' I said. 'That's why I jumped out of my skin. We've got a garden behind the house where I live in London. I'll be a lot more careful now when I walk around out there.'

'You really don't have to worry. A grass snake would bite you only if it thought you were attacking it. The bite would be unpleasant but not dangerous. Adders are more aggressive and can certainly give you a nasty bite but again, only if you appeared to threaten them or surprised them. No snake likes to be cornered. Give it an escape route and it will slide away at once. Adders prefer heathland. If you find anything in your London garden it's more likely to be either a grass snake or a slow worm or blind worm as they're sometimes called. Slow worms are often wrongly believed to be snakes by the general public. In fact they are a legless lizard and aren't blind. Their eyes are very small but they are sighted. They are also able to blink, which a true snake, like Arthur there, cannot do. Also, like lizards, slow worms can shed their tails if trapped. You are unlikely to find a smooth snake, the other British snake. They are very rare.'

Arthur lay unmoving in the grass while Paul told me rather more about snakes than I wanted to know. He seemed unbothered by the removal of his shelter. He was tangled up like a pretzel so judging his length was difficult. Certainly he wasn't on the scale of the python the exotic dancer had brought to her audition at the club. Arthur, I guessed, would straighten out to be between eighty and ninety centimetres long. He was greenish-grey and shiny with faint barred markings and a yellowish patch at the back of his head. He wasn't my idea of a pet. I realised I was expected to make some comment but for the life of me I couldn't think of any way one could express admiration for this knotted length of living hosepipe. Nor am I into Natural History. Despite Paul's assurances, my experience has been that if there are things out there hiding in the long grass, they bite, sting or bring you out in a rash. I managed a lame question. 'Does he only eat frogs and fish?'

'Oh, no, any invertebrate, beetles and the like. They will tackle a mouse. I'm very pleased to have Arthur reside with us and like to show him off to visitors.'

'How do you know he's male?' Arthur still wasn't moving but despite that and being assured he was harmless, I was keeping my distance. His round black shiny unblinking eye seemed to be fixed on me in a sardonic gaze. Lisa was also watching me with a sarcastic little smirk on her face. She and the snake made a good pair.

'Partly by his length which hasn't increased in the time he's been here. Mature females can grow longer, up to five feet. What's that? A hundred and fifty centimetres in modern parlance?' Paul gave another of his faint smiles which I was beginning to realise did not signify mirth but rather an acceptance that there was a world outside his front door which had long passed him by and he could not hope to rejoin.

I was glad Arthur wasn't a female. He was already quite long enough.

'Besides,' Paul went on more briskly, 'I've never seen any young ones. Grass snakes like to lay their eggs in compost heaps because they're warm places. There are compost heaps a-plenty in surrounding gardens but I've only ever seen a solitary specimen, Arthur. That makes me think he is living a celibate life, all alone and occasionally receiving visitors. Perhaps that's why he and I have an understanding.'

Bitterness entered his voice. He hadn't intended it, but it slipped in there all on its own.

Lisa glanced at her father, concern showing briefly in her face, and then turned her gaze back to the grass snake. 'Dad's interested in wild life,' she said. 'That's why the garden is left like this.'

'Ah yes, the garden,' said Paul with that humourless smile. He indicated our untidy surroundings with a wave of his thin pale hand. 'The state of it distresses my neighbours. They complain that weeds invade their gardens from this one. I tell them that a weed is a plant like any other.'

At our feet, Arthur moved. Although I now knew he was harmless, the suddenness and dexterity with which he untangled himself was disconcerting. I stepped back automatically as the creature slid over the bumpy ground, heading for nearby tussocks.

'Take it easy!' Lisa said. 'He's aware of us and is getting nervous. They like to hide.' She lowered the corrugated sheet to the ground. Arthur had completely relocated himself and there was no sign of him. Never again would I tramp happily through the long grass in my London garden.

We all went back indoors. The rest of the visit passed in a haze of small talk and I took my leave as soon as I decently could. Jennifer pressed me to stay for lunch and panic entered Lisa's eyes before I regretfully refused, saying I'd promised my aunt I'd be back to have lunch with her.

Lisa saw me to the front door. 'Thanks,' she said quietly when we stood outside on the paved forecourt. 'You see how it is. My dad's got multiple sclerosis. My mum and dad never go anywhere. They've always been brilliant parents. They insisted I go out into the world and make my own way, do my own thing. They've never wanted to keep me tied to them. Mum could use my help. But she said, no, you mustn't feel you have to stay here. Dad was tickled pink about my wanting to work in the theatre. I was full of it too when I went to London. I had no idea how many other young dancers there were just like me. The first audition I went to, I found the queue stretched down the street. That woke me up with a shock from my dream world. Later, when I was broke and desperate, someone told me about Mickey hiring dancers. He paid well, they said, which turned out to be true. But the men who come to watch are just yucky. I got fed up and one day I flipped and walked out. How can I tell my parents the truth? They mustn't know about the Silver Circle. They had dreams for me and I've tried to make them come true. If the only way I could do it was by lying, well, that's what I've done. I've explained to Ned because he's the only person I can trust not to tell them.'

'You don't have to explain, really, not to me,' I urged. 'But you were foolish to let Mickey know where to find you.'

'How did he know?' She looked puzzled. 'Oxford's a big city and I never gave him my home address.'

'You told one of the other girls.'

She shook her head. 'No, I didn't. Which girl?'

'A foreign one who doesn't dance very well. She has long black hair and a liking for wearing pink. She told Mickey you had gone home to Oxford.'

'Oh, Jasna!' Her expression cleared. 'I didn't tell her a thing but I know how it must have happened. She took a parcel to the post for me once. It was addressed here. It was my mother's birthday present. I think I remember mentioning to her that's what it was. I'm surprised she made a note of the address but I'm not surprised she guessed that's where I'd gone and told Mickey. Mickey's always threatening to sack her. She's working here illegally. She's Croatian. She's scared of being deported. She'd do anything to get into Mickey's good books.'

'There's another Croatian, I think, working there,' I said. 'One of the doormen, Ivo, he's called.'

Lisa blinked. 'Oh, yes. Mickey hires all sorts. Jasna probably got him the job. I don't know. I know I was stupid to give Jasna the parcel to post for me. Working with people like that, it's best not to let them into your life.'

She sounded bitter. She realised she'd led Mickey to her present whereabouts by a simple thoughtless act of her own.

We all do stupid things. 'Look,' I said sympathetically, 'I really haven't come to make trouble. But I do need to speak to you. Can we meet somewhere private, like you were saying earlier?'

'You say you're staying somewhere near Magdalen Bridge?' she asked. 'Do you know where the Botanic Gardens are, just before you get to the bridge on this side?'

I nodded. 'There?'

'No, there's a better place. If you're coming from the Iffley Road, go over the bridge, past the Gardens, and you'll see a turning. It's called Rose Lane. Go down there and you come to some gates. They let you on to Christ Church Meadow. Joggers use it and tourists go there; no one will pay attention to us and there's so much space we won't be overheard. Go towards the river. There's a path along the bank. If you follow it you'll come to some stone steps going down to the water near a fork in the river. There used to be a landing stage there. I'll meet you there at ten tomorrow morning. I can't come before. All right?' She looked at me anxiously.

'You'll come alone?' I asked. 'I don't want Ned around. Where is he now, anyway?'

'At work.' She looked surprised at the question.

I ought to have expected her answer. Most people did work regular hours, after all. 'What does he do?' I asked.

'He's a dental technician.'

I blinked. 'He makes false teeth?'

'That's not all he does!' she retorted, nettled.

'Right, I just thought . . . He seemed more likely to be, well, I don't know, a teacher, perhaps?'

'What does it matter?' she snapped, getting stroppy

again. 'I won't bring him along. You needn't worry. I won't even tell him.'

I believed her. Ned was to her as Ganesh was to me. I could imagine Ganesh barging in if he thought I was threatened, telling me what I ought to do. She wouldn't tell Ned about our meeting because he'd insist on being there and running things.

'I'm not going back to London,' she said suddenly. 'Whatever you say, you won't persuade me to do that.'

'Mickey might settle for less than that,' I told her. 'Like a phone call and a talk.'

'Mickey never settles for less,' she said with a return of that cold flat tone. She shut the door on me.

Chapter Five

I can't say Lisa's last words hadn't made me nervous. I was only too aware that what Allerton really wanted was for Lisa to return to London. If she was right that he wasn't a man to settle for less than he wanted, I was in trouble. On the other hand, as he had indicated in my talk with him, he had anticipated I would have difficulties, not all of which I could reasonably overcome. I could only do so much. He didn't expect me to tie Lisa hand and foot, throw her in the back of a Transit van and drive her back to the Silver Circle. It did occur to me that if Lisa remained obstinate, Allerton wasn't beyond doing exactly that. But I wouldn't be the one required to do it. He paid Harry and Ivo for that sort of thing and probably several others.

In the meantime, as far as I was concerned, he would accept a phone call from her. It didn't seem to me an unreasonable thing to ask her to do. Lisa now understood that I wasn't prepared to leave Oxford and return to London and Mickey with nothing to show for my visit.

But I wasn't the only one under pressure. I'd met her family and seen for myself that she was in no position to argue with every suggestion I might make. She trusted Ned not to tell Jennifer and Paul the truth but she couldn't trust a stranger like me. I was reasonably confident I could persuade her to phone Allerton. What was said in such a conversation would be nothing to do with me. I'd have completed my task. I could go back to London and rescue Bonnie. I left the Stallard house in a fairly optimistic frame of mind.

There was Ned, of course, Lisa's friend but not mine. I hadn't seen the last of him. I was sure of that. But while he scored high points as nuisance value, as serious opposition I felt his score was much lower. Right now he was blamelessly employed in the dentures business and I told myself I could forget him for a while.

I went back to the guest house, let myself in with the key Beryl had given me, went up to my room. A little cart laden with cleaning materials stood on the upstairs landing. The door to the Americans' room was open and someone was moving about in there but probably not them. I was glad. I didn't want to run into them again.

I shut myself in my room and perched on my bed to phone Ganesh at the shop. He sounded relieved to hear my voice and asked when I was coming back. I told him things were progressing as well as could be expected, in fact rather better and, if it all went according to plan, I'd be home soon. I won't say I felt smug telling him this, but

I felt a certain satisfaction. It was nice to be able to inform him I was handling a tricky situation so well.

'I'm meeting her tomorrow morning early down by the river on Christ Church Meadow. We won't be disturbed there and can have a really good chat. I'll get her to see reason. What would it cost her to speak to the man on the phone?'

Ganesh did not sound impressed by my optimism.

'Why can't she meet you later today?' his voice asked fretfully. 'Why must you wait until tomorrow morning?'

'That's what suits her. She doesn't want to arouse her parents' suspicions and, besides, there's a friend she's keen to avoid have interfering. If she meets me in the evening the friend could find out, so it's better if she meets me in the morning. Considering the circumstances, she's being pretty reasonable,' I added before he could object. 'She and I together can sort it out, I'm sure. If I can just get her to phone Mickey I'm off the hook.'

'I hope so,' growled Ganesh down the line. 'I don't like any of this business. I don't like the story Mickey Allerton spun you. Tell him to do his own telephoning.'

'She'll hang up on him. That's why I'm here.'

'You're there because Mickey is playing some dodgy game. There's something going on, Fran, that you don't know about. Be careful, right? Be very careful.'

'Trust me,' I told him airily.

'Hah!' I gathered he didn't have that much confidence in me. 'By the way,' he said. 'I went over to that club and asked the bouncer, the bald one, if your dog was all right.'

I nearly burst into tears. 'Oh, Ganesh, you shouldn't have done that. Mickey wouldn't want you interfering in his business. He could get rough. What did he say?'

'He promised me she was fine. It seems his wife keeps a couple of pet dogs. She likes animals. They've got no kids. She took Bonnie to a canine beauty parlour.'

'What for? She didn't need a bath!' I said indignantly.

'Don't ask me. I just thought you'd like to know I checked on her.'

I thanked him again and asked him how the pink and yellow rocket was doing outside the shop. Making money?

'Not at the moment. It's bust. A guy is coming tomorrow to fix it.'

'How did it get to be broken?'

'We're not sure,' Ganesh said vaguely. 'There were some yobs outside late last night, after the pubs closed. They were horsing around. We think they mucked about with it and broke it.'

'What a shame. I expect your uncle is upset.'

'Oh well,' said Ganesh, I thought a little unfeelingly, 'if he wasn't upset about that, he'd be upset about something else. You know Hari.'

I became aware of a rattle and creak outside my door. There was a brisk knock.

'Got to go,' I said to Ganesh and cut the connection.

The door opened and Vera came in with her arms full of

towels. Behind her I glimpsed her little cart. 'I clean room,' she said firmly. No offer to come back later.

'It's not dirty,' I said. 'I don't need new towels.'

'My job is to clean. I clean,' she said.

It wasn't for me to be awkward and upset her routine. I left her to it and went downstairs.

There were sounds of someone busy in the kitchen, so I tapped on the door. Beryl opened it and, when she saw who it was, smiled and stepped out into the hall, pulling the door neatly shut behind her.

'To keep Spencer in,' she explained. 'He will jump up at people. Everything all right, dear?'

From the other side of the door Spencer barked and scrabbled at the panels. He didn't like being kept out of things.

'Everything's fine,' I said. 'But there is one thing I should tell you.' I explained that I had told people she was my aunt.

'I'm sorry,' I apologised. 'I should have asked you first if you'd mind. But I had to give a reason for coming to Oxford and I didn't want to mention Mickey. So I just said you were an aunt and I'd come to see you. I don't suppose anyone will check and find out I don't have any aunts. But I wanted you to be prepared for anyone mentioning it, if it happened.'

The person I had largely in mind was Ned, but I admit DS Pereira was lurking in my subconscious. It was a funny thing, but just as I knew Ned would pop up again, I had this nasty feeling so would Pereira, if only to wave me goodbye as I set off back to London. Pereira didn't want me on her patch. I made her nervous. She made me nervous. This is not an unusual situation between me and the police. We treat one another with distant caution. Even Inspector Janice Morgan, on whose manor I live back in Camden, and who is by far the fairest copper I've ever met, has a way of studying me every time we meet as if assessing my relevance to any situation she might be handling. It's as if I were some strange object found at a scene of crime and she's debating whether or not to drop me in a plastic bag and send me over to forensics.

Beryl was a trouper and took the news of her promotion to the status of aunt without a blink of an eyelid. 'Aunties and uncles aren't necessarily blood relations,' she observed. 'Old friends of the family get called that. That's me, then, an honorary aunt. I'll tell anyone who asks that I'm an old friend of your family.'

'Better say of my mother,' I advised her, 'I don't have any family so no one can check, but my mother, as far as I know, got around and knew a lot of people so it would be hard to disprove that you knew her. Thanks, Beryl.'

'No problem!' she said cheerily. 'I rather fancy being an aunt.'

She went back into the kitchen, closing the door again. From behind it I heard her say, 'Everything's OK.' Perhaps she was speaking to Spencer and there again perhaps she wasn't. I stood where I was listening for a few moments. I was rewarded with sounds of a chair scraping back and a man's voice, speaking quietly. I couldn't make out the words but I thought I could identify the voice. Mr Filigrew, the stationery rep, wouldn't be clocking up mega sales this trip, not if he was spending all his time hanging around Beryl.

I'd had a few twinges of conscience about using Beryl's name so her assurance was nice to have. Add to that, Bonnie was all right, even if she'd been given canine beauty treatment. I imagined her soft and scented and being fed best steak and chocolates. All this added to my general sense of wellbeing.

I now had a little free time. I ought to try and visit some of the city sights. By the hall telephone was a wooden rack with more of those tourist leaflets. I checked them over and was attracted by one which urged me to visit the Natural History museum. I hadn't forgotten my encounter with Arthur in the Stallards' garden and it irked me that I'd panicked and made a fool of myself over a harmless reptile. I'd shown myself to be lamentably ignorant about the world around us. Besides, Uncle Hari would be sure to expect me to have made some educational use of a visit to such an illustrious place as Oxford. It was already midday. I decided to have an early lunch and set out immediately afterwards.

I returned to the wine bar where I'd eaten the previous evening and despite the hearty breakfast at Beryl's I managed to make short work of a pizza. If nothing else, I'd put on weight during my stay here if I didn't do something to burn off the calories. I fished out Hari's tattered map again. He'd be disappointed if he felt I hadn't made sufficient use of it. I traced my way across Magdalen Bridge, up the High Street, through Catte Street, past the Radcliffe Camera to Parks Road and the museum. I set off on foot.

I had reached Magdalen Bridge when I was overtaken by another brisk walker and recognised Vera. She was carrying a cheap plastic briefcase of East European look.

'Hi,' I said in a friendly way.

She scowled at me and reluctantly slowed her pace. 'Hello,' she said, adding, 'Where are you going?'

I was a little surprised at being asked but decided that Vera was taking an opportunity to practise her English. 'Sightseeing,' I said. 'I'm a tourist.'

She gave me a doubtful look. 'You are not like other tourists,' she said.

This both annoyed and puzzled me. What was it about me that meant Pereira instantly identified me as someone she needed to keep an eye on and told Vera here I wasn't like 'other tourists'.

'Why not?' I asked her.

Vera shook her mop of hair. 'Not enough luggage,' she said. 'No guidebook in your room. You should have suitcase or big backpack. You only have little bag and not many clothes, also no camera or camcorder. All tourists have camera.'

'Hey!' I said indignantly. 'Have you been looking through my stuff?' I knew I'd played detective in the past but that didn't mean I liked the tables being turned and Vera playing detective among my possessions.

'I clean room,' said Vera defensively. 'I tidy.'

'Yeah, well, I travel light, OK? And I'm not interested in photography. If I want a picture of something I buy a postcard.' I decided to lob a few questions at her. 'Where are you going?'

'To library,' said Vera, holding up the plastic briefcase.

'OK. Where's that?' I asked. I wasn't bothered to know, but I wondered how far Vera would be accompanying me.

'In the Westgate Centre.'

'Beryl told me you're here to improve your English,' I said. 'Are you a student back home where you come from?'

'I am student at *filozofski fakultet* in Zagreb,' said Vera. 'If my English is good enough I can get good job, in export business or in tourist business. But I am not from Zagreb, I am from Split. My parents run a small restaurant. Before the war with Serbia we had many foreign customers, tourists, and now the war is over they are coming again. So I have seen many tourists and they are not like you.'

She seemed absolutely determined to make this point.

'Can't help that,' I said.

She gave me a sideways-through-half-closed-eyes look. 'If you visit famous buildings I can come with you. I too like to see these things.'

But I had no intention of lumbering myself with her all afternoon. 'That's all right,' I said. 'You carry on to the library. You've got better things to do.'

That gained me another scowl but she walked on and I dawdled until I was sure she was well ahead of me.

Speaking of postcards to Vera reminded me that both Hari and Ganesh probably expected some 'wish you were here' message from me. So I bought a couple of cards, scribbled a message on them and put them in my pocket to send off before I went back to the guest house. If all went well, I'd tie up things here tomorrow early and I'd probably arrive at the shop at the same time as my cards. But it's the thought that counts.

The Natural History Museum turned out to be housed in an impressively ornate building set back from the road. I crossed the dark entry, climbed a few steps and pushed at a solid wooden door, feeling I was about to breach the fortifications of some mediaeval stronghold, even if a Victorian idea of the Middle Ages. I peered in. I was faced by a huge high vaulted area with pillars and Gothic arches and an army of skeletons and stuffed things in glass cases. I sidled through and stood surveying it all with my mouth open. I was relieved to see there were other visitors here carefully making their way around, as awestruck as I was. I didn't fancy roaming around so many dead things all on my own. I followed their example and started off down one side with the intention of working my way between rows of exhibits. It was as I was rounding the skeleton of a horse that I came face to face with another visitor. We stared at one another. He spoke first.

'What are you doing here?

'Hello, Ned,' I returned politely and tried to step round him but he moved and blocked my path again.

'Look,' I said as patiently as I could. 'This is hardly the place for us to have a row. I don't want to talk to you. Please accept that and just leave me alone.'

'But I want to talk to you!' he argued, sticking out his jaw and flushing. He really was one of those people you just couldn't reason with. The expression is 'obstinate as a mule'. I thought it might have been coined for him. I'm pretty obstinate myself, in that if I decide on a course of action, I stick with it. But I do try and be a bit clever in how I go about things. Ned just had an object in view and went straight for it. What they call bone-headed.

'Not now,' I said. Not ever, actually, but 'not now' was less confrontational. See what I mean? You've got to work round an obstacle.

'Yes, now!' said Ned.

'Why aren't you at work?' I asked him, 'making teeth.'

His flush deepened to brick red. 'Actually I do high-precision work—'

'Ned,' I interrupted. 'I just don't care, right? It's all the same to me if you're in work or out of work, do the most fascinating job in the world or the most boring. You could be a – a trapeze artist or a polar explorer, I still wouldn't be interested.'

'I don't suppose you are,' he answered unexpectedly. 'I wouldn't be interested in you in any other circumstances. But I'm interested in Lisa Stallard and so are you and that gives us a common area of discussion, all right? So we do need to talk. If you want to know, I'm taking a late lunch. Our meeting seems sort of meant, doesn't it?'

'Spare me,' I begged. 'You'll be talking about glances across a crowded room next. All right, talk. I believe in freedom of speech. But is this really the best place?'

If I couldn't get rid of him any other way, then I'd have to give in on this point and let him say whatever he'd got prepared. I was sure it would amount to a sharp request to clear off out of Oxford and not come back. So if I had to let him say it, I would. It wouldn't make any difference. I was staying until I'd achieved what I'd come to do.

'I often come here,' he informed me. 'I work not far from here. I'm interested in bones and in teeth.'

He would be. 'I'm just doing the sights,' I said. 'I'm a visitor in the city.'

'I know what you're doing here in Oxford,' he retorted. 'And you're not a tourist. You're here from Allerton to make a nuisance of yourself.'

We were forced apart by a group of Japanese tourists at this point. When they had passed by, I took up our conversation.

'I wish you'd keep out of this,' I said. 'And so does Lisa.'

'I know Lisa better than you do!' he said angrily, a new red flush rising to the roots of his tousled hair.

A group of children in the charge of a capable-looking woman appeared and obliged us to step apart again.

'Look here,' said Ned. 'Like I said, I wanted a chance to talk to you. Let's go upstairs where it's quieter.'

I followed him up a wide flight of stairs in one corner and we found ourselves on a balcony running around three sides of the room.

'This is interesting,' said Ned, momentarily sidetracked. He indicated a glass box.

I went to look in it and, wouldn't you know, another skeleton, a human one lying rather crumpled on its side on a bed of sand. The legs were bent, the ribs partly collapsed and the head twisted to one side. I was reminded of the grass snake coiled up in a loose knot in the Stallards' garden.

'It's Romano-British,' said Ned with a note of enthusiasm. 'Look, you can see the teeth really well.'

'Some of them have fallen out,' I remarked, looking at a couple of molars lying beside the jaw on the sand.

'Excellent view of the roots,' said Ned. 'This is a young person, of course. The teeth are in excellent condition.'

'I suppose there were Romano-British dentists,' I said.

'Their teeth wore down,' Ned informed me. 'Due to the coarsely ground bread they ate.'

I turned my back to the display. 'Just tell me what it is you want to say. My name is Fran, by the way.'

'And you know mine is Ned, so that means you've

spoken to Lisa today,' he returned. He wasn't as dumb as he acted.

'All right, but I'm not discussing that with you.'

He looked away from me and at the skeleton in its glass box as if in some way he was happier addressing that. 'I know,' he said, 'what kind of work Lisa did in London.'

'It wasn't so bad.' I found myself defending her. 'There's worse. It wasn't illegal.'

'I saw the place, the Silver Circle.'

That took me aback. 'When?' I asked.

'Soon after she started work there. I was going to London on business. I asked Jennifer for Lisa's address so that I could look her up. I found her living in a horrible grubby room in a run-down council block in Rotherhithe.'

'And was Lisa pleased to see you?' I was ready to bet she hadn't been.

'No,' he said honestly. 'Not at first, anyway. I think she was embarrassed and afraid I'd tell her parents how she was living. But when she realised I wouldn't do that, she became quite pleased to see a friendly face. She was feeling really low. She hadn't been able to get proper work as a dancer. She wasn't eating enough. She told me that she'd just started work at a club, the Silver Circle, but it was temporary. She needed the money to pay her rent. She didn't have the whole flat to herself, just a room in it, but the rent was still pretty steep.'

'I bet the council didn't know the tenant was sub-letting,' I said.

'I tried to persuade her to come back to Oxford with me,' Ned said. 'But she still believed she could get real work. So I had to leave her there. But I made a point of finding out where the club was. I didn't go inside it. There was a bouncer at the door.'

'A square-built bloke with thinning hair?' I asked him, wondering if he'd encountered Harry.

'No, a tall, blond, mean-looking guy.'

Ivo, I thought. 'Did you visit Lisa again in London?'

He shook his head. 'I kept getting glowing reports from Jennifer about how well Lisa was doing, working in the chorus of all the big musical shows. So I thought things were all right, and she had found work and wasn't at the club any longer. Then, the other day, she came back unexpectedly to Oxford. She was in a bit of a state. She came round to my flat and told me that it was all a lie, everything she'd told her parents. She'd been working at the club all the time for an audience of boozy businessmen and perverts, but she'd had enough and left. Only the chap who runs the place, Allerton, took a dim view of that and he'd be sure to try and get her to come back if he found out where she was. She was terrified he would find out and when we looked out of my window yesterday in the evening and saw you talking on a mobile across the road, well, Lisa was suspicious at once. I told her not to worry, you were just someone lost and phoning for directions. But then later, after Jennifer and Paul left their house, we saw you come back and ring their doorbell so we knew then, you must be from Allerton.'

'Ned,' I told him, 'I know you mean well, but there's nothing you can do. I'm glad Lisa's got a friend to tell her troubles to. But that's as far as it goes. I don't like this situation either, but I've got a job to do. Think of it this way: it's better Lisa deals with me than with one of Allerton's musclemen.'

'I don't want her going back there!' he said desperately. For a moment he looked as if he was going to burst into tears.

'I'm not forcing her to go back. I just want her to make contact with Allerton. Leave it to me, right?'

'I don't know if I can trust you,' he said.

I told him brutally that if he trusted me or not was irrelevant as far as I was concerned. He seemed depressed but not surprised by my reply.

'I have to trust you, don't I?' he said dolefully.

'Ned,' I begged. 'Go back to work and fix some teeth, will you? I'm leaving here now, anyway.'

I walked off and left him at the Romano-British display. I had a feeling, as I ran down the wide stone steps to the ground floor, that swelling music ought to issue from behind the pillars, but there was only the chatter of children's voices and the click of Japanese cameras.

I found a post office and posted my cards and by the time I got back to the guest house it was late afternoon, I was hot and tired; I took a shower and collapsed on my bed for a rest before getting ready to go out and eat. I hoped that at least my encounter with Ned at the museum would have persuaded him to step back and let Lisa and me sort things out our way. But unfortunately this wasn't so, as I found out sooner than I could have anticipated.

I left the house around six thirty and there he was, lurking just down the road, leaning against a garage wall and looking so obvious I wondered someone hadn't rung the police to report a suspicious character.

'Now what?' I groaned.

He fixed me with a belligerent glare and folded his muscular arms across his chest. 'I've just called at the Stallards'. I knew you must have seen Lisa but I hadn't realised you'd talked your way into the place and met Paul and Jennifer too. They chattered about your visit as if it was the best thing that had happened in weeks, well, since Lisa came home, anyway. After what you said at the museum, I was prepared to give you a chance. But I was right the first time about you.'

'Ned,' I said. 'I can't stop you ranting on like this. But I'm pretty fed up with falling over you every time I go anywhere. Right now, I'm going to eat. You can come along and talk while I do, if you want. It won't get you anywhere. But I'm hungry and I don't see why I should stay hungry hanging about on a street corner arguing with you.'

He looked less belligerent and just a tad pleased with himself. He thought he'd won an important point. No, he'd won a minor one. He'd find out. We went to the wine bar where I'd eaten the previous evening. I had the Greek salad again and he had some pasta. Eating together has the effect of making people relax in one another's company, hence all those romantic dinners for two or business lunches. On both occasions people agree to things they might not in other circumstances.

I had agreed to listen to Ned but I hadn't agreed to do any talking. So I set about my Greek salad in silence and, after he'd pushed his pasta spirals around the dish for a while, he realised I wasn't about to speak and started himself.

'I'm going to be frank with you,' he began pompously. 'I want you to know that I think you and your employer Allerton are both slimy creeps.'

'He isn't my employer,' I said. 'I don't care what you call him. But I don't like being called slimy and, if you don't take it back, I will pick up that plate of pasta and tip it over your head.'

He believed me. 'OK,' he said hastily. 'I meant Allerton. It's probably not your fault you're involved in this. Lisa said Allerton has some hold over you.'

'He has but it's none of your business.'

'Right. I don't care what it is, anyway. I told you, I'm not interested in you. But if you won't leave Lisa alone and Allerton won't either, I'll go to London and tell him myself to back off.' He glowered. He meant it, the mutton-headed chump.

'Believe me, Ned,' I said earnestly. 'That wouldn't be a good idea. In the first place, you'd find it difficult to get anywhere near him. In the second place, one of his heavies would throw you out if you tried. They might just break your arm or your leg doing it.'

'He exploited Lisa!' Ned declared in ringing tones, gaining us some interested looks from a nearby table.

'She's a grown woman,' I said wearily. 'It was her decision to take the job.'

'She took it because she was broke and she couldn't get work in the legitimate theatre. I don't know why. She's a great dancer and she has a super singing voice.'

'So do dozens of others,' I said.

'The Stallards mustn't know. They wouldn't understand. It would destroy them. They're so proud of her. She's all they have to be happy about. You've seen how Paul is. He's an intelligent man who's a prisoner in that chair. Jennifer's life is spent looking after him. They mustn't find out.'

'They are not,' I said, 'going to find out from me. So relax.'

He'd been getting steamed up and turning red again. He did relax marginally at my words. 'I know it was her decision to take the job,' he said. 'But it's her decision now to give it up. She got sick of it. Allerton must accept that.'

'Ned,' I said. 'I understand how you feel but, frankly, your feelings don't come into this. Lisa can tell you what she likes about her job at the Silver Circle and how she feels about it and Allerton. But I've already spent more time discussing this with you than I needed to or Allerton would like. From now on, this is strictly a business matter between Allerton, Lisa and me. Got that?'

'What's Allerton told you to tell her?' he demanded, jabbing the fork in my direction and splattering tomato sauce on the table top. 'What's he threatening to do?'

'Sorry,' I said. 'My conversation with Mickey Allerton is privileged information.'

'What the hell does that mean? How can it be privileged? You're not a doctor or a priest.'

'No,' I said unwisely, but he'd been getting to me. I was fed up with listening to him lecture me and I wanted to shut him up. 'I'm a private detective – of sorts.'

It shut him up all right, for all of two minutes. During it he sat looking at me with his mouth open. I finished my salad while I had the chance.

'You told Paul and Jennifer you were an actress!' he burst out accusingly when he'd rallied.

'We say "actor" these days. I am, but, like Lisa, I've found it hard to get work. There are a lot of dancers, a lot of singers and a lot of actors. So I fill in doing whatever I can. Lisa took a job pole dancing. I don't know how to dance with or without a pole and I don't have her looks. So I undertake personal work for people.'

'How can you *do* that?' he asked, aghast. 'How can you snoop on people for *money*?'

'Oh, grow up!' I snapped. 'Perhaps if I knew how to

make false teeth, I would. I don't, so I earn a living doing what I can do. It's legal. And I don't snoop. I'm not that sort of private eye.'

'You didn't tell Lisa that, or her parents,' he accused. 'You didn't tell them you were a private detective.'

'Would you want me to tell them? Wouldn't they wonder why a private detective had come to the house looking for Lisa?'

He jabbed the fork at me again. More tomato sauce splattered on the table. He was a messy eater. 'I don't want you going to the house again, understand?'

Who did he think he was, handing out orders? I wasn't standing for that.

'I bet Lisa doesn't know you're here, talking to me,' I said. It was time to make it clear to him he wasn't getting things all his own way.

He blinked, hesitated, tried for nonchalant, but it didn't work. 'Lisa trusts me.'

'Not to handle her private affairs, she doesn't. That's why I'm not wasting another minute on you. I think we've said all we've got to say to one another.' I stood up.

'I was right!' he burst out furiously. 'You are just like your boss, Allerton, a seedy, slimy—'

I leaned across the table and tipped what was left of his pasta into his lap. He let out a howl. Heads turned.

'How dare you?' I declared loudly. 'You perv!' One or two people near us sniggered. Ned, purple with rage and embarrassment, floundered, mopping himself with his napkin and trying to smile placatingly at the approaching waitress at the same time.

In a lower tone I said to him, 'You can pay the bill. Call it the fee for my professional time.'

'Just you wait!' he hissed. The waitress was almost upon us now. 'I'll settle this my own way. I can play rough too. Allerton isn't going to pester Lisa, either through you or anyone else!'

He was mad but I was pretty cross, too, and marched off at a cracking pace heading back towards the boarding house. I hadn't gone far before I came across an incongruous sight. Mr Filigrew, still in his business suit, was progressing in a stately manner along the pavement with Spencer the poodle on a lead. Filigrew walked very upright, his head held high and his feet turned out like a dancer at the barre. He kept the lead away from him as if in some way dog and lead might contaminate him. Perhaps he worried about dog hairs on his suit.

'Good evening!' I greeted him. Spencer recognised me and began to jump about in excitement.

Filigrew turned his rimless spectacles on me. 'Good evening,' he said in a disapproving way.

'Walking the dog for Beryl?' I patted the ecstatic Spencer.

'Mm,' he mumbled, adding, 'taking a breath of air.'

I beamed at him and left him to take his constitutional. But my smile was strictly for his consumption. I wondered if and where anyone was walking Bonnie in the evening air.

* * *

Lisa and I had fixed to meet at ten the next morning. I had decided to set out early partly because I needed to find the place and partly because, when I did so, I wanted to take a good look round first.

Although I was early in the breakfast room, the Americans were there ahead of me, wrangling in their usual manner over what to do that day. There was no avoiding them so I went in and exchanged brief greetings. There was no sign of Mr Filigrew and even after I was all finished, he still hadn't showed up. As I left the house to make my way to the rendezvous, I checked the breakfast room again, but Filigrew's table was deserted and showed no sign that anyone had eaten at it. I wondered if he'd left already and was on his way to sell stationery in other towns or whether he was still there and breakfasting in private with Beryl. Possibly there was someone like Beryl in every town on his regular route. I fantasised briefly that he was a bigamist, married to some of these ladies. He was an unlikely looking sex symbol but those are the ones you need to watch. A certain type of woman falls for a man of mature years in a business suit and that flashy tie hinted at hidden depths.

It was a beautiful morning. The sun glowed against the honey-coloured stone of Magdalen College on the other side of the road to the Botanic Gardens. The square baroque building inside the gardens looked gracious if a little knocked about. There was a timelessness about the whole place. In any other circumstances I would have enjoyed being here. Perhaps, if I was lucky and Lisa agreed to speak to Mickey Allerton on the phone, I could wrap up my business here today and linger a little longer before going back to London. Not going round any more old buildings, I'd had my fill of that. But just sitting out somewhere nice and quiet and watching the world go by.

I felt a stab of guilt when I found myself thinking this. What of Bonnie? I had to rescue her at the first opportunity, not loaf round Oxford taking in the dreaming spires. But if all Ganesh had led me to believe was true, Bonnie was doing fine.

The opposite scenario to all this was that Lisa would refuse to speak to Allerton and I'd have to go back to London to admit failure. Things might not then turn out so well. Despite Mickey's assurance that the only retribution he'd deal out was to refuse me any further payment, I couldn't be sure he might not think up something nastier. I was sure he didn't like people letting him down. I still feared Bonnie might pay the price of my failure.

I found Rose Lane, went down it, through the metal gate and found myself on the edge of a huge open area of grass and trees and a fenced playing field, traversed by gravelled walkways. In the hazy morning sunshine I could see the roofs of the surrounding buildings as a distant fringe. That such a place could exist in the middle of a busy city shut away from the hustle and bustle and untouched by any development seemed amazing. But then I always think the same thing of London's parks.

The tourists had yet to arrive in any numbers and there were comparatively few people around apart from early-morning joggers. Two of these padded past me heading in the opposite direction. They moved as a unit, keeping step and panting in unison, holding their elbows out at identical angles. That and the Oxford connection made me think of Tweedledum and Tweedledee. A woman in faded jeans, a striped top and colour coordinated waistcoat – the sort of outfit which looks thrown together and actually costs a three-figure sum – walked a spaniel dog. Two more men of academic appearance strolled by deep in discussion. I followed the tree-lined path to the river and set out along it. It was amazingly calm here and very beautiful. Sunspots played on the rippling surface, dotted with leaves fallen from overhead branches. Waterfowl bobbed along as buoyant as corks, darting in and out of the reeds and vegetation at the water's edge. The trees rustled gently overhead and cast a shade which was welcome even at this relatively early hour. Already clouds of midges swarmed about my face. The only sound was that of my footsteps crunching faintly on the gravelled track.

I looked at my wristwatch. It was only nine forty, twenty minutes to go yet before my meeting with Lisa, if she showed up. She might have decided to cut and run as she'd done from London and be halfway across the country by now. I hoped she showed. I didn't want to tell Mickey

I'd made a complete mess of things. Besides, if she didn't appear, I'd have to call at her parents' house again. I'd much prefer not to do that, not because I worried about Ned, but because every meeting with Paul and Jennifer would require an increasing degree of mental agility to obscure the truth. So far I'd told them nothing that wasn't more or less true. Any more conversation with them and I'd have to start telling outright lies. From then on you have to remember what you've said. It can turn out tricky.

Ahead of me the river took a fork away to the left. Alerted, I kept my eyes peeled and soon came upon the stone steps. They looked solid enough but slippery and the lower ones were underwater. The boat which must once have been moored here had gone, but instead something else nestled against the bottom steps. The river caressed this object gently and the undulating current brought it momentarily up to break the surface hump-backed before descending again to be almost completely submerged, a hazy outline beneath the river's green veil.

I stopped, took my hands from my pockets and stared down in numb disbelief. The object rose again, breaking the surface, and there was no doubt about it. A human being floated face down in the river. The water streamed away from the white glistening shoulders. The legs still trailed down in the depths. I couldn't see the face.

I felt the blood draining from my cheeks. I couldn't move, frozen by an ancient innate terror at the sight of death. I was in a silent world in which no birds sang and the river ran without noise. I almost seemed to be someone else, an onlooker observing both myself and the object of my paralysis.

Then the blood rushed back into my face so that it glowed with heat. The birdsong returned, unnaturally loud. The gentle river sounds seemed those of a roaring torrent. Following numbness my brain went into a frenzy of activity, sending conflicting messages until my whole thinking process was completely clogged. I struggled to disentangle them. It had to be some kind of optical illusion, a mistake. This was impossible. Surely some prankster had tossed a dummy in there as a sick practical joke. Then, after shock and incredulity, my brain told me that at least it wasn't Lisa. She hadn't struck me as being the suicidal type but one never knew. This, whatever it was, real or not, but increasingly I feared it was real, was both too big to be a dummy figure or to be Lisa. For that at least I felt a spurt of relief. This in turn helped to steady me and enable me to take another look.

It – he – was almost certainly a man, a big bloke at that. His legs, clad in what looked like red silk running shorts, trailed in the water, his upper body wore a sodden running vest clinging to the skin. His arms were spread out to either side of him. His face was well down in the river, only the back of his head showing, covered with wet short-cropped blond hair.

I tried to persuade myself, although instinct told me it was untrue, that he wasn't dead. He was a swimmer. Why he should be swimming in the river in such an awkward pose, how he could breathe without snorkel apparatus, these things I thrust briefly to the back of my mind. Then reality hit and with it panic. I stumbled back and tripped over a fallen branch; my feet became entangled in it and I lost all balance, landing painfully on my backside.

The pain brought me to my senses. Pull yourself together, Fran! I ordered myself. I needed to call the police. I had Ganesh's mobile phone on me. Dial 999, that's all I had to do, and wait until help got here.

Then I remembered Lisa again. At any moment now she'd be walking down that riverside path towards me – and the thing in the river. She mustn't see it. She mustn't get involved, be a witness and have to make a statement to the police when they got here as I would have to do. Mickey would be furious and he'd blame me. Think, Fran, think! Call the cops. Then go back the way I'd come and head her off before she got near enough to see anything. I pulled out the phone and hesitated. Ought I to try and drag him to the edge, raise his head from the water? If he'd just gone in, he might yet be saved.

I descended the steps cautiously, crouched and stretched out my hand. Water lapped about my feet and suddenly, on the step's coating of green slime, I lost my footing. I had no time to save myself and, with a resounding splash, tumbled head first into the murky green river to join the drowned man.

The mobile phone slipped from my grip and sank to the

river bed almost without my realising it. I threshed about in panic. I can swim but swimming with a corpse was a new experience. Horribly I bumped against him. The body rose on the swell of the disturbed water, the face appeared briefly and I found myself staring into Ivo's dead eyes before his features sank back out of sight in the green soup.

I struck out for the bank and as I did I became aware of an approaching sound, a creak of wood and swish of water, signifying company. A punt was approaching, a girl sitting in it, the boy standing and manipulating the pole.

Seeing me struggling in the water he stopped propelling his unwieldy craft and I saw they were my fellow guests at Beryl's, the two young Americans.

'Hey!' the boy called out. 'You all right there?' Then he saw the partly submerged form beside me. 'How about your friend, is he OK?'

He realised this was a foolish question even as he spoke. He turned, passed the pole to the girl and was obviously preparing to jump into the water in some sort of rescue attempt such as had hazily entered my mind and led to my present predicament.

'Stay there!' I yelled.

The girl had seen the body now. She let out a piercing scream which sent the river fowl flapping away in panic. The punt lurched and swung round as she stood up. 'It's a body!' she shouted, pointing. 'Ohmigod, it's a body!' Then pointing wildly at me she added, 'What happened here? What have you done?'

Chapter Six

'I haven't done anything!' I spluttered at her. 'I fell in.'

'How?' she demanded, fixing me with a no-nonsense look.

It occurred to me she was a person who concentrated on details and managed to miss the big picture. Why did it matter how? There must have been a dozen possible ways and any one of them would do. In the meantime, I was floundering in the river with a corpse. But now the girl moved on with inexorable logic to how Ivo had fallen in. That was of interest to me, too. I'd be doing a lot of thinking about that. But later, not right now.

'Were you with him?' she pursued in her one-track way. 'How did he get there? What were you two doing, fooling around? You shouldn't do that, close to water. Don't you know an adult can drown in four inches of water? All you need to be is face down.'

I suppose I could have stayed there until I drowned too, just to satisfy her with a practical demonstration. But I couldn't be bothered with all these questions at a time like this and I didn't need their help to get myself to safety. I struggled to the steps and crawled out, soaking wet, smelling less than fragrant and feeling sick. I'd swallowed a pint of river water and I'd been sharing my unwanted bath with a drowned man. I staggered towards the trees and threw up violently.

By the time I was able to pay attention to what was going on behind me, the American boy had managed to get his punt to the bank. He climbed out and secured it and was talking crisply into a mobile phone. That made me realise I'd lost Ganesh's. It was down there in the water beneath Ivo and if the police searched the area of the river, as they well might, they'd find it and they'd trace it back to Ganesh. The girl had also managed to get ashore and was standing well back from the river edge, arms folded. Her look of dismay had been replaced by one of suspicious reproach, like my old headmistress when I was called up before her yet again for some misdemeanour.

You again, Francesca . . .

Yes, me again.

'Hey,' said the boy. 'You'll catch cold. Take off that shirt. You can have my jacket. Just a moment.' He knelt on the bank, reached down into his punt and pulled out a blue cotton top, handing it to me. She was all theory but he was a practical type.

I struggled out of my wet shirt, while he averted his eyes in a gentlemanly manner, and pulled on the jacket. It improved the situation but not much. The girl gave him a look which clearly said, 'You won't see that jacket again or, if you do, it will be unwearable.'

'I called the police,' he said. 'My name is Tom, by the way. I know you're also staying at our guest house. This is Maryann.' He indicated the girl.

Maryann was standing there, arms folded and still in inquisitorial mode. 'How did he fall in?' she demanded again.

She wasn't going to let it go. She had me tagged as prime suspect, that was clear. I decided that either she belonged to some fundamentalist sect which believed in public confession or she was a student of psychiatry and believed you should dig your secrets out of the closet and face them. What she'd be good at was playing one of those interrogators in thrillers who shine lights in captives' faces. It would be the sort of thing, I felt, which would come naturally to her.

'How the hell should I know?' I snapped back. 'He was in there when I found him.' I turned from her to her boyfriend, who at least had spared me stupid questions. 'My name's Fran,' I told him.

'What we have to do now, Fran,' said Tom with what seemed to me ill-placed confidence, 'is to secure the scene. We apparently have here an unexplained fatality.'

'Tom's dad is in homicide,' chimed in Maryann, fixing me with a grim eye. She said it as she might have said Beryl was in the guest-house business and Mr Filigrew in office supplies. Did she mean he was a hit man?

No, it turned out he was a detective in the NYPD, one of New York's finest. And yes, Tom knew all about keeping people from trampling the area and destroying evidence.

'Although,' he said, 'it's probably an accident.'

'Perhaps he was mugged,' said Maryann, still staring at me.

Now I had it worked out. These two were playing a version of good cop, bad cop. But even Tom had had enough of her techniques.

'Heck, Maryann, who mugs a guy in running shorts? Where'd he keep his wallet? He probably had a heart attack and toppled over. These guys who work all day in an office, they suddenly think they'll get fit and start a running regime. They don't monitor their pulse or anything. One day they're jogging along and—' Tom clicked his fingers. 'Over they go.'

'He looks kind of fit already,' said Maryann, peering towards the floating body with an expression of distaste. 'I think he was mugged. Probably the attacker was on drugs. He could be a homicidal maniac. Maybe a serial killer. Have they had any other unexplained deaths lately around here?'

'Maryann, listen to me, willya? These guys drop dead in Central Park all the time.'

While all this was going on, I was keeping a nervous eye open for the approach of Lisa and the police, though preferably not in that order. If the police got here first, they wouldn't let her get near the scene. Tom was right about that. This was an unexplained death and they'd secure the area as a first procedure. But I'd also been through this before. I realised everything would be frozen as they found it. Nobody in. Nobody out. That meant that if Lisa was already in the vicinity when the police turned up, they wouldn't let her leave. They would put yards of blue tape round everything, crawl all over the ground looking for clues and signs of a struggle and take statements until their little notebooks were all filled up.

If I was sure of anything at this moment, and I wasn't sure of much, it was at least that Mickey Allerton didn't want Lisa making statements to the cops. That was why I was praying the police arrived first.

Someone was coming, not uniforms but the two academic types I'd seen earlier. They were still strolling along deep in discussion. Tom moved to intercept them by standing on the path and spreading out his arms.

'Don't come any further, folks, there's been a little accident. Now it's nothing to worry about. The police are on their way. Just stay right there. Don't mess up the scene.'

Predictably, this didn't have the intended effect. Neither of the men liked having their conversation interrupted by a complete stranger and neither of them, from the look of them, was used to taking orders.

'Nonsense,' said one of them sharply. 'What kind of accident?'

145

'Somebody drowned,' called Maryann. 'He's in the river, there.' She pointed.

The academic gentleman took off his glasses and peered in that direction. 'Ah yes, I see. Pull him out. We should try artificial respiration.'

'He's dead, sir, I'm afraid.' This from Tom the ever-confident.

'How do you know? Are you a doctor?' The academic type was disposed to dispute.

A couple more people arrived and wanted to know why the path was blocked. They were told there was a body in the river. Voices were raised in a well-bred English sort of way. This was Oxford, after all. Oh, how dreadful! Where was it? Ought not we to pull him out and try artificial respiration? It was remarkable how long someone could be submerged and still be resuscitated.

'He was mugged,' said Maryann. Presumably she had reached this conclusion by her own lurid processes of deduction.

'We don't know that, Maryann,' said Tom wearily. I wondered if their relationship would survive this morning's events.

But she had successfully stirred things up and that, I reasoned, was what she wanted to do.

More people, tourists, arrived. Cameras whirred. Voices rose in a babble of tongues. The English ones demanded, What? Had the police been called? This was a very quiet area. Muggings were almost unknown. Where was the mugger? Someone then observed me, standing damply to one side. Who was the other young woman? Had she also fallen in the water? She looked rather wet.

'We ought to pull him out and try and resuscitate him.' This was the first man, ignoring the questions raining in from all angles. Whatever Maryann thought of me, he obviously considered I was of no importance whatsoever. 'There is, of course, always a possibility of brain damage after a certain time. Speed is of the essence.'

There was a murmur of agreement although no one seemed disposed to leap in the river and manhandle the body ashore. As for me, whatever passing interest I had provoked in the crowd, it had been displaced. One soggy female couldn't be expected to hold the attention in the way a genuine corpse could.

'He probably had a heart attack.' Tom was sticking to his guns. I also suspected that he wasn't going to relinquish his role of Person in Charge without a fight. The academic gent responded with alacrity.

'Young man, you seem very fond of giving medical opinions. I ask you again, are you qualified as a doctor?' The academic gentleman had metaphorically rolled up his sleeves. He resented Tom taking charge. That, he clearly felt, was his role in life.

'No, sir, I'm a computer—'

'Oh, really? Studying computers? At *this* university?'

'No, sir, at—'

'Oh, *not* at this university. A pity. Which university? Oh, an American one. I see.'

The crowd was increasing. Considering there had been so few people about when I'd arrived earlier, now they were coming from all directions and were growing ever more excitable and fractious. Tom, like Horatius on the bridge, kept them all back.

At that moment my searching gaze landed on Lisa. She had joined the fringe of the crowd and was standing there, her mouth open in puzzled dismay. I managed to catch her eye and frowned ferociously at her. She got the message and melted away. I heaved a sigh of relief. It wasn't a moment too soon. The police had arrived.

There were two of them. They were surrounded in an instant by a jabbering crowd of helpful onlookers. A couple of the women in the crowd decided it was the moment to become upset. One of them burst into tears, her bosom heaving melodramatically. Her friend, clearly annoyed that she hadn't managed to burst into tears first, led her to one side with a consoling arm round her shoulders.

'Quite so, my dear,' said the academic gentleman to the lady with the heaving bosom. 'Feeling faint, I dare say. Sit down and put your head between your knees.'

She stopped sobbing long enough to give him a remarkably dirty look. I left them to it and went to sit down on a convenient log. One of the officers took off his boots and jacket and lowered himself into the water. He pulled Ivo to the bank, as I'd hoped to do, and with the help of his partner got him ashore.

An ambulance was now bouncing its way towards us

across the grass. The police were trying to sort out who had been on the scene when the body was found and who had just turned up later. They got rid of the sightseers with the exception of the academic gentlemen, the talkative one of whom insisted he was allowed to make a statement about being prevented from trying artificial respiration on the deceased by a person qualified only in computers.

They promised they'd talk to him in a minute.

'Who found him?' the drier of the coppers asked, staring at Tom and Maryann. 'Was it you?'

'She says she did,' said Maryann, pointing at me. Though fond of giving her opinion she was shy of taking responsibility. There are a lot of people like that.

'This is Fran,' said Tom in his chivalrous way. 'Come right over, Fran, and tell the officer what you saw.'

Step right up, little lady, and take part in our show.

'Your name is, miss?'

'Fran Varady. I'm just a visitor to the city. I'm staying at the same guest house as Tom and Maryann. I was walking along the path here and I saw him in the water.'

'She isn't with us. She was in the water with him,' said Maryann immediately. 'She wasn't on the path like she said. She was right there in the water up to her neck. She was by the body, up real close, and manhandling it.'

'I fell in!' I fairly yelled at her. I turned to the police officers. 'I thought if I could grab his ankle I could drag him up the steps there, sort of rescue him. I know it was daft. I lost my footing on the steps and fell in. I was going to call nine-nine-nine. I had my mobile phone in my hand.'

'She didn't have a cellphone in her hand when we came by,' said Maryann. Had I done something before this morning to upset her? I wondered.

'Look,' I snapped. 'I dropped it when I fell in. It's down there somewhere at the bottom of the river. I was floundering in the water when Tom and Maryann came along in their punt.'

'I thought it seemed kind of odd, seeing someone swimming about in the river like that, fully clothed and so early in the morning,' declared Tom in a masterpiece of understatement. 'But I recognised Fran. I called out to ask what was wrong and then I saw the John Doe there.' He indicated Ivo over whose still form two paramedics were now crouched.

'He would not allow us to attempt artificial respiration,' boomed the academic man from a few feet away. 'Now, of course, it's far too late.'

'Fran?' asked a voice at my elbow.

It was DS Hayley Pereira. My troubles were complete.

Pereira drove me back to the guest house. Beryl met us in the hall and after a first startled look, only said, 'You'd better get out of those wet trousers, love. Had a bath you didn't want?'

'I fell in the river,' I said.

Pereira had me by the elbow. She gave me a little push. She didn't want me discussing what had happened with anyone until she'd talked to me first. 'Where's your room?'

'Upstairs, at the back,' I said. 'I'll go and—'

She acted on my information and ignored what I'd been about to add. She was coming too. We got upstairs to my room in record time.

'Do you have a change of jeans?'

'Yes,' I said, annoyed. 'I have a change of clothing. You sit there if you want.' I pointed to the chair with arms, 'I'll go and change in the bathroom.'

She hesitated.

'Oh, do me a favour!' I exploded, even angrier. 'Let me get out of these wet things before I catch pneumonia? What's your problem? I'm not carrying any banned substances. Look!' With an effort I pulled my soaked jeans pockets inside out. I also pulled off Tom's jacket, which left me in my bra, and tossed it on the bed. 'You can take a look in that, but it belongs to Tom, the American, and if you find anything in there, it's his. Although I had my hands in the pockets and they're empty. Anyway, he's the type who, if he ever did smoke anything, didn't inhale. I can't contact anyone because I haven't got a mobile phone. It's in the river. If you find it, it's registered to Ganesh Patel, the friend who lent it to me. I'll leave the door of this room open and you can see the bathroom, right across the corridor. I can't slip out.'

'OK,' she said smoothly. 'But leave the door open, both doors.'

I stomped away in a bad temper, ostentatiously pushing both bedroom and bathroom doors open to their fullest extent and wedging them. I wondered, if I couldn't shut myself in the bathroom, whether I could position myself out of her direct line of sight. But that was difficult. There was a mirror hanging on the wall right opposite the door and she could probably see me wherever I stood. The best I could do was turn my back to her as I peeled off my sodden jeans with great difficulty and got into dry ones. I also pulled a clean T-shirt over my head. I rubbed my hair with a towel and peered in the mirror. I looked like something that had been dragged up from the river bed. Heck, I *had* dragged myself up from the river bed. Over my shoulder, I could see Pereira back in my room, perched on the chair I'd offered her, with her ankles crossed like they told us to do at the private school for young ladies I went to. It made me wonder where Pereira had gone to school. Her face was expressionless but her eyes were fixed on me. No way was I getting the chance to drop anything down the lavatory pan or conceal it behind the cistern.

'How are you feeling, Fran?' she asked kindly when I got back. She'd decided for the sympathetic approach having realised I was pretty nervy.

'Like I nearly drowned and I've been eyeball to eyeball with a dead bloke,' I snarled.

'Shall I ask the landlady for some tea?'

'I don't want tea!' I growled ungratefully and plumped myself down on the edge of the bed.

'Can you tell me about it?'

I do so hate it when the police are being nice to you. They adopt a friendly, cosy tone which isn't reflected in their eyes. I'd rather they just behaved like their usual surly selves.

'Yeah,' I mumbled.

She took out a notebook and pen. She was going to write it down.

I'd had time in the bathroom to put together a sort of story which I'd stick to. I began it with, 'On my walks from here into the town centre I've been going over Magdalen Bridge and I noticed there was this big sort of park area behind it. So this morning, I thought I'd go down there and have a look round.'

Pereira didn't say anything, just scribbled in her book.

'I found the river path and I was walking along that. It was nice, very quiet.'

'You didn't see anyone else?' She looked up and raised her eyebrows, pen poised.

'No, not on the path. I saw some people earlier when I came through the gate at the end of Rose Lane. There were some joggers but they were heading away from the river. There was a woman with a dog and two men who came along the riverside path later after I'd found – found it. One of them later insisted on speaking to the police because Tom, that's the American, hadn't let him try artificial respiration. Well, I don't think he was offering to do it. I think he wanted someone else to do it. But Tom said the man in the water was certainly dead. I think he was right.'

'Oh?' Pereira said. 'What made you think he was beyond resuscitation?'

'Because I had some crazy idea of trying to drag him out although I probably couldn't have done it. But I fell in, trying to catch his legs from the stone steps there. I splashed about and the – the body rocked in the water. His head came up and I saw his face. His eyes were open and sort of glassy. I reckoned he was dead. Then Tom and Maryann came along in their punt.'

'Yes, the two young Americans. I'll have to talk to them next.'

'Well, that's it, then,' I said. 'Tom took over. His father is an officer in the homicide department of the New York police.'

'Is he, indeed?' said Pereira wearily. I supposed people who reckoned they knew the drill ended up causing more problems than those who knew they were amateurs.

'Tom gave me his jacket so I could take off my wet shirt.'

Pereira handed me her notebook. 'Can you read that through and, if you agree with it, sign it?'

I took the little book, scanned my statement and scrawled my name at the bottom.

She took it back and looked at it. 'Varady?' she said.

'It's Hungarian.'

'Mine's Portuguese,' she said. 'Nobody knows how to spell it.'

'Nobody knows how to pronounce mine,' I said. 'They say Var*ady*. It's *Var*ady.'

'Nor mine. I've been advised to change it but I don't see why I should.'

She gave me a sympathetic grin inviting me into the club of those who struggle with the burden of a foreign surname. I wasn't joining it.

'Up to you, I suppose,' I said.

'Right,' she returned briskly, knowing she'd been rebuffed. 'I need a permanent address for you. That will be in London?'

I gave it to her.

She sat back and looked at me thoughtfully. I waited for her to ask the question I dreaded which was, had I recognised the dead man? But she didn't. If she had I would have told her I didn't know him even though that would have put me in the position of telling a lie. Although I can lie with confidence if I need to – my dramatic training, you know – if in some way she later found out, I'd be for it. But if I confessed I knew Ivo, I'd have to explain how and why and when and bring Lisa into it. The fat would be in the fire and Allerton would be longing to turn me on a spit over it. What was it the Greek sailors found themselves between? The whirlpool and the moving rocks, Scylla and Charybdis, that's it. A good education always throws up these useless nuggets of information at inappropriate moments.

Then I thought, why should she ask if I knew him? I was a stranger in Oxford, she knew that. The dead man hadn't been identified and there was as yet no reason to suppose he wasn't a local keep-fit enthusiast. Nor had she any reason to suppose his being in the river was anything but an accident. He'd collapsed while jogging, possibly with the heart attack Tom had wished on him. Perhaps, I thought wistfully and I feared in vain, it would be put down as an accident at a future coroner's inquest. But not if they couldn't identify him. Then it would start to look suspicious. If he lived in Oxford, someone ought to notice he wasn't there and come forward to report him missing, even claim the body. A totally unidentifiable man in running kit floating in the river, that's weird. Where were the rest of his clothes? I frowned. Ivo couldn't have travelled down from London early that morning in running shorts, surely?

The whole thing stank nearly as badly as I must do. I couldn't see it being an accident myself. Not with the dead body being Mickey Allerton's doorman. What on earth was Ivo doing in Oxford? Had Mickey sent him along to watch over me? Ganesh had been right, of course. Mickey hadn't told me the entire story. There was something going on and I was in the middle of it like a woman lost in thick fog. Once I got rid of Pereira, I would need to do some serious orienteering.

Instead of the question I'd feared, Pereira asked, 'The two joggers you saw when you came from Rose Lane on to Christ Church Meadow – they were jogging away from the river, you say?'

'Yes, but I didn't mean they'd come immediately from the river. I was just indicating the direction they were taking, jogging away from me down the gravel drive towards the town in the distance. I don't know where they'd been before that.'

'Hm,' she tapped the notebook with her pen. 'Can you describe them?'

'Not really. They were youngish. Both white male, of middle height and both fairly stocky in build. They wore running shorts. I only saw them from the corner of my eye and didn't pay that much attention. I can't even be sure they were young. I didn't look at their faces. They jogged like young men, bouncing along full of beans. Not like older ones, making hard work of it.'

A smile played across her face for a second and I wondered if my last words suggested someone to her. She made a note. I could see where her mind was headed. She needed to find people who had seen the dead man before he went in the river, probably running. The joggers were obvious as possible witnesses if they could be tracked down. I began to wonder about them, too. I wish I'd paid more attention to them. I didn't think Ivo had fallen in the river all by himself. Nor did I subscribe to the theory he'd had a heart attack. As for mugging, if a mugger had tackled

Ivo, he'd soon have found out his mistake. He would have been the one found floating in the water. What kind of person could take on Ivo in a physical confrontation and come out the winner? Someone who was as strong as he was, obviously. Or someone who was . . .

Pereira was speaking again. She had folded her notebook and tucked it away in her black leather shoulder bag. She wasn't wearing her short skirt and cherry-red jacket today, perhaps that was London wear. She wore what looked like designer jeans, a peacock-blue top and expensive trainers. The only other policewoman with whom I had any close acquaintance, Inspector Janice Morgan back in London, dressed like a bereavement counsellor. It was a pity Morgan couldn't adopt some of Pereira's style. But if they dressed differently, their minds worked much the same way.

'You know, Fran,' said Pereira, rising to her feet. 'I can't help feeling that you're not keen for me to know your business.' (Translate as: you are holding out on me.)

'Should I be?' I snapped.

She shrugged. 'No. But I sense more than usual reserve. Did you find your friend?'

Heck. I remembered telling her I'd come to Oxford to track down a friend.

'No,' I said. 'I thought she might be staying at this guest house but she wasn't. But as I'd come, I decided to stay on for a few days and see the sights.'

'And have you?' asked Pereira. 'Seen the sights?'

'I went to the Natural History Museum yesterday,' I was able to tell her with perfect truth.

'Oh? That's an interesting place. What did you like about it? Anything in particular among the exhibits?'

I gave her a tired look because I'd be daft if I didn't know she was checking on what I'd told her. 'The architecture of the place is pretty eye-catching,' I said, 'all those Gothic arches. There was a very interesting Romano-British skeleton in a glass display box on the upper gallery. But I didn't know I'd end up seeing another body today. I didn't expect that to be one of the sights of Oxford. Perhaps it would have been better if I'd gone home when I didn't find my friend.' It still sounded thin. But it was the best I could come up with. I hoped I wasn't asked to explain my deep interest in Natural History.

'Don't go home, will you?' she said. 'Not without letting me know.'

'I can't hang around waiting for an inquest,' I objected.

'Of course not. You must have a job to go back to.'

'I'm an actor,' I said. 'I'm resting. I was working as a pizza waitress but the restaurant folded.'

'That's a pity,' she said. 'An actor? So if you're between acting roles, you must be willing to take almost any job going.'

'I'm working part-time in a newsagent's.'

'And yet you have enough money to come on holiday to Oxford?' She raised an arched eyebrow.

'I'm not broke,' I said. 'I told you, I was working.'

'Living in London is expensive, though.' She wasn't giving up.

'I live in a place with a controlled rent,' I returned. 'The house belongs to a charity.'

'You're lucky,' she said, I thought sarcastically.

'Not really,' I muttered. Some luck.

She decided to let me off the hook for the time being. 'I just need you to stay around, if you can, until I complete my inquiries. It ought not to take long.'

I thought she was leaving, but at the door she paused and looked back. 'We do have a drugs scene in Oxford, Fran, but we work hard at tackling it.'

'Leave it out, will you?' I shouted at her. 'I'm not a druggie and I'm not a pusher!'

'That's all right, then.' She smiled at me and was gone.

I didn't know whether to laugh or cry. She suspected I might be in Oxford on dodgy business and thought I was some sort of runner for a drug baron. She'd seen my request to change in the bathroom as a ploy to empty my little packs of white powder down the loo. But she didn't have grounds yet to search me or my belongings. I just hoped that, when they got Ivo on a slab down at the morgue, they didn't find any puncture marks in his arms. Pereira would be back here like a greyhound out of the trap. It's not much fun being the rabbit.

Chapter Seven

As luck, or the lack of it, would have it, Pereira had barely left my room and started on her way downstairs when Tom and Maryann returned to the guest house. They must have met up in the hall because I heard their voices and Pereira's in conversation. Pereira was introducing herself, offering her ID. Tom was protesting they had already made statements.

Pereira uttered those words beloved of coppers. 'Just a couple of points, sir. It won't take a moment.'

'Yes, but we . . .' Maryann joined in.

Abruptly the sound of their wrangling was cut off and at the same time I fancied I heard a door shut. I ventured out of my room and hung over the landing banister. The hallway below was now empty and silent, the only movement that of the dust particles dancing in the shaft of light entering through the transom window above the front door. The air held the lingering odour of breakfast bacon overlaid with lavender room freshener and a whiff

161

of small dog. Through the closed breakfast-room door I could again hear the murmur of speech, although much as I strained my ears I couldn't make out any words. Prudence advised against creeping downstairs and listening at the door. I felt sure Pereira had all the instincts of a natural hunter and would know I was there, however careful I was.

I guessed Tom and Maryann were repeating their version of events at Pereira's request. That meant Tom would be giving his view of it and Maryann was probably interrupting at intervals to accuse me of being a violent mugger. I thought wryly that Pereira hadn't brought them upstairs to their room as she had me to mine. She didn't want them walking into me.

I went back to my room and lay down on the bed. I was exhausted. My limbs were weak and felt disjointed. I must have resembled a puppet whose strings had snapped. I didn't know how I was going to get out of this. I didn't know if or when they'd identify Ivo. I forced the image of his floating corpse into my mind although my deepest wish was to blank it out. I strove for any tiny detail which might give me a clue. All I could remember was that he'd worn shorts and a cotton top. I couldn't recall seeing any jewellery like a chain and medallion round his neck, or one of those identity bracelets, anything distinctive. It could take a long time before they found out who he was and by then I'd be back in London. They couldn't keep me here indefinitely. In theory, they couldn't keep me here at all.

They had my London address. They'd check it out, of course they would. But once they confirmed it was all in order, well, there was nothing to stop me leaving.

Except that I hadn't done the job Mickey Allerton had sent me here to do. I'd met Lisa, I'd spoken to her, and she knew I came from Allerton. But I'd yet to persuade her at least to call him. I reckoned there was no chance of persuading her back to London.

I pushed myself up to a sitting position, dragged the pillows into a mound behind my back and tried to work out some plan of action. Did I go looking for Lisa? Or, in the circumstances, did I stay away? Did I phone her? She'd seen the crowd and she'd got my telegraphed message to clear off out of it, but had she learned from a bystander why the crowd had gathered? That a body had been discovered? Even if she had been told, she hadn't been near enough to see it. She couldn't know it was Ivo. Did I tell her? She'd freak out if I did. She'd bolt away from Oxford and I'd never find her.

There was a tap at my door, heralding Beryl with a steaming mug of tea and some chocolate biscuits. 'For shock,' she said briskly. 'When the Americans came back, they said you'd found a body in the river. Shame,' she added thoughtfully. 'Bloody nuisance, that.'

'Too right, Beryl,' I agreed. Her use of the word 'nuisance' showed that she had her priorities in strict order and I wasn't first on the list. Mickey Allerton was. She knew I was here on his business and a police inquiry would not be welcomed by him. Any inconvenience to me personally was a secondary issue. Not that Beryl lacked sympathy for my plight, as the tea showed. I was glad of it, despite having refused Pereira's offer to fetch some.

Beryl put the tray on my bedside cabinet. 'Eat the biscuits. The sugar's good for shock and chocolate gives you a boost,' she ordered.

'I will,' I promised, 'thanks. Beryl, I need to contact Mickey Allerton. I've lost my mobile phone. I don't want to use the public phone in your hall. I can go uptown and find a kiosk . . .'

She shook her burnished auburn helmet of hair. 'No, no need. When the copper's gone, come down to my flat and use the phone there.' She stared at me thoughtfully and sat down on the chair vacated by Pereira, her false leg stuck out awkwardly in front of her. I realised how difficult it must have been for her to bring the snack upstairs for me and felt embarrassed as well as grateful.

'Listen, dear,' she said, 'I'm not asking your business or Mickey's. All I'm asking is, the phone call you want to make to Mickey, is it about your finding this dead bloke in the river?'

'Yes,' I admitted.

'Is it likely to worry Mickey?'

'Yes,' I agreed.

'I see.' She bit her lower lip and scarlet lipstick smudged her top teeth. 'Well, dear, in that case, I've got a suggestion.

Before you go phoning Mickey, you'd better have a word with Mr Filigrew.'

'Oh, Gawd . . .' I groaned, falling back on my pillows. 'He's Mickey's tail on me, isn't he? I thought he was a dodgy sales rep with a woman in every port of call.'

'Oh, yes?' said Beryl, giving me an old-fashioned look. 'Think I can't recognise one of them when they turn up?'

'Someone should have told me,' I said grimly. 'Either you or Filigrew or whatever his name is. What is he? Some sort of solicitor?'

'A proper one!' said Beryl earnestly.

'Hah! So, did Mickey think I might fall foul of the law? If so, why?'

'No need to worry you, dear,' she soothed. 'Mickey was acting for the best. Mr Filigrew is only here in case you had any trouble.'

'Yeah, well you can tell him I've got lots of that.' I picked up my mug of tea. 'And tell him I don't want him phoning Mickey before I do!'

'You can trust Mr Filigrew,' Beryl assured me before hobbling away.

I considered that the first blatant untruth she'd told me although perhaps she believed it at that. I knew I couldn't trust Mr Filigrew. I wasn't paying him. Nor did I think his presence in Oxford meant he would lend me a helping hand if I had trouble. He was here in case Lisa had any.

I paused with the tea halfway to my lips. 'Why should Lisa have any trouble requiring a dodgy lawyer?' I wondered aloud. 'Or is Mickey worried she might make damaging allegations of some sort?' Was Filigrew here to pay off Lisa, if need be? How many mysterious ingredients were mixed into this brew?

When Pereira had finally left and Tom and Maryann clattered upstairs and past my room, still arguing, I slipped down to Beryl's basement flat.

'Ah, there you are, dear,' she greeted me cosily, as she opened the door at the foot of the stair, just as if I'd dropped by for a nice chat. 'Come along in, then. Spencer! Behave!'

Spencer was bouncing around in his demented fashion, jumping up at me. I scratched his ears and thought again of Bonnie. I heaved a sigh. Whatever happened, I had to get Lisa to make that phone call to Allerton and then they could sort out their differences without my further help. I could go home and reclaim my own dog. That was all that mattered to me. The police could sort out the business of Ivo in the river. That was their job.

Beryl's flat displayed an extension of the style in which my room was done out. It was all frills and flounces and cute ornaments and photographs of Beryl in her heyday including one in which she was dressed up like Marlene Dietrich in a top hat and fishnet stockings.

'I wasn't bad, was I?' asked Beryl, seeing me study it.

The sound of a throat being cleared prevented my reply. Mr Filigrew was sitting bolt upright in an armchair wearing what I supposed were his off-duty clothes, that is to say he'd taken off his jacket and replaced it with a navy-blue knitted cardigan. On his feet were leather slippers. A newspaper on his knees lay folded at the crossword puzzle. Quite making himself at home. He still wore the flashy tie.

Seeing that my attention was turned to him, he took off his rimless specs, polished the lenses with a little bit of yellow cloth and invited me to, 'Sit down, my dear.'

Now there are two things I don't like and he managed to score both of them in one short sentence. I don't like being called 'my dear' by any person I don't look upon as a friend. I don't like it when people assume an authority they don't, in my view, possess. This was Beryl's flat and any invitation to sit down should come from her. Moreover, he was attempting to take the initiative in any conversation we were to have. He didn't know me. He soon would.

'My name is Fran,' I said coldly. 'All right if I sit here, Beryl?' I indicated a funny-looking chair with no arms and a floor-length flounce all round it. It looked as if it might dance away across the carpet.

'Anywhere, dear,' said Beryl. It was all right when she used the endearment. I did count Beryl as a friend. She was Mickey's friend before she was mine, of course, but I felt she was well disposed towards me.

Filigrew, or whatever his real name might be, I sensed was not well disposed towards me – or, probably, towards anyone. He had that dyspeptic look which holds the world at fault. He'd taken my snub by baring his long discoloured

teeth in a curious grimace, not a smile and not a snarl. He
just wrinkled up his upper lip and let me see he needed to
visit a dental hygienist. There was something very unsettling about the whole thing and suddenly I knew what it
was. Some dogs do that when they aren't sure of you. They
sidle up, baring their upper teeth in a sort of canine grin.
Their body language is subservient but the teeth display
isn't unintentional. They are hedging their bets.

Speaking of dogs, Spencer liked me. He settled down at
my feet and looked up at me, pink tongue lolling and
button eyes bright with expectation.

Filigrew cleared his throat again but I got in first. 'Beryl
tells me you act for Mickey Allerton.'

He replaced his spectacles and surveyed me through
them, his mouth pursed. 'That depends,' he said.

'Either you do or you don't,' I told him crisply. 'If you
don't, I'll leave now.'

'I represent certain of Mr Allerton's interests,' he
snapped. Now he actively disliked me, but so what?

'I need to phone Allerton,' I said. 'But Beryl suggests I
listen to you first. I'm prepared to listen, but make it brief.'

He put both hands to his spectacles and removed them
again. His fidgeting with them was beginning to annoy
me. It was his way of gaining time – and he who gains time
gains the initiative. He knew he'd lost it at the outset, but
he was going to get it back again, by hook or by crook.

He blinked watery eyes at me. 'I need an assurance
from you that this unfortunate incident, I mean of course

your discovery of a body in the river . . .' Here Filigrew paused and murmured, 'T-t-t . . .' in the manner of a man who'd just discovered something nasty sticking to the sole of his shoe. 'You could, I suppose, have avoided finding it?' His voice was heavy with reproach.

'How?' I asked him, amazed. 'Do you mean, having found it, I should have run away before anyone else turned up and pretended I knew nothing about it? Isn't that an offence? Aren't we supposed to report something like that to the proper authorities?'

'You might have been forgiven for thinking you were mistaken about the man being dead. You might have thought he was swimming. There would be no offence in making a genuine mistake. You should have phoned here and asked my advice.'

'I didn't know about you, did I?' I retorted. 'You didn't tell me you represented Mickey. That's your fault. Mickey's not going to blame *me* for that!'

'Then you should have phoned Mr Allerton and asked him what he wanted you to do.' Filigrew glared at me. He knew as well as I did that Mickey would seek to blame someone for introducing an element which could seriously screw things up.

'Don't talk daft,' I said to Filigrew. 'I didn't have time. There were other people around.'

He conceded the point. 'Well, well, perhaps you might be excused for not seeking advice.' He rallied. 'But that means there was all the more reason to get out of there before other people arrived. People, incidentally, who could safely have been left to find the man themselves.'

'I found him, me, right? All by myself,' I said bleakly. 'It wasn't by choice but that's what happened. There was no possibility he was swimming. Stop bleating about what I might have done or should have done. If I had tried to run away, it would have been worse, because the Americans came along in a punt just moments later and they would have seen me disappearing into the distance. Someone who runs away is a lot more suspicious than someone who stays. Anyway, I fell in the water.'

'That,' said Filigrew sharply, 'could certainly have been avoided.'

'What's this assurance you want?' I demanded.

'That the police will not be seeking to interview the young lady.'

'You mean Lisa Stallard? No, they won't, because by the time she arrived there was a crowd. I managed to catch her eye and send her a message to clear off. She did.'

'Good.' He looked relieved. I don't think he was any happier at the idea of giving bad news to Mickey Allerton than I was. 'You haven't yet spoken to the young lady, I mean about Mr Allerton's request?'

I wished he'd stop referring to Lisa as the young lady. I was sure he'd never refer to me like that. 'I've spoken to her,' I told him, 'but it was difficult as most of the time her parents were present. She doesn't want them to know about her working for Allerton. That's why she agreed to meet me down by the river so we could sort things out. I still hope to persuade her to phone Mickey. I want my dog back.'

'What dog is this?' asked Beryl, who though taking no part in our conversation had been listening.

'I wasn't going to tell you, Beryl,' I said. 'Because I know Allerton's your friend. But he's got my dog and is holding her hostage – or rather, he's given her to one of his musclemen to keep until I return.'

'Oh, I don't think Mickey would hurt an animal!' protested Beryl.

'I didn't say he'd do it himself,' I snapped. No, his idea had been that Ivo should take care of this bit of business. Mickey was shrewd enough to guess what Bonnie meant to me. At least, I thought, now Bonnie won't fall into Ivo's hands, whatever else happens.

'No one has hurt her – yet,' I went on more calmly. 'But I'm not going to see her again if Lisa doesn't phone Allerton. That's it in a nutshell. You don't like this situation and I don't like it. I didn't want to come on this errand in the first place and I don't know why Mickey chose me.'

'Oh, that's easy,' said Beryl unexpectedly. 'Mr Filigrew has been telling me about it, about the dancer who left the club without a word to anyone and how Mickey asked you to get her back because he's concerned about her. These girls who want to be dancers . . .' Beryl clicked her tongue. 'They've no idea what a tough life it is and how uncertain. You want to be an actor, don't you? Well, that puts you and this girl Lisa on much the same wavelength. You're both young and stage-struck. She'd talk to you.'

'I'm not stage-struck!' I defended myself. 'I *am* an actor. I've worked as an actor. I don't like being used by Allerton. I don't like being talked about and I don't like any of this!'

'To return to the body in the river.' Filigrew drew the conversation firmly back to the main matter. 'Your feelings are immaterial. If the young lady is not going to be involved, then perhaps we don't have to trouble Mr Allerton about it. It's not his concern, after all, it's yours. You took the job, whatever your reasons, and all this is your responsibility.'

Filigrew was as worried about Mickey Allerton as I was. He wasn't working out how to get me out of trouble, but how to extricate himself. The look of contempt on my face must have warned him. He essayed his unattractive smile again.

'The police are not being difficult, are they? You are not under any kind of suspicion? I am on hand to give you any necessary advice and you can, if they wish to question you, ask that I be present.' His watery eyes blinked at me again.

He really was a solicitor. But not in a thousand years would I ask for him to be there. He wouldn't be representing me; he'd be representing Allerton and himself. The very request for a solicitor would alert Pereira. That I, a stranger in town, could call one up at a moment's notice would make her even more suspicious. Last, but by no means least, I didn't want Filigrew sticking his nose into my business.

'I've already made a statement to Sergeant Pereira,' I said, 'and signed it.'

He looked worried. 'What did you say? I wish you'd spoken to me first.'

'We've been through all that,' I pointed out. 'I didn't know you were Allerton's mouthpiece. Anyway, there was no chance. DS Pereira brought me home and we went straight to my room.'

'Fast work,' said Beryl with grudging approval. I guessed she wasn't entirely unfamiliar with police methods.

Filigrew muttered, 'Pereira,' and wrote the name down in the margin of his paper, by the crossword. 'Detective sergeant, you say?'

'Yes. I don't think she's bent, so don't go offering her a holiday in Tenerife to lose her notes, will you?'

I didn't really think he'd do that. It was a sort of joke on my part. But his neck flushed as red as a turkeycock's and the colour rose up his pale cheeks in a crimson tide. He even gobbled like a turkey. 'That is an outrageous suggestion—'

'She's winding you up, Mervyn,' said Beryl easily. She winked at me on his blind side.

'Really?' snapped Filigrew, glaring at me. 'You are extremely ill advised to do that, Miss Varady. You may need me.'

He could be right, after all. I had enough enemies in

this cruel world without adding him to the number. 'Take it easy,' I said. 'My nerves are shot to bits. I'm hysterical.'

At that they both looked at me in horror. 'Drop of brandy,' said Beryl, getting awkwardly to her feet. 'That'll do the trick.'

'Look,' I said to Filigrew. 'I don't know what suspicions she's got, if any. The police don't take me into their confidence.'

Filigrew relaxed and seemed also to be considering that he and I had to get along somehow. 'So,' he said cautiously. 'It is a purely local event, a piece of bad luck and bad timing. You found this man in the river. You made a statement to DS Pereira. There is no need to trouble Mr Allerton.'

'Yes, there is, because the dead man works – worked for him.'

'What?' shouted Filigrew, completely losing his cool and bouncing to his feet.

The newspaper fell to the floor, sheets separating and spreading out across the carpet. The crossword with Pereira's name in the margin ended up by my feet. Spencer leapt up and barked. Beryl shushed him and scooped him up in her arms where he wriggled furiously. Beryl's eyes were popping at me like ping-pong balls. I hadn't told her that.

'How do you know?' snapped Filigrew, sitting down again. He was annoyed that he'd twice lost control in front of me. He smoothed his sparse hair, put back his specs on his nose and glared at me.

'I recognised him. His name is Ivo. He was a doorman at the Silver Circle.'

'Lumme,' breathed Beryl.

'You can't be sure of this!' Filigrew was sweating. It was warm down in this basement but not that warm.

'Yes, I'm sure. I told you, I fell in the river, right by him. I saw his face.'

'Ooh, horrible,' Beryl shivered.

'You can't be right!' objected Filigrew but he didn't sound half so confident.

'I'm right and I suggest that, when I've told Mickey, you have a chat with him yourself. Because it seems to me that Mr Allerton has been holding out on both of us!'

Filigrew pulled himself together at that. He stood up and announced, 'Wait here. I'll speak to him first.'

Then he stormed out.

'Has he got a mobile?' I asked Beryl. I couldn't see Filigrew communicating with Allerton via the phone in the entrance hall.

'I expect so,' she said comfortably. 'Nearly everyone has, haven't they?'

'I had one,' I said. 'But I lost it in the river, like I told you. The police will probably dig around on the river bed looking for anything which might have been Ivo's. They'll find it. They'll trace it to a friend of mine. I'll have to warn him. Is it all right if I phone London while old Filigrew is talking to Mickey?'

Beryl hesitated.

'I'll pay for the call,' I assured her.

'Not that, dear.' She seemed awkward. 'Best wait for Mr Filigrew to come back, eh?'

I understood her dilemma. She wanted to do the right thing by Allerton and she'd only my word that the person I wanted to call was the owner of the phone I'd lost.

I told her, all right, and we settled down to wait for Filigrew's return.

'Tell you what, dear,' said Beryl suddenly. 'Let me get you that drop of brandy.'

'Thanks, but no. I don't drink spirits,' I said gloomily. 'I'm strictly a wine and beer person. If I start knocking back brandy now I'll be in no state to speak to Allerton.'

'I've got a bottle of white wine open in the fridge?' She put Spencer on the floor and prepared to make for the kitchenette.

'Honestly, Beryl, I appreciate it, but no – well, later, when I've got my phone call done, perhaps?'

The door opened and Filigrew returned. I was right about the mobile. He held it out to me. 'He wants to talk to you,' he said.

I took the phone gingerly and put it to my ear. 'Mr Allerton?' I hoped my voice didn't sound as nervous as I felt.

'What the hell is going on, Fran?' Mickey's voice crackled in my ear.

'Ivo's dead. Honestly, I don't know anything about it.'

'What was he doing in Oxford?' crackled the voice.

'How should I know?' Allerton was Allerton but my nerves were frayed and I was losing my awe of him. All this was his fault, whichever way you looked at it.

'I want Lisa kept out of this!'

'She is out of it. Believe me, Mr Allerton.'

'You'd better be right, doll.'

'Mr Allerton? Do you still want me to try and persuade her to phone you?'

There was a pause. 'Yeah, I do. But be careful. Give it a day, see what the cops do.'

'I don't want to stay here,' I said miserably.

'And I don't want my bloody doormen turning up in rivers!' snarled the voice down the line.

'If you didn't send him,' I retaliated, 'didn't you miss him? Shouldn't he have been at work?'

'He said he had a cold.' Even Mickey Allerton seemed to realise that he'd accepted the feeblest of excuses for Ivo taking time off. 'If the stupid bugger wasn't dead already,' he said with more emotion than I'd ever heard him use, 'I'd screw his ruddy neck myself!'

That I did believe.

'I think I will have that brandy, after all, Beryl,' I said when the phone link had been disconnected.

'I'll join you,' said Beryl. 'How about you, Mervyn?'

'Yes,' said Filigrew, straightening his tie with nervous fingers. 'Make it a double, Beryl. This is going to get worse before it gets better.'

* * *

As it turned out, I didn't need to phone Ganesh. He phoned me. Thames Valley Police, the local Oxford lot, had sent a diver into the river that same day. He'd found the phone and, hoping for an identity for their corpse, they'd traced the owner at once and got on to the Met. They'd sent someone round to the shop.

'Hari's a gibbering wreck!' yelled Ganesh down the line to me.

I was taking the call in the hall and hoping neither Tom nor Maryann appeared.

'We had a couple of flatfoots from the local copshop here, saying Thames Valley colleagues had informed them I'd drowned in flipping Oxford. I had to prove who I was. Look, I said to them eventually, this guy who's been found in the river in Oxford, is he Asian? So then they checked back with the police in Oxford and it turned out the drowned man is blond and blue-eyed and it isn't likely his name is Ganesh Patel.

'You'd have thought that was that, but no, it got worse. Oxford police had found a mobile in the river and traced it to me. That was why they'd got on to the Met about me. So then they asked, had I been in Oxford that day or recently? No, I perishing well hadn't, I told them. They just looked at me and asked if I was sure, which means they thought I was lying. So I had to prove that, too. Hari swore I'd been in the shop all day, of course, but they didn't believe him because he's my uncle. Fortunately the cook from the Greek restaurant across the road had been in the shop twice during the day and remembered me. Did they leave after that? What do you think? They moved on to a new lot of questions. What was my phone doing in the river with a dead guy in Oxford? I told them I'd like to know that, too! You must have some idea, they said, how your phone got to Oxford without you. Did the description of the drowned man mean anything to me? Had I, perhaps, lent him my phone? Because it was found directly underneath the body and it did not have the appearance of having been in the water very long. No, the description didn't mean a flipping thing to me! I told them. But they kept on and on so I had to tell them something. I nearly said I lost the phone, because I didn't want to drag you into it. You'll note, I hope, that even in the difficult situation I was in myself, my immediate instinct was to protect you from awkward questions whereas you, on the other hand, have no scruples in dropping me right in it!'

'I hope you didn't tell them you lost the mobile,' I interrupted anxiously. 'Because I told the police here I'd borrowed it from you—'

'Yeah, well, luckily I've always believed in being straight with the law. Unlike some people I could mention. So I said, I'd lent it to you but *you'd* probably lost it. Still trying to protect you, see? Fran, what is going on? How did my mobile get into a river?'

'You won't like this, Ganesh,' I warned.

'Ho, ho, ho. What a surprise. Won't I? Fran – *what have you done now?*'

'Why,' I wailed in despair, 'does everyone always assume I've done something?'

'Francesca,' said Ganesh in that lecturing voice he sometimes assumes, 'has it never occurred to you that things happen to you that just don't happen to other people?'

'It does cross my mind, from time to time, as it happens. Cut it out, Gan, will you? I'm in enough trouble without you getting at me. How is Hari now?'

'I told you, a wreck. He's drinking herbal tea and phoning every relative we've got. My dad's coming up to town tomorrow. My mum's had hysterics. Usha and Jay have both been round here asking me if I need a good solicitor because Jay's got an uncle who's a top-notch lawyer. Jay ruddy well would!'

The last words were snarled. Jay is the sort of upwardly mobile professional Ganesh wishes he was. But he drew the short straw and ended up working for Hari.

'Get his name and number,' I advised. 'I might need him.' After all, Filigrew hadn't struck me as being any Perry Mason.

Ganesh groaned. 'Spill it.'

'You remember I told you about the bouncer at Mickey's club, not Harry, but the really weird bodybuilder? He's dead – here in Oxford. He's the man the two coppers from the Met were describing to you. I was walking by the river and there Ivo was, floating along. That's not quite true. He wasn't drifting; he was resting up by some stone steps. I fell in the river trying to pull him to shore. That's when I lost your phone.'

There was a silence. 'You know,' Ganesh said in an odd sort of voice, 'I sometimes think all this happens to me because of something rotten I did in my previous existence.'

'Please don't turn religious on me, Ganesh.'

'I am not. I am just looking for an explanation. I'm a quiet, law-abiding newsagent. I'm a good son and nephew. I'm vegetarian and I don't drink – well, only the odd pint. I don't smoke or do drugs. I've never had so much as a parking ticket against me. So, why me?'

'What do you mean, why you?' I snapped, losing it. 'It's not you, it me! I'm the one in trouble!'

'Somehow, at this end, it doesn't feel like that. Or perhaps I only imagined those two coppers round here today giving me the third degree and giving my uncle a nervous breakdown? He'll never get over it,' concluded Ganesh passionately. 'Neither shall I.'

'What about me? I'm sorry Hari's upset and I'm sorry I got you involved, but I'm the one who found the stiff. *I'll* never get over it!' I yelled down the line.

'You see? That's what I mean. Why do you do these things, Fran? Find bodies—'

I slammed the phone down on him and turned away.

Vera the waitress was sitting on the stairs watching me with interest, her chin propped in her hands and her mop of black hair falling over her forehead.

'What are you doing there?' I snapped. I do snoop myself

when it's required in a good cause but that doesn't mean I accept being snooped on. 'Don't you know it's rude to listen to other people's conversations? How long have you been there?'

She considered this, frowning beneath the fringe of hair. 'I only came now, just one half a minute ago. You were shouting. I think something is wrong. I came downstairs to find out. Something is wrong?'

'Yes.' I made an effort to calm down. 'I'm sorry I was shouting and disturbed you.'

'Is all right,' said Vera. Her snub nose twitched and her brown eyes peered up at me bright with curiosity. 'You have trouble? What have you done?'

'Oh, not you, too . . .' I groaned.

Chapter Eight

I spent a sleepless night haunted by visions of Ivo's blank staring eyes and white, waxy skin. In my memory the first signs of rigor had made the eyeballs bulge and retracted his lower jaw. The flowing current washed into his nostrils and gaping mouth and river flotsam decorated him with grotesque confetti of leaves and twigs. Perhaps my imagination painted the scene as even more lurid than it had been in reality. Certainly my mind began to sprawl in a dozen different directions but at the end of every new alley was Ivo. I began to imagine him, not just as I'd seen him last, but as he must be now, lying in a steel mortuary drawer, neatly slotted away with a tag tied to his big toe reading 'unidentified'. But no, perhaps that was wrong, too. Perhaps by now the post-mortem examination had already been carried out. That was a nightmare too far. I thrust it away.

To escape the images which formed in the darkness, I switched on the bedside light. I hadn't brought a book with me and the only available reading matter was the stack of tourist leaflets and an old copy of a women's magazine on the lower shelf of the cabinet. I read the article on nutritious and economical meals but it featured a large picture of a dead fish, which brought me back to Ivo. I tried the fashion pages and the beauty hints and even 'this month in your garden'. I read the short story and completed the crossword puzzle. I studied the readers' letters. Nearly all of them were from women in unhappy twosomes. I wanted to say to the writers: 'Why not just dump the guy?' But they wouldn't because rather than face a new situation they wanted to cling to the imperfect one they had. I thought that, ramshackle and unpredictable though my life was, I'd rather have it than mind-numbing routine and relationships which were clearly going nowhere but down the pan. The agony aunt replied with predictable words of advice which couldn't be implemented. Why not talk it over with him? Because the creep is a liar and a conman, that's why.

Now I wasn't so sure that their sad lives were any more fraught than mine. They at least knew in their hearts what the end of their problem would be. He'd leave, either with a new love or to go back to his wife if he'd got one. Nothing so straightforward would solve my dilemma.

In the way that Ivo refused to leave my head, I now began to wonder what Jasna would do when she heard of his death. Had they just been co-exiles or closer? What of Ivo's family back home in Croatia, assuming that to be his country? Perhaps he had a dear, grey-haired old mother and venerable father, depending on the wages he sent home— stop it, Fran!

It's easy to wonder about people and come up with the wildest scenarios. People wonder about Ganesh and me. But we're friends. Yes, of course it could go further if we let it but we don't. We like what we have and we know the dangers of tinkering with it. Ganesh's family like me but they would never see me as bride-material. I wouldn't want to be the one to come between him and them. He grumbles about his family but he's very much a part of them all. One day, I suppose, we'll have to make a decision. We put it off. Worrying about things doesn't help. In the end, most decisions make themselves.

I studied the advertisements in the magazine. I didn't want two skirts with elasticised waists for the price of one. I wasn't yet in line for a stairlift and I couldn't afford a home foot spa. Anyway, I'd spent enough time in water, thanks.

I put aside the magazine, lay back with my hands behind my head and stared up at the ceiling. What was Ivo doing in Oxford? If Mickey hadn't sent him, who had? If he was down there on Christ Church Meadow it could only be because he was spying on me and on whomever I might meet. But how did he know I'd be there? Somehow or other, if I could rearrange all the pieces, it would make sense. But it was like doing a jigsaw with three or four vital shapes missing. There was a gap in all of this, a missing link. I wondered if Darwin had felt similarly frustrated. I fell into fitful sleep, tossing to and fro, unable to get comfortable, unable to rid myself of Ivo's unwished ghostly presence, wondering what would happen next.

By the time morning came I was stressed out, I had bags under my eyes and I longed to talk to someone friendly and on my side, not Allerton's. I bitterly regretted having quarrelled with Ganesh. On my way down to breakfast, I rang the shop from the hall telephone. Fortunately, he answered it and not his uncle. I hadn't really prepared what I might say to Hari who, by all accounts, was in a worse state than I was.

'It's me, Fran,' I said in a subdued tone.

'Oh, hello, Fran,' said Ganesh, 'everything all right?' He sounded a whole lot calmer than he had the previous evening and I guessed he also regretted the spat.

'So far,' I said. 'Give it time. It's early yet.'

'Are you coming home today?'

'Well, I've still got something to do . . .' Vera had appeared from the kitchen carrying two plates of eggs and bacon. She rushed past me into the breakfast room. 'You know,' I said to Ganesh when she had gone, 'I've still got to carry out my original assignment.'

'No, you don't,' he said stubbornly.

'Yes, I do. I won't get Bonnie back otherwise.'

'Allerton can't expect you just to carry on as if nothing has happened!' Ganesh was outraged and the emotion was building up in his voice again.

'Yes, he does. I've spoken to him on the phone.'

'That man is unreasonable.'

'Tell me something I don't know. Tell him.'

'I think I shall!' snapped Ganesh.

That panicked me and I spent the next couple of minutes making him promise he'd go nowhere near the Silver Circle.

'This call is costing me a fortune,' I said. 'I've got to hang up and go and have my breakfast.'

I drifted into the breakfast room. Mr Filigrew was sitting in his usual seat and shaking pills from a little tube on to the tablecloth. He looked up at me and radiated displeasure.

'Good morning,' I bid him politely.

'Good morning to you,' he retorted icily. He lined his little white pills up on the cloth, counted them, and screwed the cap back on the tube.

'Indigestion?' I asked sympathetically. 'I expect it's the fried food. Perhaps you ought to stick to cornflakes and toast.'

He looked as if he was going to choke so I left him and found my own table. Next door sat Tom and Maryann. Tom greeted me with a friendly, 'Hi, how are you doing?' Maryann looked baffled as if she couldn't understand why I wasn't in gaol.

'I'm doing all right in the circumstances,' I told him. 'How are you, Maryann?'

'We made a statement to a police officer,' she said.

'It's interesting to see how those guys work in this country,' said Tom, a man who always took a practical view.

Vera appeared by my table. 'Full English?'

I was surprised that I felt hungry but I did and said, yes, please. Maryann looked as if my healthy appetite merely confirmed her worst fears that I was a hard-boiled emissary from the criminal underworld.

'Like you said,' I told her. 'It comes with the room and it's a pity to waste it.'

Mickey had told me to carry on trying to contact Lisa but he'd also advised me to wait a day. I didn't think delay was a particularly good idea. If I were Lisa, I'd be planning to leave, or even have left already. I wouldn't wait around for me. I decided I'd first go back to the scene of Ivo's unexpected demise and snoop around, hoping to find some clue to the mystery, and then take the bus up to Summertown and try and see Lisa again. I didn't relish the prospect of either task. I had another reason for returning to the scene of the drowning. I didn't want to spend a second night imagining Ivo in the river. I needed to see the place without him and looking normal. I wanted my last sight of it to be picture-postcard perfect, all the horrors gone.

Christ Church Meadow was restored to calm and nearly deserted. I looked to see if the two joggers, Tweedledum and Tweedledee, who'd been here the previous day, were here again but there was no sign of anyone resembling them. I walked down the river path until I came to the submerged steps. Access was now barred by a strand of blue and white police tape. A notice had been tacked to a tree requesting passers-by who might have been in the area on the given date and noticed anything unusual to contact the local police station, the address and phone number of which were displayed. In particular the police were anxious to talk to anyone who might have noticed a white male of about six feet in height, fair-haired and well built, in red running shorts and white running vest, jogging along the riverside track.

I didn't know when they'd been down here to tack up the notice but this tangible sign of an investigation in progress unsettled me even further. I wondered if they already realised they would have difficulty identifying the corpse. My longing for a picture-postcard scene was foiled. When I'd first come here, yesterday, I'd been struck by how peaceful and pleasant the place was, before I found Ivo. Now on another just as quiet sunny morning the location seemed eerie. The water, murmuring softly as it rippled past the stone steps, held sinister secrets. I was jumpy not only because of the memory the scene provoked, and the thought of the police ferreting about, but because this place could be dangerous for me. Like it or not, I was connected with the Silver Circle, too. I should have heeded Ganesh's wise words telling me I had little idea what was really going on here, but I knew I needed to find out. I'd no wish to join Ivo in the river and the best way to avoid that was to put myself fully in the picture. No more unpleasant surprises. If I wanted to uncover the real story, this was the logical place to start. But what should I be looking for? The river whispered and chuckled at me. I tried to make out in which direction it flowed but that proved unexpectedly difficult. Here, at the point where the two branches met, it seemed to eddy round. Could Ivo's body have drifted? He hadn't looked as if he'd been in the water that long. But was I an expert? The river knew but I couldn't make it disgorge its secrets.

I prowled around the area which was now pretty well trampled, still unaware what I was looking for. If there had been anything significant to be found, as I told myself crossly, the police would have done so by now. The fallen branch which had tripped me when I'd started back on first seeing Ivo's body in the water still lay to one side of the path. As I stepped over it my toe snagged in it and that annoyed me. It was stupid to be angry with an inanimate object but I grabbed the branch and shook it violently to relieve my feelings. Then I stopped and studied it. Was it possible he had been jogging along the path and had also tripped over this innocent-looking piece of debris, resulting in a loss of balance and a fall into the river? It was highly unlikely. Even if he had fallen in, he'd have struggled out, as I'd done. If he was conscious, that was. But he could have struck his head on the steps and been knocked out. It was an outside chance but freak accidents happened.

However, supposing he wasn't conscious when he went in, then someone had rendered him unconscious. How? I considered the branch. It was long, thin and pliable. The thicker end fitted neatly into my palm and then it became progressively more spindly until it forked at the other end into two even spindlier arms. It didn't have enough weight to be an adequate weapon and I thought it would be too unwieldy at that length. If you want to cosh someone, you need some short, heavy implement especially if you mean to attack a physical specimen like Ivo. A piece of wood could do it; but not this piece of wood. I tossed it aside with a sigh.

What had brought Ivo here in the first place? And was I going to tell Lisa the identity of the dead man? I could imagine her reaction.

'Fran?'

The voice was quiet but it made me jump and my heart leap into my mouth. I whirled round and saw Hayley Pereira a short distance away, standing with her hands in her jacket pockets, watching me. I had no idea how long she'd been there. I cursed my bad luck. She probably thought I was returning to the scene of the crime as all good assassins are supposed to do. To me it sounds a daft thing to do and perhaps murderers only do it in books.

'Hello,' I said, because there wasn't much else I could say.

'What are you doing?' she asked.

It was a simple enough question but I needed to take care how I answered it. 'I was thinking about it all last night,' I said. 'I kept imagining the man in the water. I thought, if I came back, and saw the river like this, normal, with no body floating in it, it would help.'

She nodded. 'You've had a bad shock.'

'Do you know who he was?' I held my breath. Had I sounded normal as I asked the question?

'No, not yet.' She shook her head.

I wonder how far I could push asking questions before she became suspicious of the amount of interest I was showing. I decided to act dumb. 'What happens in a case like this? Will there be a post-mortem?'

'Oh, that's been done already,' she replied. 'Last night.'

I was taken aback at this news. 'Oh,' I said. 'Tom, the American, thought he might have had a heart attack.'

'There was no sign of that.'

'And Maryann, Tom's girlfriend, thought he'd been mugged, stabbed or something.' Tom and Maryann were proving unexpectedly useful to me.

Pereira almost smiled. 'No, at least, there's no sign of any injury consistent with a mugging, nothing violent.'

'Nobody bashed him on the head with a baseball bat, then,' I said.

She looked startled and I remembered I'd been talking of Tom's heart-attack theory. Quickly I moved to re-establish my naïve persona. 'Sorry. I live in London. We hear a lot about that sort of thing.'

'I see.' She nodded. 'No. The cause of death was drowning.'

'Poor chap,' I said, hoping the relief I felt hadn't escaped into my voice. I knew now he had no head wound, the obvious injury I'd have looked for. Floating in the water as he'd been when I found him, any blood would have washed away but post-mortem examination would have revealed any cranial injury immediately. Yet at the same time the mystery deepened. He had entered the water alive. How could a young fit man like Ivo drown in a relatively placid river? We weren't talking foaming rapids here. Had he gone in willingly? It was difficult to imagine an assailant powerful enough to force him.

But there was one person who could have done it. Ned, Lisa's white knight: young, fit, strong. He'd issued threats when we'd last met. He'd do anything to protect her. Anything? Even murder?

Pereira spoke, interrupting my line of thought. 'I agree, it's a very sad incident but also a puzzling one. We are keen to know just how he came to fall in. It's not very deep by the bank. Even if he wasn't a good swimmer, he'd only need to keep afloat and scramble out either on this side or over there, up that slipway.'

I saw now that opposite the steps on the further bank was a concrete ramp. Lisa had mentioned some sort of ferry. Pereira had turned away and I found myself walking back with her towards the rear of the botanical gardens and the gate out into Rose Lane.

'This is a beautiful spot,' she said. 'I'm sorry you have to associate it with a nightmare.'

'Yeah,' I mumbled. 'I had nightmares all right.' I glanced at her. 'How about you?'

'Me?' She looked startled. 'Did I dream about the dead man?'

'Well, not him specifically. But you must see some bad sights. Do they haunt you?'

'The ones that haunt me,' she said, 'are the things which happen to the innocent and helpless or those who should be innocent: battered babies, mugged old people, eight-year-old girls passed round as sex objects.' She glanced at me. 'And we get the odd baseball bat attack here in Oxford, too. London hasn't got a monopoly on these things.'

'I guess so,' I said. 'I thought I'd go back to London tomorrow if that's all right with you.'

'I should think so. We have an address for you. We found your mobile phone, by the way. You seemed worried about that. I should say we found a phone belonging to a Mr Ganesh Patel. The Metropolitan Police contacted Mr Patel and he confirms he lent the phone to you.'

'I know,' I confessed. 'I spoke to him last night. He's mad at me for losing the phone and because his uncle, whom he lives with, is upset. His uncle's a very nervous man.'

'He should be glad it wasn't you in the river,' Pereira said.

He probably was, and so was I, but I didn't say so to her.

Pereira's car was parked just over the bridge. She offered

me a lift to the top of the High Street but I declined it, saying I'd rather walk.

'Let me give you a number to reach me on,' she said, 'just in case you remember something else. You're still in shock, but when it wears off you might recall seeing something or someone around before you found the body.'

She pulled out her notebook, scribbled out a phone number, tore off the sheet and handed it to me. I glanced at it. It was for a mobile. She wanted me to speak to her, if I remembered some detail, and not to one of her colleagues. Detectives work as part of a team but it seemed Pereira was keen to make her mark. If I told her anything, she'd have to pass it on, but she wanted to be the one to come up with the new evidence. I understood this. It was a human enough failing. But it put me in the position of being her private information source. Where I come from, that sort of thing is viewed with extreme disfavour by the populace at large.

'Thanks,' I said briefly and stuck the noted number in my pocket. I doubted I'd be calling it. When I left her she was standing by her car watching me as I marched away.

In the centre I caught a bus to Summertown and went to the Stallards' house. Jennifer answered the door. She looked harassed and said she was sorry, but Lisa had gone out early.

She sounded fretful as if she could have done with Lisa being there. Suddenly she blurted out, 'Do come in for coffee!'

'Really,' I said, 'that's all right. I just wanted to speak to Lisa. Do you know where she's gone?' I held my breath, hoping the answer wouldn't be that she'd left Oxford.

Jennifer shook her head. 'To see a friend, perhaps? I got that impression . . .' She bit her lip. 'Won't you come in for coffee? Are you sure? Just come and say hello to my husband.'

I recognised an appeal for help and it was difficult to refuse. I sidled unhappily indoors after her.

Paul was in the back room, reading the morning paper. I was again struck by the dark cluttered ambience of the place and its stuffy air of defeat. There was another atmosphere, too, which had nothing to do with stale air. Paul looked frail this morning but beneath the frailty he simmered with frustration and hopeless rage. I could sense it coming off him in waves. Before he saw me, he asked petulantly, 'Who was that?'

Invalids aren't saints. Who would be, stuck in a chair like this, surrounded by the same four walls day in and day out? Frustrations boil over. They can make life hell for devoted carers. Probably, now his daughter was at home, Paul had perked up a bit. But she'd gone out and this morning things weren't going well. No wonder Jennifer had welcomed the sight of me as a possible diversion.

Certainly Paul brightened as soon as he saw me. Jennifer bustled away to make the coffee and I settled down to make small talk, mostly about the theatre and my ambitions. It was a difficult and strained occasion and the longer it went on the clearer it became to me that his life was so completely empty that he latched vicariously on to any evidence of a 'real life' outside the four walls of this house. While, owing to my own lack of starring roles, my experience of working in the theatre has been limited, I do at least have a good idea of how it goes. Paul didn't. His ideas were drawn entirely from reading about famous actors. He leaned heavily for information on the autobiographies of elderly stars of stage and screen, some of whom had turned up their toes years ago. It was clear to me that his idea of theatrical life was impossibly glamorous, all showbiz parties and wealthy upper-class stage-door johnnies panting to drink champagne from satin slippers. I got the impression he saw a future for Lisa in which some wealthy admirer showered her with flowers and diamonds before carrying her off to marriage and possibly even a title.

I tried hard to get the conversation away from his fantasies, from myself and from his accounts of his daughter's (entirely fictional, did he but know it) success on the London musical stage. I asked about his collection of books. We discussed old films we'd both seen on television. I even, in desperation, asked how Arthur was that day.

'I called in on him earlier this morning,' said Paul. 'But he wasn't at home. He's probably out shopping for slugs and worms.'

I realised this last reference was a joke, but it didn't stop it being dismally and embarrassingly revealing of the emptiness of his existence. For him Arthur was as good as a human neighbour. I wondered they didn't get themselves a livelier pet, like a cat. But perhaps cats and grass snakes didn't mix.

Eventually I managed to get away, feeling that I was abandoning them but knowing there was nothing I could do except help keep Lisa's secret. No wonder she depended on Ned as a shoulder to cry on. She could never bring any problem home. Home was a nest of inbuilt problems already.

'I'm sorry you've missed Lisa,' said Jennifer at the front door. 'I'll tell her you were here.' She reached out and took my hand. 'Thank you so much for giving us a little of your time,' she said quietly.

For the first time I took a good look at her. She had a faded prettiness and a strong resemblance to her daughter. But there were dark shadows beneath her eyes and lines of strain around her mouth. Her hair was short and neat and she'd had time, even so early in the morning, to apply powder and lipstick. She was keeping herself together with the desperation of one who has no alternative. I felt sorry for them both and sorry for Lisa who had to carry on her shoulders the burden of being the one ray of light in their dull world.

I was too transparent. She read my thoughts. 'Parents often talk of children being a problem,' she said. 'But parents can be a problem too, can't they?'

'Lisa loves you,' I insisted. 'You're not a problem to her, neither of you. You mustn't think that. It isn't true.'

She made a little dismissive gesture. 'Are you close to your parents, Fran? What do they think of your choice of acting as a career?'

I flushed and explained awkwardly that my parents were dead. 'My dad died when I was just fifteen. My mother—' I didn't want to explain about my mother. 'My mother died not so long ago,' I said.

'Oh, Fran, dear, I am so sorry!' She was overcome with embarrassment and sympathy. She took my hand and patted it.

'It's all right,' I assured her. 'I'm used to being on my own. As for whether they approved of my acting ambitions, I think Dad did. My mother was quite interested.'

How to explain that my mother's interest in what I was doing had been of a superficial and painfully brief nature. We'd spent so little time together at the end and it had been dominated by other things than what I wanted of life. But in so far as she had been able to give her attention to me, lying there on her bed in the hospice, I think she was mildly interested and wished me well.

I broke free of Jennifer with a few more awkward words and bussed my way back to Beryl's guest house. Here I took out the keys I still had and let myself in. But Beryl was aware of my arrival. She must have been listening out for it. As I shut the front door, the kitchen door at the back opened and her helmet of bronze hair popped out.

'Hello, dear,' she greeted me. 'You've got a visitor. She and I are just having a coffee in here.'

Oh, no, I thought. Pereira has come back! It could only mean bad news if she had. I entered the kitchen trying for the nonchalant look and probably really looking as shifty as they come. But it wasn't Pereira. It was Lisa who sat at Beryl's table, drinking coffee and nibbling on a chocolate digestive.

'I've got some things to do down in my flat,' said Beryl cheerfully. 'You two stay here and make yourselves at home. Make yourself a coffee, Fran.' She hobbled away.

I pulled out a chair and sat down opposite Lisa. 'I've just come from your house,' I said. 'Why didn't you ring and let me know you were coming over here? I'd have waited in for you.'

She put down the half-eaten biscuit. She'd tied back her blond hair with a pink scarf and her face looked white and drawn except for the end of her nose which was also pink. There was something pet-mouselike about her, but an angry pet mouse.

'What do you mean, you went to my house? I told you, I didn't want you around my parents! It's risky! What happened? Did you see them?'

'Yes, I saw them. I had coffee with them.'

I thought she might throw her coffee at me. 'You had no right! They're going to start suspecting—'

'Not if you and I both act natural. We're friends in London, right? I had coffee with them the other day. Why shouldn't I stop and have another with them when I call for you and find you out?'

Sulkily she asked, 'What did you talk about?'

'About the theatre. I think your mum was pleased to see me.'

'I know Dad's having a bad day. It isn't anything unusual. Mum copes. I lend a hand when I can. I can't be there all the time. They don't expect that. It's just a bad situation. There isn't a way out.'

She sniffed and rubbed at the end of her nose with a handkerchief she pulled from her sleeve. She was wearing another of those woolly chain-mail sweaters which looked as if they'd been knitted on a pair of snooker cues. This one was soft green in colour.

'Anyway,' I said. 'The reason I went to your house is because I've still got to talk to you about Mickey Allerton. That's another bad situation and you're already out of it. But I'm not. If I can spend time sitting with your dad, you can help me out with Mickey. It's only fair.'

'I came to Christ Church Meadow yesterday morning to talk to you about him, like I promised!' she snapped. 'But when I got there, half Oxford was milling about. People were saying someone had drowned and the local radio station last night reported someone drowning there. Was that what it was all about?'

'It was.' I hesitated. 'I found the body.'

She stopped rubbing the end of her nose with her hanky

and stared at me, eyes popping. 'Shit,' she said. 'That was bad luck.'

'Yes, and it was a bit worse than you might think,' I said. 'I recognised him.'

She frowned and looked suspicious. 'I thought you didn't know anyone in Oxford.'

'This wasn't an Oxford acquaintance. It was a London one and you know him, too. It was Ivo, the doorman at the Silver Circle.'

She'd had little colour in her cheeks but now even that drained away. 'So you lied!' she gasped. 'You said you hadn't brought anyone with you from the club!'

'I didn't. I didn't know he was in Oxford and I don't know what the hell he was doing down there in the river!' I snapped. My nerves were frayed. I'd had enough.

Lisa looked terrified, as well she might. Her fingers gripped the mangled handkerchief so tightly her knuckles showed up as white bony protuberances beneath the stretched skin. Her lips moved soundlessly. When she could speak she whispered, 'Mickey sent him. He sent him to check on you and me.'

I shook my head. 'I spoke to Mickey on the phone yesterday and he didn't seem any the wiser about what Ivo was doing here than I am. He didn't send him to check on me. He sent a guy called Filigrew to do that, a weasellylooking type in a business suit.'

She bit her lip and stared at me while she thought it

out. 'Then he came here on the same job as you're doing, to try and get me back to London!'

'Mickey sent me to do that. Why would Ivo take it upon himself? He'd be more likely to mess things up.'

She was shaking her head furiously. 'Ivo wouldn't think like that. He's not very bright. Neither is Jasna but put the two of them together and it's the sort of dumb plan they'd come up with.'

'Jasna?' I recalled my late-night mental meanderings. 'Right, that's the girl who works at the club, the one who squirrelled your home address away in her memory and gave it to Mickey. Or that's what you said you thought must have happened. Is she Ivo's girlfriend?'

'I still think that's what must have happened!' she said impatiently. 'Look, Ivo and Jasna are just mates as far as I know. They're compatriots, both Croats. I shouldn't think either of them is working legally. Jasna's been scared Mickey is going to sack her. She's a lousy dancer. I don't think she ever had any training. She's vulgar. Mickey doesn't like that.'

I thought of Lisa in her cowgirl outfit and something of my doubt must have shown in my face.

'There's erotic and there's plain vulgar,' Lisa said. 'You should know that. Mickey likes his acts to have class. I bet she knew Mickey had sent you here to bring me back to London and she told Ivo, if he could do it, then Mickey would be grateful and Ivo could ask for Jasna to keep her job.'

'All right,' I said. 'I'll buy that for now. But it doesn't explain Ivo being in Christ Church Meadow the morning I'd arranged to meet you!'

'Well, I don't know how he got there, do I?' she shouted. She pulled out her hanky again and rubbed furiously at her nose.

'Got a cold?' I asked sympathetically.

'Hay fever,' she snapped.

I made a lunge across the table, seized her wrists and yanked her hands towards me. I pushed up one of her sleeves and then the other. There were no needle marks.

She was yelling at me and swearing fit to turn the air blue. I released her. She snatched back her arms and pulled her long sleeves down, still swearing.

When she ran out of breath, I said. 'OK, so you don't mainline. But you snorted a line or two before you came out this morning.'

'Wouldn't you?' she asked bitterly. 'If you were stuck in a bloody awful situation like me?'

'I've been stuck in any number of bloody awful situations and I'm in one now,' I retorted unsympathetically. 'I've always got by without drugs. Where did you get the coke?'

'This is Oxford,' she mumbled. 'You can buy anything.'

'I don't care what you do,' I said. 'I really don't, except in one respect.'

'I'm not going back to London,' she said, and she meant it.

'All right, then phone him and say so. But just speak to the guy, will you? Then I've fulfilled my commission, done the job to the best of my ability. He won't pay me but he won't be mad at me, either.'

'I'm not contacting Mickey Allerton in any way. I'm not speaking to him on the phone.' Her mouth was set in a thin obstinate line.

'Then I don't get my dog back,' I said.

She boggled at me.

'My dog means a lot to me,' I said. 'I'm not being sentimental. She's a real part of my life and she's Mickey's prisoner. Look, I'm asking you nicely. Phone Mickey and speak to him. What have you got to lose?'

'He'll only say I have to go back.'

'You haven't *got* to. Even Mickey must know that. What's the hassle? Look, he's not insisting you go back to London. He says there's some job lined up for you in Spain.'

'Yeah, he mentioned it,' she said. 'Like, he didn't tell me the details. It was just, "How would you like to work in Spain, doll? Live in a nice place out on the costas?" I don't, right? I don't want anything that has Mickey Allerton attached to it.'

We seemed to have reached an impasse but she was eyeing me thoughtfully. 'Fran, we could do a deal on this.'

I didn't reply. If she wanted to talk, let her. If she had some bright idea, I needed to hear it. I didn't need to commit myself in advance. I should have shut up about

Bonnie. She probably guessed I'd do anything halfway legal.

She leaned across the table. 'I've got a way out of this, for the time being, at least. A friend rang me last night. She's a dancer like me but she works on the cruise ships. Those ships run a cabaret every evening for the passengers. She's signed up for the summer with a company sailing the Norwegian fjords but she's hurt her ankle. The ship's at anchor in Amsterdam waiting to sail out again. It leaves the day after tomorrow. If I can get out there I can be a temporary replacement for my friend until her ankle gets better.'

'So go,' I said. 'What's stopping you?' I felt numb. She didn't need to do any deals. All she had to do was go to Amsterdam on a budget flight and for six weeks or so she was safe aboard doing nightly dance routines as part of a group. Six weeks was way long enough for Mickey to lose interest and give up. So what had brought her here to see me? She could cut me right out of the loop.

'I haven't got my passport. I left it behind in London when I decided to chuck it all in. I took off in such a hurry, I just forgot it.'

The penny dropped. 'Ah,' I said. 'You want me to fetch it for you.'

'Fair's fair,' she retorted like a child. 'I want my passport. You want your dog. You get my passport for me. I phone Mickey for you.'

'The other way round,' I said. 'If I do it, you phone Mickey first.'

She sulked again but gave in. 'OK.' She pulled the hanky from her sleeve once more and snuffled into it.

'But I don't see why you can't go and fetch it yourself,' I added.

'Mickey knows where I live, doesn't he?' She started getting angry again. 'He's probably got someone looking out for me, just in case I turn up. They won't know you.'

Like everything else about this business, I didn't like it. But I agreed. It seemed straightforward enough.

Now we'd come to an agreement, I said, 'We'll phone Mickey right now. Have you got a mobile?'

She reached down to a canvas sack at her feet and pulled out a dinky little model with a puce overcoat.

'Let's have it!' I invited.

She handed it over. I tapped in the number Mickey had given me and waited.

'Yes?' He didn't need to say more.

'Hello, Mr Allerton,' I said. 'It's Fran. I've got Lisa here. She doesn't want to return to London but she'll speak to you.'

'Then put her on!' he said. 'Why am I wasting time with you?'

Such a nice man. I handed the phone over. Lisa scowled and, holding it gingerly, as if Allerton could somehow jump out of it and join us in the kitchen, said, 'Hello? This is Lisa.'

I watched her as Allerton said whatever he said. He took his time about it. She listened, stone-faced.

'I don't want that,' she said at last when Allerton had presumably paused for breath.

Another long spiel at the other end.

'I've told you,' Lisa's voice rose plaintively. 'I don't want to go to Spain. I told you when you suggested it before.'

More from Allerton. Now they were in conversation I ought not to eavesdrop, at least not openly. I got up and tactfully left the kitchen. I stationed myself in the hall, ear pressed against the door panels.

'I'm not bloody going and I'm not bloody coming back to London! I've quit, got that? I've quit!' I heard Lisa yell.

There was a lot more I couldn't make out. They were obviously having a real barney over the phone.

He must have changed tactics because eventually she seemed to calm down. The last thing I could make out was, 'Just give me some time, can't you?'

Was she weakening? Was she seeking to string Allerton along until she could get away on the cruise ship?

I pushed open the door and slipped back into the kitchen.

Obviously the last answer hadn't pleased Allerton and he had gone off the deep end again. Even I could see the phone was nearly jumping out of Lisa's grip as he expressed his frustration and fury. Eventually she handed the phone back to me, still stone-faced. 'He wants to talk to you.'

'Fran!' barked Allerton. 'You can come back to London. I'm washing my hands of that little cow!'

'What about my dog?'

'Dog?' He seemed taken aback as if he'd forgotten Bonnie. 'Oh, yeah, you can have your dog.'

I handed the phone to Lisa who cut the connection and shut it down. She dropped it back in her bag. 'All right, then? You'll go to London, now, this afternoon?'

'All right,' I said. What was there left to worry about? I'd got Lisa to speak to Allerton. He'd washed his hands of her. He'd promised my dog would be returned. A quick trip to fetch Lisa's passport seemed nothing.

We both stood up. Just then the kitchen door opened and Vera marched in. She stopped, looked at me, looked at Lisa and then turned and bolted out again.

'What . . .' I began.

But Lisa had turned from white to red in the face. She pushed back the table with a teeth-grinding screech on the tiled floor and hurtled towards the door.

'You just come back here!' she was yelling.

But Vera had made good her escape and it was Lisa who returned, panting.

'You didn't tell me about her!' she charged, glaring at me.

'Tell you what? She makes the breakfasts and the beds. Her name is Vera.'

'Yeah,' stormed Lisa. 'And she's another mate of Jasna's, isn't she? Another Croat! They all hang together! I've seen her waiting outside the club for Jasna and they've gone off to do the shops, excited like a couple of little kids.'

I remembered Vera with her little cleaner's cart outside my bedroom door while I was speaking to Ganesh on the mobile, telling him I had arranged to meet Lisa at Christ Church Meadow. I recalled finding her sitting on the stairs eavesdropping on another of my phone conversations with Gan.

'She snoops,' I said.

'You bet she snoops!' said Lisa viciously. 'She's like her pal, Jasna. She listens and she stores stuff away in her head because one day it might be useful.'

'Well,' I said heavily, 'I suppose that's how Ivo came to be down at Christ Church Meadow yesterday morning. He's been hanging around here somewhere with Vera feeding him details of my movements. Listen!' An idea struck me. 'Perhaps she's been listening to us, talking in here about my going up to London for your passport?'

Lisa looked doubtful. 'You went outside while I was talking to Mickey. Was she there?'

'I didn't see her,' I admitted. But then, I hadn't been looking. I'd been doing my own bit of eavesdropping.

'I don't think she knew I was here,' said Lisa, after some thought. 'Because she came marching in just now. She wouldn't have done that if she'd known. She would have been afraid I'd recognise her – and I did! You will still go up to London, won't you? The job on the cruise ship won't be repeated. I must get over to Amsterdam. Go now, go today.'

'Mickey says he's washed his hands of you,' I said. 'You could go yourself.'

'I'm still scared of him!' She thrust her angry little face into mine. 'You *promised*! It was a deal. I spoke to the bloody man and in return you said—'

'Oh, all right,' I interrupted. She was wearing me down. Good luck to the fellow members of that dance troupe, stuck on a cruise ship with her for weeks.

Lisa cheered up. 'That's wonderful. I'll go now and book a cheap flight. It's all working out fine.'

I was glad she felt that way. I saw her out of the place and then climbed the stairs. On the first landing, where the guest rooms were located, I paused. Then I made my way to a narrower stair at the end of the corridor and climbed up again, to find two tiny attic rooms. The door of one was ajar. I looked in. It seemed to be a boxroom. The other door was shut.

I tapped at it. 'Vera?'

There was no reply but I knew she was there. An empty room and a room with someone in it, even someone holding her breath, feel different.

'Come on, open up,' I said. 'It's me, Fran. Lisa's gone home. I promise.'

There was a shuffling and rattling and the door opened a crack. Vera peered through it. 'What do you want?'

'I want a chat with you, Vera. Let me in.'

She pulled the door open and stood aside sulkily.

The room was furnished quite nicely: a bed, a sofa, a little table with a television on it, another little table with an electric kettle and necessities for making coffee, a wardrobe built in under the eaves. Cosy. I walked over to the built-in wardrobe and pushed the sliding door aside.

'What are you doing? Is my room!' Vera shouted at me.

She darted towards me. I ignored her and, when she grabbed my arm, I shook her off. I reached into the wardrobe and pulled out a sports bag. I unzipped it while she watched me resentfully.

'I've been reading a fashion article in a women's magazine,' I said conversationally. 'But it didn't say women had started wearing these.' I held up a pair of Y-front briefs.

'Sod you,' said Vera chippily. 'Is not your business.'

'Oh yes, it is. You had him hidden up here, didn't you? Ivo, I mean. How did he get in and out of the house without Beryl seeing him?'

Vera bit her lip and sulked some more. 'Fire escape,' she said at last. She nodded towards the window.

I went and peered out. Surely enough, there was an iron fire-escape staircase which started up here and wound its way down the back of the house into the garden. My gaze fell again on the little door in the back wall. There must be an alley behind the houses in this street. I remembered my first night here and the shadow I'd thought I'd seen move against that rear wall. I shivered.

Ivo had stood there, silent and still, watching me outlined in my window.

I recalled too the glimpse of someone in pink on the platform at Paddington. Jasna had trailed me to the station and watched to see me board the train. She'd gone back to the Silver Circle and told Ivo to get straight after me. If my eye hadn't been taken by Pereira, I might have noticed Jasna at Paddington and so much might have been different.

Vera was watching me, her eyelids flickering. 'What you do now?' she asked nervously. 'I need this job. I must get my English good enough or I won't get really good job in Croatia.'

'I'm not going to tell Beryl, not if you cooperate. You have caused a lot of trouble, Vera. Ivo's dead. Or do you know already? Did you hear me talk about that when you snooped on my phone call?'

I saw at once that she hadn't known. I thought she was going to pass out. Her face drained of all colour and her eyes looked enormous. She opened and closed her mouth a couple of times before she could speak and, when she did, her voice was hoarse.

'No, is not possible.'

'It's possible. It was on the local radio last night. He's been staying here. Didn't you wonder where he was when he didn't come back yesterday? His clothes are here. All he wore was running shorts. Where could he be for forty-eight hours just wearing those?'

'I don't know, I don't know where he was,' she whispered. 'I think perhaps he was looking for that girl, that one who was downstairs in the kitchen. She is a lot of trouble, that girl. The boss at the club wants her back. Ivo thought, perhaps he could take her back.' She ran her tongue over her lips, wetting them. 'The police know this?'

'They don't know about Lisa. They know they have a dead man on their hands. He drowned, by the way. They don't know who he is yet, and they won't give up until they do. Then they might well find out you hid him here and they'll want to know why you didn't come forward. I'll tell you what you're going to do. You're going to the police—'

'No!' she interrupted vehemently. 'No police!'

'Are you here illegally?'

'No, I have work permit, one year. I work for Beryl. It's nice here.' She began to snivel.

'That's all right, then. No reason for you to worry about the police. Here's the story. You tell them your boyfriend came from London and stayed here. You don't want the landlady to know but you're worried because he's missing. He went out jogging yesterday morning and hasn't come back. Well, he wouldn't, would he? Because I found him in the river. They'll probably ask you to identify him.'

Vera wrapped her arms around her upper body and rocked miserably to and fro. I felt sorry for her but this wasn't the time for concern about someone else. Somehow I had to satisfy the police that the reason Ivo had come to Oxford had nothing to do with me.

'Was not my boyfriend,' she said sulkily. 'Only friend of a friend. She ask me, I give him place to sleep.' She pointed at the sofa. 'He slept there. Really.'

'I don't care if he slept hanging upside down from the rafter with his bat's wings folded,' I said. 'Just get down there and identify him or I tell Beryl you've been sneaking men in.'

I thought she was going to cry again but she nodded.

'Good. Just do it, right? Now. But before you go, you listened at my bedroom door, didn't you? You heard me arrange to meet someone by the river?'

'I not listen at doors,' said Vera obstinately. 'I don't know what you say.'

'But you knew why Ivo came to Oxford?'

'I only know he came to find that girl for his boss.' Her voice rose. 'Is not my fault he is dead. I know nothing, nothing!'

She'd agreed to go to the police and identify him, because she needed the job, as she said. But she wasn't about to admit anything else and, if I pushed her too hard, she might turn awkward. I had to settle for what I'd got.

'All right,' I said. 'I'm going to London this afternoon and I'll be back this evening. I'll expect to hear you've been to see the police and you've identified Ivo's body.'

She began to cry then, snivelling unattractively and rubbing tears and snot over her face with her forearm.

'You don't understand, none of you understand. There is no work for people at home. There was no work for Ivo.

215

He trained for professional sportsman but no team took him. He want to make movies but no movie company take him. He doesn't have much education, only his strength. His parents are peasants. He doesn't want to spend his life working on the land. Jasna is a cousin, a sort of cousin. She wrote to him to come to London and she can get him a job at her club. The big boss there needs strong men at the door. So Ivo came. But the big boss doesn't like Jasna and he doesn't like Ivo much either. They are frightened because both of them can get the sack, don't you understand that? They were frightened! Now I am frightened too!'

I didn't have time to play nursemaid or to discuss East European labour problems. I left her to it and set out for the station. I didn't tell Beryl what Vera had done and I didn't tell her I was intending to be away from Oxford that night. She wasn't around anyway. Neither was Filigrew. I wondered what he was doing and decided that probably I didn't want to know. I was in the process of extricating myself from Mickey Allerton's business. Just this one last little errand for Lisa and I was home and dry.

Chapter Nine

It was five o'clock when I got back to London and well into the rush hour for traffic. People were streaming into Paddington Station and I had to fight my way against the flow through the crowds to go down into the Tube. The underground air was stuffy and warm, heavy with human sweat and dust. Individuals cease to exist in such throngs. They meld into an amorphous mass that is drained of colour except for monochrome shades of grey. Faces are tired and puffy. Even those with companions don't speak. They are anxious to be home and fearful of missing trains. They clutch briefcases full of work they are taking with them and laptop computers. They carry this mobile office as a snail carries its house on its back. The air is filled with the patter of their feet as they scurry along the corridors and the creak and rumble of the heavily laden escalators which carry them upwards to the anthill of the station concourse. However insecure my lifestyle, I have never wished to join them.

Not that I was without worries of my own. I could have gone first to the address Lisa had given me but I wanted to make sure that Ganesh and I were really back on our old friendly footing and I directed my steps towards the newsagent's. I also wanted to bring him up to date on what had happened and talk it over with him, just as I normally did. I wanted to be with him and Hari, people I knew were my friends, who might criticise but would always stand by me and who never asked me to do the impossible.

The shop stayed open until eight or eight thirty if things were busy, but not after that. They had to get up very early in the morning for one reason; another was that late-night trade brought with it additional risks. With a busy street scene outside as active as in daylight hours, unwelcome visitations increased. They already got them by day: grubby old winos cadging a handout, light-fingered pilferers and outright nutters who simply wanted to be there and talk. At night it could turn nasty. They closed the shop before some druggie, desperate for a fix to see him through until morning, burst in demanding the contents of the till or drunken yobs decided to round off the night by smashing up an Asian shop.

The pink and yellow space rocket was still outside. A sad little handwritten notice hung round it to tell anyone interested that it was still, or again, out of order. I wondered if the technician had been to fix it.

I pushed open the door and the bell jangled. Hari looked

up from behind the counter, a look of alarm on his face. I couldn't see Ganesh and supposed he was in the stockroom.

'It's OK, Hari,' I said. 'It's only me.'

'You are in Oxford,' said Hari, still looking alarmed as if I were an apparition from the spirit world.

'No, well, yes – but I just popped back to London for a few hours to do something. I'm going to Oxford again tonight.'

He came out from behind the counter. I can't say he looked terrifically pleased to see me. But then, there had been a little upset here while I'd been away and I'd caused it.

'Look, Hari,' I began. 'I'm really sorry I lost Ganesh's phone in the river and the police found it and contacted—'

He waved his hand, dismissing all this. 'No, no, my dear. Only that you are safe, that is the most important thing. But I did tell you to stay away from the river there.'

'No, Hari, you told me not to go in a punt. I didn't go in a punt. I was just walking . . .' It struck me that his face was still puckered in a worried frown. 'Where's Ganesh?' I asked. From the stockroom Ganesh could have heard my voice. He should have appeared. It began to dawn on me something was wrong and it hadn't to do with Oxford.

'Has something happened?' I asked sharply.

Hari drew himself up to his full five foot two. 'Now, Francesca, my dear, you must not worry.'

'Where's Ganesh?' I shouted. 'What's happened to him?'

He raised both hands, palms outwards, in a calming gesture. 'He is perfectly all right. But there has been a small misfortune . . .'

'What is it?' I yelled.

Hari looked doleful. 'Such a remarkable animal.' He shook his head.

'Hari,' I said as calmly as I could. 'If you don't tell me exactly what's been going on immediately, I shall scream very, very loudly.'

I don't know whether he ever would have got round to telling me. At that moment the bell jangled at the opening of the door and Ganesh walked in. Not seeing me at once he began, 'I've put notices in all—'

Then he saw me, stopped with a look of dismay on his face and said, 'Oh, damn. It's you. Why aren't you in bloody Oxford?'

Ganesh isn't given to swearing, even mildly. This was clearly a moment of great stress. And why did no one want to see me?

'Come upstairs,' Ganesh went on quickly, taking me by the arm. 'I'll make us a cup of tea.'

I allowed him to bundle me upstairs to the flat but before he could escape to the kitchen I barred his way and said bluntly, 'Come on, all of it.'

'Don't freak out!' he begged.

'I shall,' I promised him, 'if you don't tell me straight away what's wrong.'

He drew a deep breath. 'The bouncer at the club, not

the one you found floating in the river, the fat bald one with the wife who likes dogs. She's been looking after Bonnie. Well, this morning early she thought she'd take the dogs, hers and Bonnie, for a run in Regent's Park before it got hot. Her dogs are little hairy things, they don't like the heat. So she took them to the park and when she got there she let them off the lead, all of them, Bonnie included. She thought because Bonnie got on well with her dogs, she'd stay with them. But she didn't. She ran away.'

'Where?' I asked dully, the word dropping into a long deep silence.

'I don't know, do I?' Ganesh snapped. 'The woman looked all over the park. She asked all the other dog-walkers. She asked the café there to put a lost dog notice in their window.'

I realised he was tired and worried and upset because he had dreaded giving me this news.

I sat down suddenly on the sofa. 'Bonnie's been in Regent's Park before, with me,' I said, trying to sound calm so that Ganesh wouldn't get more agitated. 'She knows the place. Perhaps she's run back to my place, looking for me.'

'I've been there,' Ganesh said. 'No one's seen her but the other tenants all know. They're all keeping an eye open. And I've put a lost dog notice in the window of every Asian newsagent's and grocer's in the entire area. I've even told the police and the RSPCA.' He sat down beside me, his shoulders slumped in dejection. 'I can't do any more, Fran. I've walked all over the area looking for her.'

'It's not your fault, Gan,' I consoled him. 'It's the fault of that daft woman letting her off the lead. Bonnie's gone looking for me. She probably ran back to the flat, found I wasn't there, and is running round all the other places I go. She might turn up here.'

'Hari's watching out,' he assured me.

'Right,' I said, slapping my hands on my knees. 'I'm not going back to Oxford until Bonnie's found.'

'What's happening in Oxford, anyway?' Ganesh asked. 'Why are you here? Have you come back for good? Is it all over?' A note of hope entered his voice and I realised how much he'd been worrying about me in Oxford, too.

I felt selfish and was sorry to dash even this faint ray of optimism. But I couldn't just forget about Lisa and her passport. I explained it to him as briefly as I could. For good measure I told him about Vera and how she'd hidden Ivo in her flat and that Lisa had recognised her.

'I promised Lisa I'd fetch her passport,' I concluded. 'She kept her part of the bargain and phoned Allerton. But the honest truth is I'm fed up with Allerton, Lisa, Vera, Filigrew, Ned . . .' I sighed. 'All of them, even Beryl.'

'Who is Ned?' asked Ganesh.

'Lisa's friend, the one I mentioned to you. He's all brawn and not much brain, but devoted with it.'

'Devoted enough to push Ivo in the river?'

'Don't ask me,' I said. 'I've considered it. But let Pereira find that out. It's nothing to do with me. Provided Vera does as I told her and tells Pereira Ivo came to Oxford to see her, Pereira will lose interest in me. Ivo's death will go down as a mugging or an accident. Perhaps it really was one of those. I don't care any more.'

'Who is Pereira?'

I stared at him. 'Didn't I tell you? She's a copper. I'm sure I told you about her.'

'Fran,' Ganesh said firmly, 'you tell me next to nothing. The first I know about anything is when the police turn up here telling Hari I've drowned in Oxford and the Oxford plods have retrieved my mobile from the bottom of the river.'

'I've told Hari I'm sorry about that. I am sorry I lost your mobile.'

Ganesh indicated a leather holder clipped to his belt. 'I've borrowed Usha's. I've given the number to everyone I've told Bonnie is missing so that, if they see her, they can ring me wherever I am.'

'I can't go back to Oxford tonight,' I objected. 'I must stay at my place here in case Bonnie comes home.'

Ganesh went into the kitchen and began making the tea. 'Listen,' he called to me from there. 'Why don't you go over to your place now and check it out? If she's not there, you can go on to Lisa's flat and get the passport – where is this flat, anyway?'

'St John's Wood.'

Ganesh came back, a mug of tea in either hand. 'Blimey,

that's a bit upmarket for a pole dancer, isn't it? I'd have thought the rent was out of her league.'

'What do I care where she lives?' I demanded. Then I broke off and stared at him. 'All this has scrambled my brain,' I said. 'I've just remembered Ned told me that when he went to London to see Lisa, before she started working at the club, she lived in Rotherhithe in a rented room in a council flat. She must have been earning an awful lot of money at the Silver Circle to be able to move from there to St John's Wood.'

'Dodgy,' opined Ganesh. 'The whole thing has been dodgy from the beginning. Don't say I didn't warn you. I suggest you go and get the passport and take it back to your flat. Stay there tonight. Then take the train to Oxford first thing tomorrow morning. Drop off the passport at Lisa's house and afterwards come back here. After all, once you've given her the passport, you don't need to stay in Oxford any longer, do you?'

I shook my head.

'So, do it. Then you're in the clear.'

That's why I like talking things over with Ganesh. He makes everything sound so simple.

After I'd drunk my tea I went to my place but there was no sign of my dog. The flat is on the ground floor of a double-fronted house. Each floor has two flats on it except for the attic which is a single conversion. There are also two basement flats with separate entrances. Although Ganesh had already done the rounds there, I knocked on all doors and asked about Bonnie, or pushed notes underneath giving Beryl's phone number in Oxford. Erwin the drummer, who has the other ground-floor flat, promised to ask all his mates to keep a lookout. I didn't hold out much hope from this. I'd met some of Erwin's mates, most of them musicians, affable souls puffing joints at all hours of the day and night and given to memory lapses. Erwin insisted he would keep them looking and I appreciated his wanting to help. There wasn't anything else I could do, so I set out for Lisa's flat.

It was getting late in the evening when I got there, about eight. It was pretty quiet everywhere. Lisa had given me a set of three keys. One was the key to the main entrance to the flats and another opened the flat itself. The remaining key was a small one which locked the drawer in which she kept the passport. It was in a bedside cabinet, she'd told me. I couldn't miss it. It all seemed straightforward.

The flat was in a low-rise block built, by the look of it, some time in the thirties. I let myself into the downstairs hall and shut the door quietly behind me. But not, as it appeared, quietly enough – or else she'd seen me approach.

She popped out of her door, the ground-floor flat to the left, and stood smiling at me. She was eighty years old at least, nearing ninety at a guess, and five feet in height. Her hair was dyed an alarming black and she had piled it on her head and attempted to fix it there with pins. Wisps of hair escaped all over and dangled wildly around her face which was puckered and plastered with lavishly applied pancake make-up. Her mouth was a wobbly scarlet line of lipstick. As for her clothes, she gave the impression she had been hunting in a box of jumble and pulled out things at random. A drooping skirt in Indian cotton hung to her ankles and her feet were thrust into gold Turkish slippers.

'You are visiting somebody here?' she asked. She had a strong accent which I thought I recognised. She sounded a lot like my grandmother Varady and didn't look unlike her.

I pointed upward towards the first-floor flats and attempted to edge round her. She shuffled sideways and continued to block my access to the stairs.

'Mrs Betterton?' she asked. 'I think she has gone to visit her son. He lives in Hendon.' She peered up into my face. Her eyes were sharp little black roundels on a yellowish background.

'No,' I said. 'Not Mrs Betterton.'

'Ah,' she said cunningly, 'the young lady. But she is not there. She has also gone away visiting.'

If she was anything like my grandma, she'd go on asking until I explained myself. I decided to save time and tell her more or less what I was doing there.

I held up the keys. 'I've come to check the flat for her. All right? Make sure there are no leaky taps or anything.'

She looked alarmed. 'There is a problem with the plumbing? The water will come through my ceiling?'

'No,' I said patiently. 'I just used that as an example. So if you'll excuse me, I'll pop up and see.'

This time I moved too quickly for her, got past her and was halfway up the stairs before she could react. She didn't give up, though.

'I can come with you?' she called, putting her hand on the banister and preparing to haul herself up after me. 'In case it is the plumbing?'

'No need!' I called back firmly. 'I'll let you know if it's the plumbing.'

I'd reached the upper landing. Lisa's flat was indeed to the left directly above the remnant of the Austro-Hungarian Empire. I got the door open as fast as I could, scurried in and shut it behind me, just in case she had decided to follow me upstairs.

The atmosphere suggested the place had been closed up a while. Scents which had been trapped there when the door was shut lingered in furniture and curtains: a stale smell of cigarettes, fried food and lavender bubble bath. I went to the window and opened it to clear them all out. Then I took a look around me.

Ganesh was right: this did look an expensive hang-out for a pole dancer, even one earning good money. I was in the living room, which had a parquet floor and was furnished with two huge white leather sofas. They faced one another across a glass coffee table of aggressively modern style. There was a large painting of a nude on the wall. The girl in the picture was turned away from the observer but looked back over her shoulder. She wasn't Lisa but probably a professional artist's model because the painting was a genuine original and looked as if it had cost a bit. Even I could see it was an extraordinarily erotic picture and it made me feel uneasy. This wasn't because I'm a prude but because I doubted it would have been a woman's choice of décor. Those two monster leather sofas also had a masculine look. I wondered if I was in the right flat.

I took a look in the small kitchen which had been left clean and tidy and smelled faintly of good quality coffee and pepperoni pizza.

I turned my attention to the bathroom. There were a lot of used towels stuffed in a wicker basket awaiting laundry day. A large bath towel was draped carelessly over the edge of the bath. I touched it. It was damp. There was still water in the dip surrounding the plughole. Ought it not to have dried up by now? Lisa had been days in Oxford.

I opened the door of a mirror-fronted cabinet and was confronted with an array of cosmetics and toiletries all crammed together, and a man's electric razor. I closed it and turned my attention to a small pedal bin. It contained a lipstick-stained tissue and a torn piece of thin white printed card. I picked it out of the bin and scrutinised it. It was all that remained of a small box of the kind that one associates with chemist's shops. Little of the print remained intact but there was enough for me to make out what it had once contained. My unease increased.

But I was here to get a passport and I'd better hurry up and do it. The need to get out of here was becoming overwhelming. I found the bedroom, but only after opening the door to a small boxroom which Lisa had apparently been using as a dressing room. Her clothes hung on the sort of rail on wheels you see in shops. Every kind of outfit was here, not just her professional ones with their spangles and lurex. She had the sort of brimming wardrobe most young women probably only dream of and nothing was cheap. Shoes were lined up by the wall. I counted twenty pairs. Trainers and high boots jostled Jimmy Choos and Manolo Blahniks. Some looked as if they'd never been worn but were the result of a no-holds-barred spending spree.

The bedroom was dominated by a king-size bed decked with a satin quilted throw and numerous fancy cushions, just like you see in the display in a furniture-shop window. There were matching bedside cabinets both with lockable little drawers. I tried the nearer one with my little key but the drawer was empty. I went round to the other side and tried again. The same key worked and the drawer slid open. A jumble of envelopes lay within. I riffled through them until I found one containing a small red booklet. The passport! I pulled it out and opened it. Lisa's face stared blankly at me in the sort of mugshot you get from one of those photo cabins. I slammed the drawer shut, hastily relocked it and turned towards the door.

As I did the bell rang. Damn, I thought. Old Mother Hubbard downstairs had finally creaked her way up determined to find out what I was doing and why I was so long about it. I wasn't going to let her inside. Anyway, I'd got what I'd come for. I thrust the passport into my pocket and set out for the bedroom door. I'd stretched out my hand to pull it open when I noticed for the first time the dressing gown hanging behind it. There was something about it didn't look right and not just the colour, which was dark brown. It was made of silk or a silky type material and patterned with an oriental design.

I hesitated and unhooked it. The doorbell rang again. I ignored it and shook out the dressing gown, revealing the dragon crawling up the back. Not only was it far too big for Lisa, it was the wrong style, or put another way it was designed for a different sex. This was a man's dressing gown. I put my nose closer to the thing and sniffed. I didn't think Lisa smoked cigars but the wearer of this did.

For the first time I turned my attention to the built-in wardrobe. If Lisa kept her extensive wardrobe in a separate dressing room, what was in here? I slid back a door. A row of suits and jackets confronted me. On a shelf were neatly folded sweaters. The cigar smell, which had been trapped in there, oozed out and assaulted my nostrils. No wonder Lisa had chosen to house her own clothes elsewhere.

The doorbell squealed a lengthy frustrated peal. The

old lady must be leaning on it. I hurried across the living room, pausing to slam shut the window I'd opened, and pulled open the flat door.

Two people stood there, both totally unknown to me, a woman and a man. She was tall and thin and had turned forty although she dressed like a twenty-year-old in tight white trousers and a cropped top which revealed her bare midriff. The skin of her face and arms and the midriff were all evenly tanned and suggested regular use of a sun bed. Her hair was bleached and cut short in a feathery style and her eyes sparkled either side of her pointed nose in a challenging expression.

He was shorter but, to make up for it, broader, giving the impression he was square. He had dark coarse hair, a pock-marked skin and pouched dark eyes. He wore a navy blazer and cream-coloured chinos and a lot of heavy gold jewellery. His dark eyes watched me expressionlessly. I had the feeling he was some sort of minder. Behind them both I could glimpse the old lady from downstairs. She was halfway up the staircase clinging to the banister, a look of triumph on her wizened face. Whatever this visitation was, I reckoned the aged one was responsible for it.

The woman in the doorway took the initiative. 'About bleedin' time,' she said. 'What you been doing in my flat?'

It was a difficult moment but my life has been spent dealing with difficult moments and the first rule is not to let anyone see they've caught you on the hop.

'It's not your flat,' I said, blocking the door as she made

a movement forward. I had to let her see that, if she wanted to get in, she was going to have to push past me. Either she or the gorilla with her would be capable of doing that, but my failure to fold in the face of her aggression threw her momentarily on to the back foot. 'If it was your flat, you'd have a key,' I went on.

She blinked. 'All right,' she said. 'It's Mickey's flat. But I've got a right to it and that little tart he keeps here certainly isn't getting to keep it. It's part of the settlement. My lawyer says so.'

Now I was the one thrown into confusion and could only hope my face didn't show it. One thing was shockingly clear to me. This flat belonged to Allerton. He had decorated and furnished it as a bowerbird does its nest and installed Lisa, his mistress, in it. Mickey chose the white leather sofas and the provocative nude painting. Mickey relaxed here in the dragon dressing gown and kept his clothes in the built-in wardrobe. Mickey had paid for the unworn shoes and designer label dresses. If I hadn't been so anxious to get out of the place, I would have worked that out for myself instantly and not had to have it signposted by this woman. A shiver ran up my spine. Mickey had bathed that morning in the bath and left the water and the damp towel. It might easily have been Mickey who had turned up here now and found me going through the place.

Lisa's decision to bolt and leave Allerton now appeared in an entirely new and intimate light. This was a lot more than a dancer who'd got fed up with working in a seedy club. This was the end of an affair and a shared lifestyle. This was shouts and threats and tears and bruised emotions. This girl hadn't just worked for Mickey. She had been sharing his bed and his life and in return he had given her everything she wanted. As a result, he had thought he owned her. Perhaps that was what had led to Lisa deciding to call an end to it. Mickey had become too possessive, perhaps jealous. More shoes and clothes than she could wear didn't compensate for lack of all freedom. Nor, let's face it, was Mickey the sort of boyfriend she could take home and introduce to Paul and Jennifer.

I sighed. Ganesh had said I hadn't known what was going on and obviously I hadn't. Mickey hadn't been frank and neither had Lisa. If either of them had told me the truth I wouldn't be here now. I'd have run a mile. I'd have tracked down Bonnie and kidnapped her from Harry's wife and hidden us both away until the combatants in this lovers' battle had concluded it. I had been a fool to imagine this whole thing was a business matter. It was as upfront and personal as it could get.

It was probably even more complicated. The woman hovering impatiently in the doorway had mentioned a lawyer. A sinking feeling made itself felt in my chest.

'Who are you?' I asked, guessing what the answer would be.

'I'm Julie,' she retorted, staring at me.

'Great,' I said. 'I'm Fran. You don't know who I am and

233

I still don't know who you are. If you think you're coming in, you're going to have to tell me. Even if this flat belongs to Mickey Allerton, Lisa has been living here.'

'I know that!' she snapped. 'I'm Julie Allerton, Mickey's wife.'

Oh, shit, I thought. She would be, wouldn't she? Not just a discarded girlfriend but the legal trouble-and-strife. Never had rhyming slang appeared so apt.

'Soon to be ex-wife,' she added.

Double disaster.

'And this is my friend, Donald.' Julie concluded her introduction by waving a scarlet-tipped nail at the simian type beside her who still remained silent and stared at me as if I were part of the furniture.

'Perhaps you'd better come in, then,' I said.

She marched past me, Donald lumbering after. Julie paused and looked around her critically. Donald just stood there without any apparent interest in his surroundings.

'I never furnished it like this,' Julie said. 'Mickey must have chosen it all or he got someone to do it for him. That little scrubber didn't do it. I had it really lovely, you know, tasteful. Now it looks like a knocking shop. What's he done with all my furniture and curtains and my beautiful white carpet? If he's sold them off then he owes me the money. Bloody hell, to change it all and never one word to me!' She turned to me and I got the critical look. 'Do you work for my husband?'

'Not at the club,' I said. 'I'm just running an errand for Lisa.'

'I didn't think you'd work at the club,' she said dismissively.

Very rude, I thought. All right, I'm not the glamorous type, but there's such a thing as tact.

She went to one of the sofas and sat down, crossing her legs and swinging her foot. She wore strappy sandals with very high heels and her toenails were painted to match her fingernails. The action indicated not so much nervousness as a pent-up frustration ready to burst out and wreak havoc. 'Sit down, Donald,' she ordered.

He shambled across and sat down beside her, hitching up his cream chinos to reveal white silk socks and flat white loafers. I wondered whether the look he was aiming for was nautical. I closed the flat door and took a seat on the opposite sofa facing the pair of them. We must have looked like three passengers in a train.

'I've got an arrangement with Mrs Kovacs downstairs,' Julie confided. She began to rummage in a capacious white leather bag and pulled out a packet of cigarettes. 'You smoke?'

'No, thanks,' I said.

'I'd give up,' she said, 'if it wasn't for the stress. I've had a lot of stress. Divorce isn't easy and Mickey is being a real shit.'

Donald moved to pull a lighter from his blazer pocket and thumb it into flame. Julie leaned towards him and lit her cigarette. He put the lighter away without attempting to light up himself. Julie looked round her.

'Got an ashtray in here?'

'I'll look in the kitchen,' I said. It was strange, playing hostess to these two in this flat. I couldn't see an ashtray in the kitchen but I found a saucer and brought that back, putting it on the glass coffee table.

'Ta,' she said and tapped out the already long column of ash.

'Mrs Kovacs,' I said, 'would be the old lady who lives in the flat below this one.'

'That's right. She keeps an eye open for me. See, I know Mickey's trying to diddle me over the divorce settlement. Well, I'm not having it!' She nodded and blew a cloud of smoke in my direction.

I coughed meaningfully and waved it away.

'Sorry, dear,' she said attempting to dispel the fumes with a wave of her scarlet nails. 'Well, old Ma Kovacs, she lets me know what goes on up here!' Julie nodded. 'Of course, I know anyway. I'm not daft. You know what? I've got it worked out and you can tell Mickey so if you see him. Or you can tell that Lisa so. She's not having my flat. She's not having anything of mine. Well,' Julie reflected, scowling into the spiralling cigarette smoke, 'she can have my husband and welcome to him, but she's not having anything else.'

'Mrs Kovacs,' I said, sticking to my own line of conversation, 'phoned you to let you know a stranger had turned up with the key of the flat and was up here.'

'That's it, dear. So Donald and I jumped in the car and came over from Hampstead. Didn't we, Donald?'

Donald nodded silently.

Perhaps Julie noticed that I eyed Donald with a slightly puzzled look. At any rate, she felt she had to explain him. 'Mickey himself might have turned up and I didn't want to face him all on my own. I wanted, you know, moral support.' She nodded at Donald.

Donald looked more like strong-arm support to me, but, either way, Julie had probably been prudent. The idea that Mickey might just walk in on the three of us was an unsettling one. But there was safety in numbers, if he did.

'So,' said Julie. 'What are you doing here, anyway?'

'Look,' I said. 'This business of your divorce and whose flat this is and all the rest of it, it's nothing to do with me, right? I didn't even know Mickey Allerton was married.'

'Well, he soon won't be,' said Julie crisply. 'Where's the bimbo?'

'If you mean Lisa,' I said, 'she's had to go and visit her family. Her father suffers very bad health and he's in a wheelchair.' Julie stared at me. 'On the level,' I said. 'She asked me to pop in and check out the flat because she left in a hurry and she doesn't know when she'll be coming back.'

Julie stubbed out her cigarette and leaned towards me. 'You can tell her from me that she's not never coming back here, right? I'm getting in a locksmith tomorrow to change all the locks. My lawyer says I can.'

'Like it's nothing to do with me,' I persisted.

Julie leaned back, arms folded, and surveyed me. 'But you know my husband?'

'We've met,' I said.

'She's got him twisted round her little finger,' Julie said.

Not to the point where he took it quietly when Lisa decided to end the affair. It was no use telling Julie that Lisa had had enough. She wouldn't believe it and I couldn't blame her, not with all that expensive schmutter in the dressing room. My mind was now running in a new direction. Mickey had invested heavily in this little love nest. He was trying to persuade the flown lovebird back into it. But if she really wouldn't listen, wouldn't come back, it might not end with only Ivo floating in the river. I'd read about crimes of passion. I had to get out of this whole thing.

'You know the trouble with my husband?' asked Julie conversationally as she lit another cigarette. A haze of blue smoke was beginning to fill the air between us and my eyelids itched. 'You know why he's got himself into this mess with that girl?'

'He didn't realise age difference mattered?' I ventured since she seemed to expect an answer.

'He's not that old!' she snapped. I realised she and Allerton were probably much of a generation and my implication that Mickey was verging on the elderly hadn't gone down well. Studying her now I could see how the skin round her eyes was beginning to sag and her jaw was losing its firm line. She hadn't yet resorted to plastic surgery but the day would come if she wanted to stay looking the way she did now. Even so, I thought with some sympathy, it wouldn't do her any good. Mickey had already found a way to recapture his lost youth. Lisa had the key to this flat and the visitor didn't.

'Well, no,' I said hastily. 'And he's looked after himself. He's a very attractive man.' I added, 'Not my type! But I can see he would be for a lot of women. Still, it's got to be twenty years between them.'

'Age doesn't matter,' said Julie firmly. 'Does it, Donald?'

Donald appeared surprised at this unexpected appeal to him for an opinion on matters of the heart. His bushy eyebrows shot up and he uttered a kind of grunt which could be interpreted any way you wanted.

'Mickey's problem,' said Julie, 'has always been that he's a bit of a dreamer.'

Now I must have looked surprised because a dreamer wasn't how I'd have described Allerton. A well-groomed thug who exacted value for every pound spent and didn't like being crossed, yes. Wandering lonely as a cloud, no.

'You can believe it.' She gestured at me with the cigarette. 'Now I give Mickey his due. He's done well for himself. For a long time I could have said he'd done well for both of us because we were together then.' Julie leaned forward and through gritted teeth uttered, 'Twenty-four years. Next year I was looking forward to our silver wedding. I was planning a big bash. I won't say Mickey had never let his fancy stray. But it was nothing that mattered, not until little Miss Plum-in-her-mouth turned up. What was a girl like that doing, asking for a job at the Silver Circle?'

'She wanted to be a dancer,' I said.

'Then she's as daft as he is,' said Julie, sucking furiously on the weed. 'You know what Mickey's dad did for a living?'

'No idea,' I said faintly.

'He worked for the council, environmental health they call it now. Rat-catcher in chief, that's what he was. It was a respectable living, mind, and we'd all be worse off without rat-catchers, but Mickey, he wanted to be in charge of his own life. He didn't want anyone telling him what to do and he wanted glamour. You don't find any glamour down drains.'

I nodded agreement. It had occurred to me I should encourage her to unburden herself. Anything she told me about Mickey might prove useful. Know your enemy! 'Go on,' I invited.

She was more than willing. 'When I met Mickey he was running a pub and all his family was real proud of him. Then he scraped enough together to stop working for the brewery and go independent. His mum told everyone her son was a successful businessman. So he was. But Mickey, he had dreams far, far beyond pulling pints. He turned the pub into a club. It was just a starting point. He sold up and moved on to something bigger and in a better location. Then he took on a second place. It was like everything he touched turned to, you know, gold. Like that bloke in the story.'

'King Midas,' I said. 'It ends badly, that story.'

'So does this one. No matter how well things were going, Mickey wanted to do better. The thing that triggered all the trouble, as I see it, was when he bought the villa.'

My mind was running ahead of her now. 'In Spain?' I guessed.

She nodded. 'It's a lovely place, Fran. It's got a kidney-shaped swimming pool.'

'Nice,' I said.

'You bet it is!' she retorted. 'But we started mixing with a different set of people and Mickey, he started to get really big ideas. He wants to open up this really posh nightclub in Spain, the sort of place where you get stars to come and sing for the punters. All upmarket décor and no week-in-the-sun holidaymakers but the real high rollers. "Mick," I said to him. "Stick to what you know." He wouldn't listen to me. But it was good advice, wasn't it, Donald?'

Donald grunted again. I wondered if he could speak.

'Then along comes Miss Lisa, all nicely spoken and easy on the eye, a bit of real quality totty. And Mickey loses any common sense he ever had just like that, overnight. I'm out: she's in. We'd bought this flat as an investment because there's good money to be made renting out furnished accommodation around here. But then Mickey pinched the keys and moved Miss Lisa in. I might, just might, have put up with that if I'd thought it was temporary. Mickey's at a funny age for a man. They do silly things. I don't mean you, Donald.' She patted his knee.

Donald looked alarmed at this intimacy and then puzzled as if he wasn't sure he was being paid a compliment or insulted.

Julie took up her tale. 'But that wasn't the end of it. Oh no, Mickey thinks he's going to sell up here and move out to Spain, taking her with him. They'll live in the villa and open up this big fancy club and run it together.' Julie bared her teeth in what was intended for a smile. 'Over my dead body,' she said.

Now I didn't like to point out to her that it might come to just that. She knew Mickey better than I did. But he'd been married to the woman for twenty-four years and he'd probably realised it wouldn't be easy walking out. She wouldn't settle without a fight. It was ironic, really. He couldn't get rid of Julie and he couldn't keep Lisa. I found it sad. Julie wasn't sad or, if she had been, she'd got over it. Now she was out for everything she could salvage from the wreck of her marriage. That was all that mattered to her.

'Oh, I'm a realist,' she was saying. 'I can't stop him doing it. He'll come to grief but that's his problem. Mine is getting what's owing to me for twenty-four years' loyalty. That's why I'm getting a divorce. I'm getting a court to tell him what's due to me. He can argue with me but he can't argue with a court, right?'

'Right,' I said faintly. 'I see your point. After so long together . . .'

She surged on. 'Do you know? We lived above that pub when we were first married. We were childhood sweethearts, you know that?' She fired the question at me.

I shook my head.

'No, of course you don't,' said Julie suddenly sounding lachrymose. 'But we were. I was eighteen when we got married and he was twenty-two. Only a couple of kids really but we were as happy as larks. The only furniture we had was bits and pieces our families gave us or we got from second-hand shops. But from the start Mickey was full of ideas how he would make it big-time and we would both be living in luxury. He did it, too. And we were still happy even though we didn't have any children. Funny, you always think you'll have your own kids. But it didn't happen for Mickey and me. The doctor said there was nothing wrong with me. I would've liked a baby, but Mickey said, it didn't matter, we had each other.'

Merry hell. I'd be in tears if she kept on like this.

Luckily Julie reverted to her aggressive mode. 'Now not only he doesn't want me, he wants to cheat me out of this flat and anything else he can stop me getting. He says I can have the house in Hampstead. Big deal. He knows I'm living there and he'd have a devil of a job getting me out of it. But trust Mickey, he found a way to turn even that to his advantage. "You're getting that big house," he says, "and it's worth a good bit, so I don't have to give you any more. Fair's fair," he had the nerve to say. "You get the house, I get the rest." '

She spluttered to a halt, took a deep breath and began again. 'Fair? The bastard doesn't know the meaning of the word! I gave him the best years of my life. I could tell him, he's not the only one who isn't fair. Life isn't fair! Men, they mature like a good wine, eh? A woman . . .' She broke off again and cast a slightly nervous glance at Donald. But he sat there looking so blank it was difficult to tell if he was even listening. He'd probably heard it all before, anyway.

She turned practical. 'I realise I won't get the villa in Spain and there's not much I can do about that. But I'm having this flat as part of my divorce settlement. After all, if Mickey sells both clubs he'll be pretty well set up and I don't suppose I'll see any of the money because he'll spirit it abroad. Mickey's good at doing that. So I should have the two residential properties in this country. That's only fair, isn't it?' she appealed to me. 'My lawyer says it is. I worked for years in the pub behind the bar for nothing and I worked as receptionist in the first club for a couple of years until Mickey reckoned now we'd moved house to a swankier area, it wouldn't do for me to work in a club. I had to be, you know, a proper lady and stay home going to coffee mornings and making friends with the sort of people Mickey wanted us to be thick with. I worked hard at that, too. I chatted up the wives and then Mickey got to meet the husbands. Everything I've done in my whole life,' she concluded passionately, 'I've done for Mickey Allerton!

Stupid, that's what I was. Well, I've stopped being stupid now! You can tell him that from me.'

I thought about all those unhappy letters to the agony aunt I'd read in Beryl's woman's magazine. When the worm turns, it does so with a vengeance.

'Julie,' I said placatingly, 'I don't know anything about divorce. But perhaps you ought not to do anything rash. You and Mickey should sit down and talk it over in a week or two. The situation might have changed by then.'

'You don't sit and talk things over with my husband,' said Julie bitterly. 'Mickey doesn't worry about other people's feelings. He doesn't discuss things. He makes up his mind and that's it.'

'He might not go to Spain with Lisa,' I ventured, wondering how far I could go.

Julie shrugged. 'Whether they go or stay, I hope she takes him for every penny, but not every penny that belongs to me.' She squashed out the remains of her cigarette and stood up. 'Well, let's take a look around, since we're all here.'

'You look,' I said. 'I'm leaving.'

But Julie had pulled open the door to the dressing room. 'Strewth!' we heard her exclaim. There was a silence, broken only by the rustle of cloth. She was rummaging along the dress rack. Then she came out, her face set white and furious, and marched past both Donald and me, without a word, into the kitchen. There was the sound of a drawer being dragged open, a clatter, and she came out holding a wicked-looking knife.

I scurried behind Donald but it wasn't me she was after. She went back into the dressing room and the ensuing tearing and ripping sounds indicated she was busy shredding all that designer wear into tatters. In between her efforts we could hear her muttering to herself, 'Little bitch! You won't wear that again! Look at this! Must have cost a couple of grand! Well, you'll be able to use it for dusters now, Miss Lisa!'

'Donald,' I whispered, edging out from behind the sofa. 'Don't you think you ought to stop her? Isn't it criminal damage or something?'

Donald, still relaxed on the sofa without any sign of being about to move, proved he could speak.

'You don't never argue,' he wheezed, 'with a woman holding a ruddy great carving knife.'

Fair enough. I tiptoed out of the flat, leaving Julie to it.

Chapter Ten

'Do you know what?' I asked my audience at large. 'I thought Mickey Allerton was older, well into his fifties. But if Julie's telling the truth, he's not more than forty-six. He looks pretty good, mind you, but still at least ten years older than he is.'

My listeners consisted of Ganesh, his sister Usha, her husband Jay and – ostensibly busy in the background with a stack of invoices – Uncle Hari. We were all gathered in Hari's flat over the shop and, for the most part, sitting in near darkness. Hari had an old-fashioned green-shaded reading light on the desk where he was working. It cast a white glare on the paperwork and virtually no light anywhere else. The rest of us had to make do with sulphur-yellow street lighting seeping through the chink in the window curtains and the glow from the flickering television.

Originally we were bathed in the dim radiance of the dusty chandelier in the middle of the ceiling directly above our heads. It held three forty-watt candle bulbs in glass bowls filled with dead flies. But we had been denied even this when Hari had pointed out that if we were watching television we didn't need it, and had we any idea of the size of his electricity bill? So we switched off the light and sat in the gloom, even though none of us was taking much notice of the television, thus effectively getting the worst of both worlds. The telly offering was a long drawn-out whodunnit in which the detective appeared to have so many personal problems to deal with I wasn't surprised it was taking him so long to work out who did the murder.

Jay and Usha did not appear to mind either sitting in the near-dark or the rubbish on the television as they were far more interested in my adventures. Usha was particularly keen to hear the details of the Allertons' marital difficulties. Ganesh, having heard my story before, sat mutinously introspective with his arms folded, glowering at the turgid police drama as the detective struggled through yet another row with his wife or female colleague or some woman or other. On telly or in real life, you couldn't escape the battle of the sexes. But I had a feeling that, in his mind, Ganesh had substituted Uncle Hari for the victim in the screen story.

'Living the sort of life he's led,' opined Jay in reply to my observation, 'I'm not surprised Allerton looks older than he is.'

I've always got on well with Usha. I like Jay too although he can be a bit pompous. He was squeezed next to his wife on the old sofa and I wondered, when the time came for them to leave, how they were going to extricate themselves. Usha's baby appeared to be due at any moment; she was enormous. Jay had also put on some weight, perhaps in sympathy, and was quite a bit podgier than when I'd last met him. He looked every inch the successful accountant. Even in the dim light, I could see Ganesh kept giving him funny looks, partly wistful, partly envious and partly cross.

'It is a great mistake to do business with such people!' declared Hari, tapping madly into a pocket calculator. Hari has excellent hearing. It's always a mistake to think he's not listening.

'I didn't do business with him by choice,' I reminded him. 'He's – or he was – holding Bonnie.'

'He doesn't have your dog now,' said Jay tactlessly. 'You are no longer under any obligation to him.'

Usha dug her husband in the ribs. 'We're really sorry about your dog being lost, Fran. I expect she will turn up.'

'Everyone's looking,' I said. 'I hope she'll find her way home but I want to be there when she does. I'll have to go to Oxford first thing tomorrow morning to give Lisa the passport. Then I'll consider I've done my bit and I'll come back to London and concentrate on finding my dog.'

'I'm coming with you to Oxford,' said Ganesh in a loud firm voice.

No one looked at him. We all looked at Uncle Hari, who dropped his pocket calculator and rose to his feet.

'No argument, Uncle,' said Ganesh. 'I've not had any time off for ages.'

'Tomorrow it will be very difficult!' protested Hari. 'Who will go to see the suppliers?'

'It's an emergency!' insisted Ganesh.

Hari gestured wildly, sat down and picked up his calculator. I fancied he hadn't given way but was just waiting until he got Ganesh on his own to argue it out.

'I think it's a good idea for Ganesh to go with Fran,' said Usha loyally. Ganesh was her little brother and she still stood up for him in any scrap. 'She shouldn't be on her own. There's a killer loose out there in Oxford.'

'A killer?' yelled Hari, leaping to his feet and sending the pocket calculator flying. 'No one should go to Oxford, no one! Not you, Francesca, and not Ganesh. Most certainly not Ganesh. It would be most irresponsible.'

'There might not be a killer, Mr Patel,' I said as soothingly as I could. 'Perhaps Ivo just tripped and fell in the river.'

'One should not leap to conclusions,' declared Jay. 'I dare say this was an accident, you know. Just as Fran said, the fellow was jogging by the river, slipped and fell in. Possibly he could not swim. Not everyone can swim,' he added a touch self-consciously.

There was an awkward silence. Hari sat down again, muttering to himself. To get away from the subject of the proposed journey, I returned to the subject of Mickey Allerton.

'I wouldn't like to be in Mickey's shoes when his wife catches up with him. She's really on the warpath. She's determined to get her fair share of Mickey's assets and funds by hook or by crook.'

This was financial talk and Jay came into his own. 'Disentangling their finances will be very difficult.' He shook his head. 'Probably they have made no clear arrangement for such an eventuality. If he has property overseas it will be difficult for her to get a share of it. Also if, as she suggested to you, Fran, Allerton has been sending money out of the country . . .' Jay shook his head disapprovingly. 'It suggests he may not have been putting in accurate tax returns. Who are his accountants?'

'I don't know,' I said. 'Perhaps he does his own accounts?'

Jay looked deeply shocked. 'No wonder,' he said loftily, 'his affairs are in such a muddle.'

'What does she look like, Mrs Allerton?' asked Usha, more interested in the human element.

'Pretty good. I think she must diet all the time.'

Jay passed a hand over his spreading midriff, perhaps without realising he did it. 'Why do you say this?'

'She's got that pared-down, greyhound look. Usha knows what I mean.'

Usha nodded. 'Not a spare ounce of fat anywhere. When I've had the baby, I'll have to get back into shape.'

'Shape, shape!' (This from Hari.) 'All this nonsense about weight! People nowadays don't work hard enough,

251

that is why they suffer from obesity. I saw a programme about it on the television not so long ago. Everyone is getting fatter and fatter. They eat too much and sit all the time in front of the television set, just as you are doing now. That's what the programme said. It's not eating; it's inactivity, that's the problem. Nobody who works hard for his living gets fat!'

'No,' said Ganesh, 'he worries himself into a decline instead, and ruins his eyesight as well by working in insufficient light.'

'I'd better be getting home,' I said. All this was getting to be strictly family stuff. 'Nice to see you, Usha and Jay. Good luck with the baby.'

'I'll see you out,' Ganesh offered quickly, getting to his feet.

'Listen,' he said to me urgently when we were downstairs at the street door. 'I'm coming with you tomorrow, no matter what my uncle says. I'll be at your place early. Wait for me. Don't worry about Hari.'

'I don't want to be the cause of a family row,' I told him.

'There won't be a row,' Ganesh assured me. 'It's just how he is with any new idea. He always says "no". The only time I've known him agree to something without days of argument was when he agreed to put that stupid rocket ride outside the shop and look what a rotten thing that's turned out to be.'

'Don't remind him of that,' I said. 'Or he'll use it as an example of making up your mind in a hurry and living to rue it. By the way, is anyone going to fix that rocket? Has it ever worked?'

'It worked when it came but only for twenty-four hours. It's been fixed since but it's gone wrong again.' Ganesh gazed down the street where it was now dark and lamplight gleamed against shop windows, making them shine like silver mirrors.

'What's the matter with it?' I asked.

He shrugged. 'Who knows?'

'Are you sure, Ganesh? You haven't—'

'I'd better get back upstairs. See you in the morning, Fran.' He shut the door rather unceremoniously on me.

I walked home, imagining the scene upstairs in the flat now I was off the premises. Not a row, perhaps, but certainly a very lively discussion. Ganesh would get his own way, I guessed, because I knew when Ganesh had his mind made up. So did Hari probably, but he'd still put up a fight and sulk about it for days. I'm sometimes sad when I consider I don't have any family to turn to. But then, on the other hand, I'm free to make up my own mind. Reasonably free, at least, provided no one like Mickey Allerton takes a hand in things.

There wasn't much traffic about but when I reached the house where I had my flat, I saw an elderly car parked outside it. Someone had a visitor. We are not, as tenants, car-owners. Most of us are too broke and in London, anyway, who needs personal transport? I walked past it without taking much notice but then I heard the car door open and a female voice called out:

'Are you Fran Varady?'

I turned. I could only see a dark bulky shape by the car. Nothing about it, certainly not the voice, was familiar. If the voice had been male I'd have worried but a female voice appeared less threatening. All the same, I wasn't expecting a visit from a stranger.

'Could be,' I said warily.

'It's all right, love,' said the woman. 'Don't be scared. I'm Cheryl. I'm the wife of Harry who works as doorman for Mr Allerton over at the Silver Circle. I was looking after your dog.' She shut the car door and came closer. I could see her face now in the lamplight, puckered in worry. 'Has she turned up, dear? I'm that worried about her I don't know what to do. I'm really sorry . . .' She peered at me, trying to distinguish my reaction.

I had been feeling angry about the careless, as I'd seen it, loss of my dog by this woman. Now that I saw her and her evident genuine distress, my anger melted.

'She hasn't turned up yet. Do you want to come in?'

She turned back to lock up her car and followed me indoors. In my flat, I switched on the light, invited her to take a seat and went to put on the kettle.

When I came back she was sitting in an armchair but hadn't taken off her coat. I could now see she was middle-aged and plump with short dark hair cut in a mannish fashion and no make-up. She wore tight dark leggings stretched over her plump thighs and calves, trainers and a zipped-up bomber jacket, also black in colour, so that altogether just looking at her one might have doubted what sex she was until she spoke.

'I've been everywhere,' she said. 'I've been all over the park. I've asked everyone.'

'Bonnie's pretty streetwise,' I said. 'My best hope is that she'll make her way back here. I don't think she'll get run over by a bus or anything. She knows about crossing roads.'

In the background the kettle clicked off. I went to make us a cup of coffee each and brought it back. I handed Cheryl hers.

She took it and cupped her hands round the mug. Her fingers were broad and spatulate with stubby ends and close-clipped nails. Her wide gold wedding band cut deeply into the third finger of her left hand and I guessed she couldn't have removed it if she wanted to. One day she'd have to have the ring cut off.

'She got on so well with my dogs. I really thought she'd be OK without the lead. But she just took off like an arrow. No way could I catch her.' She gazed at me sadly, looking herself a little like a dog that's been caught out being naughty.

'Have you been waiting long out there?' I asked. 'You were lucky I came back. I've been in Oxford.'

She looked a bit shifty. 'I knew you were back in London.'

I was surprised and a little alarmed. 'How?'

'You won't tell anyone this?'

I shook my head, wondering what was coming.

'Well.' Cheryl leaned forward confidentially. 'Mrs Allerton rang the club to see if Mr Allerton was there. My husband took the call. Mrs Allerton said she'd seen you over at the flat. She was in ever such a state, so my husband says. Really upset. Anyway, I thought it was likely you'd come back home here tonight and not go back to Oxford until tomorrow, so I drove over and I've been waiting. Not long, not more than forty minutes.'

'That seems like a long time to me. I'm sorry.' I couldn't think what else to say. 'Cheryl, did you know Ivo, the other doorman at the club?'

Cheryl pulled a face. 'Oh, him. I met him. I always thought he was bonkers. So did my husband. He was a good-looking bloke, I suppose, but he'd got a funny way of looking at you. I heard he had an accident up there in Oxford.'

Cheryl spoke of Oxford as any true Londoner speaks of the no-man's-land north of Watford.

She frowned. 'I can't really say anything nice about him, even though he's dead. I don't wish anyone dead, mind you. Don't get me wrong. God rest his soul and all the rest of it,' she added piously and I wondered briefly if, like me, nuns had dominated her infancy. 'But he wasn't someone you'd turn your back on,' she went on. 'There was that way about him, like you never knew what he thought or what he might do. To tell you the truth he plain gave me the creeps. My husband said the boss was all set to give him the push. He'd probably have had to go anyway once the new regulations come in.'

'New regulations?' I sipped my coffee and tried for nonchalant.

'Regarding door personnel,' Cheryl said. 'It's not a job anyone can do, you know. Of course, a lot of blokes think they can, just because they're big. But you've got to have finesse.' Cheryl nodded as she produced this word, which she pronounced 'fine-ess'. 'And good judgement. Be a bit clever. I mean there are people you don't let in, right? That's pretty straightforward. Then there are people you don't want to let in but you don't want to upset, right again?'

I nodded.

'Then even when you don't let them in, or if you're escorting them out, there's a limit to what you can do. Too much rough stuff and the doorman's in the wrong. You've got to get it just right and that Ivo, well, you couldn't rely on him not to overdo it. There were a couple of incidents that didn't leave the boss any too pleased. With these new regulations, in the future doormen are going to have to go on a course to learn how to do it properly and be licensed. It'll cost money for the course and the licence. Mr Allerton says he'll pay any cost for my husband because he wants to keep him. But Ivo, he was a different kettle of fish. I don't reckon he'd have got by on any course, anyway. His English wasn't very good and, like I said, he was too quick to get nasty. He was weird in other ways, too. He was funny about animals.' Cheryl shook her head. 'I don't ever trust anyone who doesn't like animals.'

'So you're not sorry Ivo is dead,' I said. 'How did you hear, Cheryl?'

'Mr Allerton took the call in his office and my husband was there. The boss was pretty angry. He doesn't want the police coming round the club asking questions and—'

Here Cheryl grew suddenly cautious and broke off. 'Who would?' she added obscurely and busied herself drinking coffee.

'You were going to say that Allerton doesn't want the police asking Lisa Stallard questions,' I supplied. 'I do now know what was going on, Cheryl. I've been to Lisa's flat and I've spoken to Julie Allerton, remember? Allerton and Lisa have been having an affair and he was keeping Lisa in that flat.'

Cheryl put down her empty mug. 'I knew it would end in tears,' she said. 'That girl and Mr Allerton? Well, I ask you. She just wasn't like the other girls who worked at the club. I said to my husband, you mark my words, I said, that girl will go off back home to Mummy and Daddy one day. You see if she doesn't! She wasn't the type for the club. That's what the boss liked about her, I suppose, she was upmarket. But she was trouble. You could see it just looking at her. Mrs Allerton's a nice lady, you know. I keep hoping she and Mr Allerton will make it up. But I don't suppose they will now Mrs A's going for a divorce. I dare say the boss wasn't what you'd call the perfect husband.

Any man who owns a club and employs a lot of pretty girls is going to stray once or twice. Some of those girls are really beautiful, I've seen them.' Cheryl looked wistful. 'Not just good-looking but with beautiful bodies. They're dancers and keep fit. Not an ounce of spare fat.' She sighed and tapped her robust midriff. 'I can't seem to get any weight off and I'm out walking my dogs every day. I suppose we eat the wrong sort of stuff but you can't feed a man like my husband on salad, can you?'

'No,' I agreed, because she was appealing to me for support. I've never met an overweight person yet who didn't have a good reason why he/she can't slim. But something Cheryl had said caused an idea to pop into my head. It was a startling one but, before I could explore it, Cheryl returned to the matter of Allerton's extra-marital romps.

'But generally none of those little slips mean anything. They're just by way of human nature. A man is a man, isn't he? He's not the angel Gabriel. The boss was a good husband. That girl, Lisa, she's broken up a good marriage. I bet she don't care one bit!' Cheryl nodded. 'It's like all these celebrities you read about in the papers. Some girl writes a kiss-and-tell book, and half the time there's nothing to tell. But the damage is done.'

'Cheryl,' I said carefully, 'the impression I've got talking to Lisa is that she didn't want to break up any marriage. I don't think she wants Mickey Allerton, not in that way, you know. Not to be married to him.'

Cheryl leaned forward. 'That doesn't mean he doesn't want *her*, does it? It's the way it goes. If you can't have something, you want it all the more. Anyway, who knows what that girl wants? She's deep, that one. I never trusted her, nor did my husband. He remembers when she first came to the club. Someone had told her the boss was asking about, wanting to take on new dancers. She just turned up one morning looking all sweet and innocent and "oh, I'd love to work here, Mr Allerton!" The boss fell for it and he fell for her, just like that!' Cheryl clicked her fingers. 'You could see his eyes glaze over, my husband said. So he took her on and mark you, she was a good little dancer and she had that stuff what the French talk about.'

I ran this through my brain a few times and gave up. 'What stuff the French talk about, Cheryl?'

'I'm not good with foreign words,' Cheryl confided. '*Gee nee sez koi.*'

'*Je ne sais quoi?*' I ventured.

'That's it, that's what she had. But then what? She runs off.' Cheryl paused. 'A man like Mr Allerton,' she said, 'he can deal with most situations. But he's never known how to deal with that one, not from the beginning.'

This I had already realised. It was why he'd called me in.

Cheryl was looking as if she was regretting discussing Allerton so freely. She pulled herself up from the chair. 'I'll be going, dear. I'm glad I've seen you and been able to explain. I'll keep looking for Bonnie and again, I'm so sorry. You've been really nice about it. It makes me feel worse.'

I reassured her and saw her out. She'd given me a lot to think about.

I sat puzzling it out for a while and made a decision. I looked at my watch. It was gone eleven. People who weren't out enjoying themselves or doing night work would now be going to bed. But there was another category of person who sat up half the night: the Internet surfers.

I climbed the stairs to the top flat in the house. Malcolm lived there. We never saw much of him because he slept all day and came out at night, like Dracula. That was because during the night hours the rest of the world was on the Web and he could communicate with all the chatrooms and weird websites he frequented without leaving his room. On the rare occasions he did emerge he had a pale, unhealthy look like a plant that lacks sunlight. Ganesh suspected him of being a hacker busy finding his way into government records, banking accounts and any kind of place he shouldn't be. But I argued there was no reason to believe that. Malcolm was harmless, just odd and lacking a proper life. The only exercise he got was playing computer games. There are hundreds if not thousands like him.

I knocked at his door and, when he didn't answer, knocked again more loudly. I kept it up because I knew he was at home until eventually I heard sounds of movement. The door opened a crack. Like Hari, Malcolm economised on electric lighting. He didn't need it. His world was bathed in an eerie bluish colour emanating from the monitor of his computer. It gave his skin a strange white fluorescent tinge and ringed his eyes with dark shadows.

He blinked at me. 'Hello, Fran.'

'Sorry to disturb you, Mal,' I said. 'I hope you're not busy.'

Faint signs of animation crossed his countenance. 'I found this really cool new website belonging to—'

I didn't let him finish. I had a horrible feeling it would prove to be devoted to something I'd rather not know about. In the meantime there was something I did want to know about.

'Mal,' I said. 'I need your help. That is, I need your help to look up something on the Internet.'

He brightened and stood back, gesturing me past him. 'Right, come on in.'

I went in and he closed the door behind us. At such moments I do wonder why I don't tell someone else what I intend to do before I do it, just as Ganesh says I should. Too late to worry about it now. The flat smelled stuffy, of fast food represented by empty foil trays abandoned around the place, of cannabis smoked not recently but recently enough, and of overheated plastic. It wouldn't surprise me if Mal's computer didn't spontaneously combust.

Mal hovered over me, tall, thin, gangling and bearing an uncanny resemblance to an alien in one of those very old *Doctor Who* episodes. He didn't smell too fresh, either. He had holes in his jeans which might have been a fashion statement in anyone else but in Malcolm simply meant they were old and worn out. His cotton T-shirt was also washed to a faded grey; it had probably started out black. The logo of a heavy metal band printed on it had almost disappeared, only ghostly outlines of their hirsute faces left.

'Coffee?' he suggested.

'Just had some, thanks.' Mal's coffee was even more of an unknown quantity than he was.

He dragged a chair towards the screen. 'OK, then. Sit down,' he invited.

We settled down cosily and Malcolm demonstrated for me the wonders of the World Wide Web.

Chapter Eleven

It rained overnight. I lay awake listening to the steady patter of the drops against the window. When I was a kid I always felt safe, lying in bed and hearing the rain outside. But tonight I was wondering where Bonnie was and if she had managed to find shelter. I pictured her wet and hungry. Ganesh had told me he'd informed the police and the RSPCA about her. I would check with the dog pound and the rescue centre before I left for Oxford.

I was ashamed now that, when I knew Ivo was dead, I'd taken some comfort in knowing Bonnie couldn't any longer fall into his hands. My feeling had been instinctive but nonetheless selfish. In the end his death was causing me endless problems and now came Bonnie's loss on top of everything else, almost as if I were being punished for my satisfaction that a man had lost his life. I debated whether to delay my trip. But Ganesh had now arranged with Hari to take time off and he'd be at my door first thing in the morning expecting us to head for Paddington Station.

Besides, Lisa needed the passport as soon as possible if she was to get her cheap flight to Amsterdam. But what did I owe Lisa? And should I help her duck out from the mess she had created?

This led my thoughts in the direction of the information gleaned from the Internet with the help of Malcolm. I was working out a whole new theory regarding events in Oxford. The trouble was, theories are fine but I needed something to convince me I was on the right lines and not just letting my imagination run away with me.

Eventually I got up and switched on the television, made a cup of tea and settled down to watch an ancient horror movie. At some point I fell asleep because I was still there when awoken by the peal of the doorbell. I sat up with a start. Outside it was already daylight and a glance at my watch showed the time to be eight thirty. I scrambled from the sofa, yelping as my stiffened joints protested, and made a crab-like scuttle to open the door and admit Ganesh.

'You look as if you've just woken up,' he said accusingly.

'I fell asleep watching TV,' I explained as he followed me into the flat. 'Put the kettle on while I shower, will you?'

When I got back fully dressed, Ganesh had made breakfast. 'There wasn't enough milk for cereal,' he said. 'I made toast. But there isn't any butter, either. Don't you keep any basic necessities in that fridge? I found some of this.' He produced a jar half filled with scabby-looking marmalade.

'I don't need anything,' I said. 'Thanks all the same.'

Ganesh pointed at the toast. 'Eat it. I've had breakfast with Hari. You shouldn't start for Oxford on an empty stomach.'

I sat down and managed to find enough of the marmalade without odd-looking foreign objects in it to spread on the toast. 'Have you got that mobile of Usha's?' I mumbled between bites. 'Can you ring the police and RSPCA to see if Bonnie's come in overnight?'

'Done it,' said Ganesh. 'I phoned before I left the shop. No luck, I'm afraid. Not yet. She'll turn up, Fran. She's not like a lot of pet dogs who couldn't fend for themselves. Bonnie lived with her previous owner on the street before you took her in. A lot of people know her by sight. Someone will see her and even catch her.'

He was saying all the things I wanted to hear. I just hoped they were true. In the meantime, I had another matter to deal with.

'Ganesh,' I said. 'I've been having a long think about things. Also I went to see Malcolm up in the attic last night.' I pointed up at the ceiling with my knife. Immediately a distant ghostly voice in my brain, an echo of Grandma Varady, reproved me for bad table manners. I lowered the knife.

'Malcolm? He's nuts, not to mention seriously weird. Stay clear of him. What did you want to see him for?' Ganesh sipped tea from his mug and eyed me curiously.

'It's rather complicated. You see, I think I've been looking at this the wrong way all along.'

'Oh?' said Ganesh.

'I've been assuming that Lisa was running away from Mickey Allerton.'

'Well, she is, isn't she? Or that's what Allerton himself thinks and everything so far has backed it up.'

I nodded. 'But what if Allerton has got it wrong? I've been taking Mickey's version of events as being basically right because it's all I've had to go on. Even when I found out he hadn't been frank with me and Lisa is more than just another dancer to him, I still stuck with the basic idea.'

'And now?' Ganesh asked sceptically.

'Now? Ganesh, did you ever have a kaleidoscope when you were a kid?'

'No,' said Ganesh.

'We had one at home. It was really old. It had belonged to my dad when he was young. It's a tube lined with mirrors and containing lots of scraps of coloured paper. You peer in at one end and tap it. Every time you tap it you get another pattern as the paper shapes move and are reflected in the mirrors, see?'

'I know what a kaleidoscope is,' said Ganesh patiently. 'Because I didn't own one doesn't mean I don't know such things exist. I'm not ignorant, you know.'

'Sorry, I got carried away. Well, think of this whole case as a lot of coloured bits of paper in a tube lined with mirrors.'

'And?' Ganesh raised his eyebrows.

'And I just shook up the tube and I've got a whole new pattern out of it.'

Ganesh glanced at his wristwatch. 'Tell me on the train.'

As it turned out, I didn't have the opportunity to discuss things in detail with Ganesh on the train. It was crowded, and although we got adjacent seats they were on either side of the aisle and that didn't make for easy conversation. I didn't fancy shouting the details of Lisa's affair with Mickey Allerton across the gap with other passengers walking past. After a while I saw that Ganesh had dozed off. He must have got up extra early to get all his jobs done before coming to my place. I had a pang of conscience at involving him in all this. But then I reasoned it was his decision. After that, I dozed off too. I'd had a poor night's sleep, several disturbed nights as it happened, and sooner or later these things catch up on you.

It must have rained a little in Oxford overnight. The pavements were still damp although the early sun was already drying them out fast. I was wearing a denim jacket and I'd pushed Lisa's passport into the breast pocket and buttoned it down securely. I didn't want to lose it. But I was in no rush to go to Summertown and seek her out.

'Perhaps,' I said to Ganesh, 'I ought to go and see Beryl first and explain why I didn't stay at the guest house last night. She may be thinking something's happened to me and contact Filigrew or, worse, Mickey Allerton.'

Ganesh had been gazing about him at the open area before the station and a large statue of a bull, or I suppose it was an ox. Taxis and buses pulled in and out passing us and he seemed fascinated by those, too. He didn't get out of London much and I think it surprised him that anywhere else in the country functioned at all.

He pulled himself together and turned his attention to me. 'This guest house,' he asked, 'is it anywhere near the spot where you arranged to meet Lisa and found Ivo?'

'We pass it. That is, we pass by Christ Church Meadow. It's a short walk across that to the place by the river where, you know...'

I still didn't like talking about finding Ivo. Someone told me once that the human brain is programmed to blot out unpleasant events. That's how we cope with them and go on with our lives. It doesn't always work. I remember in every detail Grandma Varady's last days and how confused I was, not knowing what to do. She didn't recognise me any longer. She got out of bed in the middle of the night convinced it was morning and we had to get up. I had to wash her because she had forgotten how to turn a tap on and off. Before it happened, I'd have said it was impossible, that it's a thing you couldn't forget. But she did. She stood in front of the washbasin staring in perplexity at the taps.

'What do I do now, Eva?' she would ask, because she had got it into her head I was my mother.

I gave up telling her I wasn't Eva and trying to explain about taps. I just got on and washed her. It was like looking after a small baby. Sometimes she would sit and cry quietly because she was frightened and depressed and I couldn't help.

On the other hand, when my mother left us when I was seven, I blotted that out quite quickly. She wasn't there any more so I didn't look for her and I stopped thinking about her. It was only much later as a teenager I decided she was dead. But she wasn't dead, that was the problem, and I did meet her again. She's dead now and I'm sorry that we didn't have time to make up for the lost years. I think she regretted it too.

Life is a little like the kaleidoscope. Once the pieces have been shaken up and a new pattern formed, you can't get the old one back again. That's to say, I suppose theoretically it might be possible. I'm not a mathematician. I don't know how many permutations of design there are. It's like that idea of a monkey and a typewriter, tapping away randomly. Sooner or later, as an assemblage of letters, the monkey writes *Hamlet*. I believe some scientists tried that out once but the monkey didn't oblige them and wrote drivel before it got bored and smashed up the machine. I like to think the chimp was smarter than the guys in the white lab coats.

'I'd like to see it,' said Ganesh with suspicious enthusiasm.

I didn't fancy revisiting the spot where I'd found Ivo

bobbing about in the river but if Ganesh wanted to be put in the picture I couldn't refuse. Even so I did wonder if his motives were founded more in tourism than detection.

'I'll take you there. It's on the way to Beryl's place,' I said to him.

The warm sun on the grass was causing the overnight rain to evaporate quickly and rise in a vapour so that it looked as if the whole of Christ Church Meadow was steaming gently. Soon my trainers were covered in little bits of grass like a green fur.

'It's nice here,' observed Ganesh. 'I should have brought my camera.'

'You're not on holiday,' I grumbled.

'All right, keep your hair on. Which way to the river?'

'Down here,' I said, leading him to the left.

He strode out briskly alongside me still muttering about photographic opportunities missed and having to get a souvenir somewhere to take back to Hari.

It was quiet and very peaceful. Only a few waterbirds busied themselves about their business in the bankside reeds. I was beginning to feel easier in my own mind about being here. Perhaps it was having Ganesh with me. Then he touched my arm and asked, 'What's going on over there?'

We stopped beneath the spreading branches of a big old tree and I looked in the direction he'd indicated. Two human forms were moving about slowly, bent double and poking around in the undergrowth.

'Police?' asked Ganesh doubtfully in a low voice. He sounded depressed as if suddenly recalled to the true nature of our visit.

'No,' I whispered, grabbing his arm to stop him progressing any further. I dragged him aside under the shelter of the nearest tree. 'That's Lisa Stallard and the guy with her is Ned, her friend. I told you about him.'

Ganesh frowned and peered into the distance. 'What are they doing? Are they looking for something?'

The couple in front of us were still poking about in the long grass and bushes on the opposite side of the path to the stone steps. As I watched, Ned straightened up, the morning sunlight setting fire to his gingery-blond hair. He put his hands on his hips and said something to Lisa, shaking his head.

Lisa replied and they both resumed their search, Ned in a desultory manner which suggested his heart wasn't in it.

'Yes,' I said. 'They're looking for something and I know what it is. Come on.'

We left the cover of the trees and walked towards the searching couple. They were so intent on what they were doing that neither of them noticed us until we were upon them. Then Ned saw us and straightened up again. He looked wary but that turned to surprise when he saw me. His gaze flickered to Ganesh and the wariness returned to his expression. He looked back at me again and this time there was a familiar hostility in his face.

'What are you doing here?' he asked sulkily. 'Who's that?' He pointed at Ganesh.

'Very rude,' I reproved him. 'May I introduce Ganesh Patel, who is a friend of mine from London.'

Ned looked even sulkier and mumbled, 'Hi.'

Lisa had heard our voices and spun round. She didn't come forward to meet us but stood a little way off, glowering defiantly. She wore blue jeans and yet another of those loosely knitted sweaters she favoured, this one in pale lemon with embroidered daisies. She must have had a cupboard full of them. Her hair was attractively tousled and tumbled to her shoulders. The grim look on her face meant she didn't look nearly so pretty as usual but she was still a stunner. She was holding something in her hand: a little cloth bag of the sort dance students carry their pumps to ballet class in. The bag was clearly empty, collapsed like a burst balloon.

'Hello, Lisa,' I called to her. 'I won't ask what you're doing because I know.'

At that she did start to walk towards me. She was a quick thinker and by the time she'd reached us she'd rearranged her features into a pleasant smile. She beamed warmly at Ganesh and said, 'Hi! Nice to meet you.'

'Hello,' mumbled Ganesh and looked all daft.

Lisa obviously considered that any problem likely to be posed by Ganesh had been defused and turned her attention to me. 'We thought, Ned and I,' she said, 'that we'd investigate Ivo's death. If we came down here, we might find some clues, right, Ned?'

'Yeah, right,' said Ned obediently.

I managed not to hiss in exasperation. What was it with men? I felt myself bristle and when I spoke I knew I sounded churlish. 'What would you do if you found any clues?' I asked.

Ganesh glanced at me and Lisa blinked. 'Tell the police, I suppose. Or tell you and then you could tell the police because you've already been questioned by them.'

Ouch! 'I don't think you're looking for clues,' I said. 'I think you're looking for something quite specific. I expect your dad is missing his pet.'

She shrugged. 'I don't know what you're talking about.'

'Oh, come on, yes, you do. You're looking for Arthur, the grass snake. I've told Ganesh about that. Your father said it was missing from the garden when I saw him last. You'd like to find the creature and take it back, wouldn't you?'

'Why,' demanded Lisa, reddening, 'should Arthur be here? You're nuts.'

I shook my head. 'No, I've been a bit slow to work it out, I admit that. But now I have. You brought Arthur here with you, probably in that little bag you're holding, early on the morning Ivo died. You had originally arranged to meet me here. But then Ivo got in touch with you and you arranged to meet him here too, but earlier. You were very scared of him, weren't you, Lisa? I'm not surprised. He was a scary sort of bloke. But there was something he was scared of himself, really terrified, wasn't there? Snakes.'

'How would I know?' Lisa snapped, her eyes sparkling with anger.

'You knew because you were at the club the morning an exotic dancer turned up to audition, bringing along a python as part of her act. Ivo must have really freaked out. You saw how scared he was of reptiles, really frightened. Not just an ordinary fright but something much more, a phobia. Since then one other person had told me that Ivo was funny about animals. Even Vera told me he didn't want to go back to Croatia because it would mean working on the farm with his parents. Perhaps it was just the hard work he didn't fancy, but perhaps it was because it meant handling the livestock. He didn't like being around any of them, but snakes were really the things he couldn't stand.'

I pointed at the bag. 'It was a good idea to bring Arthur with you and hold him in your hands while talking to Ivo. I bet that made Ivo keep his distance. How did you get him to fall in the river? Just walk towards him holding out the grass snake? Just making him back off until he lost his footing?'

Ned, who had been listening with increasing unease, now burst into speech, his face red. 'Look here, Lisa didn't mean any harm. She was frightened of the bloke. That's why she brought the snake with her, like you say. If she'd asked me, I'd have come with her. But she thought she could manage it if she had something Ivo was so frightened of.'

Well, well, with friends like Ned, as the saying goes, Lisa didn't need enemies.

She turned on him savagely. 'Shut up!' she shouted. 'Shut up, you idiot! She was just guessing I was here. She couldn't know! Now she does!'

Poor Ned looked stricken. 'Sorry,' he mumbled. 'But you didn't mean any harm, Lisa, did you? I keep telling you, if you just go to the police . . .' He turned back to us. 'She didn't know he'd drown!' he said. 'For God's sake, she wouldn't have left him to drown! I keep telling her the police would understand that.'

'Will you just shut up?' she yelled again and he fell silent.

Too late, he seemed to realise the extent of the harm he'd done. It almost made me want to help him out; he looked both miserable and confused. He was an idiot but he'd meant well. I suppose meaning well is an excuse of sorts. My original diagnosis that he wasn't too bright was confirmed, however, by his words. The police would be unlikely to take the charitable view of Lisa's actions he had suggested. But stupidity isn't a crime. Lisa would argue she was stupid to leave Ivo in the river threshing about. But that's not what happened, I thought, with growing conviction.

'Perhaps,' I suggested, 'we can all go somewhere quiet and discuss this.'

'I've got nothing to discuss with you,' she told me in a small tight voice. 'All you've done is cause trouble for me. You're just Mickey's mouthpiece. I've told Mickey I want nothing more to do with him and I'm telling you now that I want nothing more to do with you. Stay away from me and from my family.'

'She's got a point,' said Ned, ever loyal. But he said it rather nervously because now he wasn't sure what he was supposed to say.

I ignored him and held Lisa's gaze. 'But I've got something you want,' I said and tapped my breast pocket.

The bright pink flush drained from her face as she grasped my meaning.

'You got it?' she whispered and ran the tip of her tongue over her lips and then stuck out her hand. 'Give it to me!' Her voice rose to an unattractive squawk.

'Manners, manners,' I said. 'I'm a woman of my word. We made a bargain, you and I, remember? You phoned Allerton and I went to London for you. If anyone here has the right to be tired of anyone else, it's me. I'm tired of you and your boyfriend – both your boyfriends . . .' I nodded to include Ned. 'I'm tired of running errands for others. But I said I'd do it, and I did. Yes, I've got it.'

'What's she got of yours?' asked poor old Ned, who really was out of the loop.

'Passport,' said Ganesh briefly. He'd been standing by as observer, looking from Lisa to Ned and back again.

Over the last few minutes he'd been showing signs of impatience and had decided to cut to the chase.

'Why has she got your passport?' Ned turned to Lisa, bewilderment written all over his bovine countenance.

'You don't tell the poor guy anything, do you?' I said. 'Well, you told him you brought Arthur here because you needed him to come and help you hunt for the snake. I'm not handing over the passport, Lisa, until we've got a few things sorted out.'

'You've got to give me the passport!' she snapped. 'It's mine!'

'Actually,' I said, 'if you read the notes inside the front cover, you'll see it's the property of Her Majesty's Government.'

'Well, you aren't the bloody government!' she shouted. 'Hand it over!' She thrust out her open palm again.

I just smiled at her.

She bit her lip and scowled at me but she had realised she wasn't in a position to call the shots. Her manner had become more placatory. 'Come on, Fran. What's it to you?'

Ned was catching up and realising there were a few things he wanted to know. 'Perhaps we *should* all talk it through without getting hot and bothered,' he said. 'We can go to my flat. I've got my car. It's parked right near here.'

Lisa looked furious but she needed to keep Ned on side. 'I'll go if you'll give me my passport afterwards,' she said.

'No deals,' I told her. 'I've made enough of them. I told you, I'm tired of it. Now we do things my way.'

Her face had turned a deathly white. 'You can't do this to me,' she said very quietly and viciously.

'Whatever I do to you,' I told her equally quietly, 'it's nothing compared with what you did to Ivo.'

I think she knew then that I really had worked it out. Her blue eyes seemed to have changed colour, becoming dark fathomless pits. She turned aside and began to walk across the grass towards the exit. We followed her.

Ned's flat was the first floor of the house next door to the Stallards in Summertown. It was at that front window I'd first noticed him, or rather noticed the curtain twitch which told me someone had seen me at the house next door. It seemed an age ago but it was only a week.

'I don't want my mum to see you,' said Lisa, as we got out of Ned's battered old car. 'Dad's not well. So make it quick, right?'

She scurried from the car to the front door and we tumbled after her in a disorderly gaggle.

'Hurry up!' she snapped at Ned as he fumbled for the key. 'Let's get inside!'

We climbed the stairs to the first floor. It wasn't a bad flat, quite roomy. But it wasn't a patch on the pad in St John's Wood where Lisa had been installed by the lovesick Mickey Allerton.

Ned offered to make coffee, which we all declined. He

looked relieved. We sat facing one another in two pairs, Ganesh and me against Ned and Lisa. The flat was furnished very much in the manner of a student let with odd furniture. It even had posters on the walls instead of pictures. Lisa took the only easy chair as of her right and lay back in it looking relaxed although her eyes were still dark and predatory.

I perched on a straight-backed dining chair of Edwardian vintage which must have been picked up in a junk shop. Ganesh got the only other available seat, a beanbag. He had to lower himself practically to floor level where he looked very uncomfortable with his knees stuck up in the air. That being the sum total of seating places, Ned stood behind Lisa's easy chair and rested his arms on the back of it so that he hovered protectively over her.

'Just tell her what happened, Lisa,' he said. 'It wasn't your fault. The guy came down from London to make her go back,' he explained to us. 'She didn't want to go. She still doesn't. Why should she?'

'No,' I said. 'She doesn't have to. Besides, she's got a job lined up, working on a cruise ship, right, Lisa? That's why she wants the passport.'

'Right,' said Lisa.

Ned looked down at her. 'You didn't tell me that.' There was a note of bewilderment in his voice. I felt sorry for him. I had an idea his world was about to collapse.

'I was going to,' she said, glancing briefly up at his face. 'I didn't get a chance.' She looked away from him quickly.

Perhaps she also had an inkling of what the truth would do to him and even a twinge of conscience.

'Don't worry,' I told Ned. 'It isn't true, anyway. There's no cruise ship, no job dancing. She just wants to get out of the country and lie low somewhere.'

Lisa then lost her cool sufficiently to address me in a manner that was extremely personal and indecent. Ned looked amazed, never having heard the like from her before, probably. Ganesh, in the depths of his beanbag, looked deeply disapproving.

'You're losing it, Lisa,' I said. 'It's all coming apart. You had it all set up nicely. But Mickey started to get possessive, didn't he? And his wife took a dislike to you. I met Julie, by the way. She's awfully cross with you. I think she's having the locks on the flat changed today. You might not be able to get back in.'

'The cow!' said Lisa.

I wondered whether to tell her Julie had chopped up all Lisa's designer wear but decided to withhold that detail for the time being.

'She's divorcing Mickey,' I said, 'and she wants the flat.'

'I didn't mean him to leave his wife!' she snapped. 'When he did it was a nuisance but not too much of a problem for me because he moved into a flat he's got over the club and lived there. But then he started bringing his stuff over to my place and staying with me. I didn't want him around all the time!'

'Mickey's the jealous type,' I explained to Ned.

'What do you mean, he's been staying with you?' demanded Ned of Lisa. All this had left him far behind.

'She's his mistress,' I said. 'I think that's the traditional term for it. And just like the good old days, Mickey installed his mistress in a plush flat in St John's Wood. Lisa's circumstances had improved a lot since you visited her in that rented room in Rotherhithe. She's been living in style.'

'But you only worked for him as a dancer, Lisa,' Ned said wonderingly, still unable to grasp the fact that she had been lying to him all along, and as yet he didn't know the half of it.

'Oh, come on!' said Lisa brutally to him. 'I had to have a stronger reason than that for leaving! The whole thing was getting so complicated! He started talking about us getting married and then we could all go to Spain—' She broke off, but too late, and stared at me aghast.

'All?' I said, raising my eyebrows. 'Just you and Mickey would make it "both", wouldn't it? But baby makes three, doesn't it?'

'Baby?' gasped Ned.

'How do you know?' Lisa demanded. Her hands gripped the arms of her chair so tightly her knuckles were white against the stretched skin the way they had been when I told her of Ivo's death. But this time she wasn't acting.

'I saw the remains of the pregnancy testing kit box in your bathroom. And I knew there had to be a really good reason why you ran away like that, especially from all that luxury. Is that why you wear all those baggy knitted sweaters? You don't have the trim waistline you had a few weeks ago?'

There was a fraught silence. Ned was shaking his head from side to side as if he'd got something lodged in his ear.

'Harry the doorman's wife, Cheryl, put that idea in my head,' I explained to Lisa. 'When she talked to me about dancers having good figures.'

Lisa said quietly but with extraordinary venom, 'I don't have to discuss it with you, Fran, or with anyone else. Please give me my passport. I've booked a seat on a flight this evening. Yes, I do want to get away from Mickey.'

'And from the police,' I said. 'You killed him, Lisa, didn't you? You killed Ivo.'

Ned burst out, 'No! How could she? You saw him. He was a big fellow. She couldn't harm him. She only . . .' but then fell silent. 'You didn't, did you, Lisa?' he asked. He sounded ready to burst into tears.

'Of course not,' said Lisa impatiently. 'He fell in the river. I didn't know he'd drown. My passport, please, Fran.' She got to her feet and held out her hand.

'Yes,' said Ned, rallying and staying loyal to the last. 'If it is her passport, Fran, you ought to hand it over.'

'In good time. First let's all go and see a friend of mine here in Oxford,' I said. 'Her name is Hayley Pereira and she's a detective-sergeant . . .'

I didn't get to finish. Lisa threw herself at me. She caught me unawares, hitting me foursquare like a battering ram. My chair toppled backwards and I crashed to the floor, Lisa on top of me. She was scrabbling at my jacket pocket, trying to tear it open and extract the passport. I was winded by the fall and struggled to fend her off. She was fit and very strong. Ganesh was struggling up from his beanbag to come to my aid but Ned darted forward and pushed him back, holding him down.

'Give me my passport, you bitch!' Lisa hissed in my face and we struggled together on the floor.

It wasn't the first time I'd been in a scrap and normally I'd have been well able to take care of myself. But this time I was handicapped by the knowledge that my opponent was pregnant. As a result, I couldn't do several things I might otherwise have done. In the end, I placed the palms of both hands flat against her face and pushed with all my strength. She tried to bite me, as I knew she would, but it isn't easy to bite a flat surface. Her grip on my jacket slackened as she took one hand from it to tug at my hands over her face. I managed to wriggle out from beneath her. Before she could turn and grapple with me again I seized a hank of her long fair hair and wrapped it round my fist.

'Ow!' she yelled as I jerked her head backwards.

'Let go of her!' roared Ned. He forgot Ganesh and leapt towards us. He hauled me away from Lisa but I still had tight hold of her hair and she was still yelling blue murder.

'Let go!' shouted Ned and brought the side of his hand down in a chopping motion on my wrist.

The pain was excruciating. I released Lisa's hair. She scrabbled to her feet and made for the door. Holding my wrist, I dashed after her. Ned and Ganesh, who had finally wriggled out of his beanbag, followed. They got wedged together at the top of the stairs while Lisa and I clattered down. She pulled open the front door and dashed out into the street with me in close pursuit.

She made for her own front door and hammered on it. 'Mum! Mum! Let me in!'

I'd caught up now and she turned and aimed a kick at me as she hunted in her pocket, presumably for her door key.

Behind her the door flew open and she catapulted back into the hallway of her family home to land at her mother's feet.

'Lisa?' Jennifer gasped.

'It's all right, Mum!' Lisa jumped to her feet. 'Just shut the door and keep *her* out!' She pointed at me.

There was a movement at the rear of the hall and another person moved forward to join us.

'Lisa Stallard?' asked Hayley Pereira.

Lisa gaped at her. 'Who are you?'

'Lisa darling,' stammered Jennifer. 'This policewoman has just come wanting to talk to you. I told her you were out. What's going on?'

Lisa was as white as a sheet, pressed back against the open front door. She looked like the trapped animal she was between Pereira and me. Jennifer, her face as white as her daughter's, put her arms round Lisa protectively.

'I didn't kill him!' Lisa squealed in a strange high-pitched voice. 'I didn't kill him!'

'It's all right, darling,' Jennifer was saying, 'it's all right. Don't be frightened. Sergeant Pereira, it's a mistake, my daughter—'

There was a squeak of wheels and we all looked up. Paul Stallard was attempting to manoeuvre his chair through the doorway at the far end of the hall. The space was wide enough but he was agitated and in his haste he was awkward. The chair struck the door frame on one side and he had to reverse and try again. This time he struck the door frame on the other side. He was growing ever more fretful and frustrated.

'What is it?' he shouted above the banging and scraping. 'What is going on? What's all the damn noise? Who are all these people? Jennifer! Come and help me with this bloody chair!'

Lisa put out her hand as if to stop him advancing any further. 'No, Dad,' she whispered. 'No, Dad, please no . . . Don't come out here. I don't want you to hear this.'

Chapter Twelve

'Well, Fran,' said Hayley Pereira. 'You haven't been exactly helpful, have you?'

Why is it the police like to be so sarcastic? They lead frustrated lives, if you ask me, and it has to find its outlet somewhere. They seldom show any gratitude, that's for sure. I had worked the whole thing out for them and was prepared to tell them all about it. Yet here I sat about to be accused of lack of cooperation.

Pereira was wearing her peacock-blue cotton shirt and a denim jacket and pants. I wondered who did her laundry. Every time I saw her she looked crisply ironed and bandbox-fresh.

I, on the other hand, looked hot and bothered after my tussle with Lisa on the floor of Ned's flat, my jeans needed a wash and my T-shirt was torn where Lisa had wrenched it. There was no mirror in here but I had a feeling my right eye was swelling. It felt puffy and when I closed the left eye, the vision in the right one wasn't as good as it had been. My wrist was painful and I hoped it wasn't broken.

Our progress from the doorway of the Stallard home to the cop shop had been interesting. When Lisa realised Pereira meant to take her in, she tried to bolt for it. I was still in the doorway and she cannoned into me. I grabbed her and so did Pereira. Ned came in to the rescue and Ganesh piled in too, although I don't think he had the faintest idea what he ought to do.

It was a real punch-up. Pereira had to call for back-up and we were all shoved into the back of a police van and sped off through the city. At the station, they separated us. After an interminable wait during which they didn't even offer me a cup of tea, Pereira had arrived and marched me into an interview room.

It was the usual dingy sort of place familiar to me from London police stations. The paint was scratched and a brand new coat was badly needed. The walls were divided into bottle-green lower halves and what had been cream upper halves. The bottle-green paint had darkened to almost black and the cream to brown. The air smelled strongly of stale cigarette smoke and I thought someone had vomited in there in the recent past.

Pereira sat across a table from me, looking quite at home even though her neat personal appearance was in striking contrast to her surroundings. But then, in a manner of speaking, this was home for her, or at least her place of work. Lying on the table between us was a folder and Lisa's passport, which I'd handed over to Pereira. Now she tapped the passport.

'You have made a claim that Miss Stallard was intending to leave the country to avoid being questioned in relation to the death of Ivo Simić.' Her voice was brisk and impersonal. But the meaning was clear. I had to back up what I said or be accused of wasting Pereira's time.

'Yes, she was, she is. She will do, if you give her back her passport. Don't believe any story she tells you about a cruise ship. Check it out. There won't be any ship. Don't believe *anything* she tells you. She's an ace liar.'

If I sounded bitter it wasn't surprising. I'd been on the receiving end of Lisa's lies as well as her fist. I still couldn't get over my first view of her in the flesh, standing in the doorway of her family's home in Summertown. She'd looked such a *nice* girl. I should have concentrated on the promotional photo Mickey had given me of Lisa in her rhinestone cowboy outfit. I wondered what her birth sign was and whether it might not be Gemini. She was two people in one, all right. Little Miss Jekyll and Hyde, I thought, a dutiful daughter whose only mistake was to be stage-struck and yet also a murderer.

Pereira looked at me like a dowager who's just seen someone eat peas off a knife. 'You've made some other statements with regard to Lisa Stallard. You've accused her of murdering Ivo Simić. She denies this, of course.'

'She would, wouldn't she?' I snapped.

'I must say I find it an extraordinary and very serious

accusation, Fran. How did she manage to do it? Also, why? There seems to be a singular lack of motive in all this.'

'I can explain it,' I said.

'I was rather hoping you would. I am also hoping you'll explain your own actions which have hardly been those of a respectable law-abiding citizen.'

'Oi!' I said indignantly. 'I haven't broken any law.'

'You knew the identity of the drowned man and you said nothing. That's called withholding information and, what's more, the rest of your actions constitute interference with an investigation.' Pereira had worked up a gear and was getting into inquisitorial mode.

'I answered all the questions you asked me and I answered them honestly,' I argued. A heretic arguing with Torquemada would have had as little luck.

She leaned forward, jaw jutting, to hold my gaze. Her own was what I believe is usually described as 'steely-eyed'. 'You didn't tell me the drowned man's identity.'

'You didn't ask that one,' I mumbled unwisely.

'Don't play silly games with me!' she snapped back. 'You should have volunteered it.'

'Sorry.' It was time to eat humble pie. She was right. I had withheld information and there really wasn't any way I could get out of it. It was up to Pereira whether she decided to charge me with obstructing inquiries. I needed her on my side. Perhaps, I thought, a touch of pathos would help.

'I was scared,' I whimpered pretty convincingly.

'You? Of what?' was the brutal retort.

'Mickey Allerton,' I said. 'He's the one who sent me to Oxford. He can be a very scary man and he was holding my dog hostage. That is, until she ran away from the person looking after her.'

'That's a new one on me,' said Pereira silkily. 'Holding a dog as hostage? But it ran away, you say. An enterprising sort of dog, then. And has this remarkable animal turned up yet?'

I shook my head and must have looked genuinely miserable because she went on more kindly, 'If what you say is true and the dog is loose in a familiar part of town it will probably find its way home eventually.'

I nodded. I was hoping the same. But it reminded me that I didn't want to be here. I wanted to be back in London tracking Bonnie down. There was a large wasp trapped against a window-pane high up on the wall of the interview room. I wondered how it had got in here since the stale air suggested the window was never opened. From time to time the insect buzzed, at first angrily and then in frustration. Now it was beginning to sound desolate. I felt a certain empathy with it. Anyone would want to be out of here. It ought not to give up. I certainly wasn't going to.

'Look,' I said, 'you found Lisa without me.'

'Did I?' Pereira wasn't going to help me out.

'You were at her house, you'd come to ask her questions. How did you get there, anyway?' My curiosity overcame me.

She lifted one eyebrow. That's a neat trick and I've never been able to do it satisfactorily. 'I am a professional, Fran, you seem to forget. Anyway, you led her to me yourself. You told a Croatian girl called Vera Krejčmar to go to the police and identify Ivo Simić.'

'Yes, I did!' I burst out unwisely. 'So I didn't withhold his identity. Vera wouldn't have gone if I hadn't insisted.'

Pereira pursed her lips. Even her lipstick hadn't smudged. I supposed she'd had time to repair it after the fracas at the Stallard house.

'It's a fine point, Fran. You made me very curious about that guest house. Not only did you live there, and the young Americans who reported the finding of the body, but Vera works there and apparently the dead man, Simić, had stayed there, although the owner didn't know about it.

'So I went and had a long talk with the owner. It turned out that, although she'd been unaware Simić had stayed in her place hidden by Vera in her room, she wasn't unacquainted with Simić's employer, one Mickey Allerton.'

Pereira hesitated. 'I then ran Simić's fingerprints through records. I should have done that earlier, perhaps, but originally I'd no reason to think the drowned runner would be known to us. But he had form of a minor kind.'

Ivo had been in trouble with the law. I, too, should have thought of that possibility sooner.

Pereira was speaking again. 'So then I got in touch with the Met and asked them to give me the low-down on a club owner called Mickey or Michael Allerton. So I do know whom you're talking about and yes, I agree with you, he would be a man to take very seriously. Armed with my new information, I went back to the guest house and interviewed both women there. They told me a story about Simić coming to Oxford to seek out a dancer called Lisa Stallard who had been working for Allerton. The common factor in all of this appeared to be Allerton and his relationship with Lisa Stallard. So I tracked down Miss Stallard.'

Pereira leaned back in her chair. 'As you know, I've just been talking to Lisa. She admits she met with the deceased, Ivo Simić, early on the morning of his death. She does not admit any part in that death.'

'She killed him!' I interrupted.

Pereira didn't turn a hair. 'That's a wild statement, Fran. There's no evidence of foul play. The body has no obvious injury. She's only a young girl and to inflict any injury on Simić . . .'

'She's just given me a black eye!' I interrupted. 'Look!' I pointed at it. 'She attacked me! Don't tell me she's a weakling who couldn't inflict any injury.'

'Do you want to see a doctor?' Pereira wasn't interested in my black eye as such, but if I walked out of there and collapsed from some unsuspected head injury then there would be an internal inquiry at the very least and she didn't want that.

'No, I want a chance to explain my theory.'

We had reached a temporary impasse. Pereira conceded a point. 'All right, she's a dancer and dancers are athletes, very fit. But although she might handle herself very well in a scrap with you, she'd be no match for Simić. To suggest she killed him is fanciful.'

'So why did he drown?' I demanded. 'He was over six foot tall. The river's probably only about that depth, if that, by the bank.'

'Perhaps he hit his head?' Pereira suggested. 'Unconscious, he might have drowned.'

'You just told me there was no obvious sign of injury on the body. If he hit his head there would be an abrasion, some sign. Does the forensic report refer to anything?'

Pereira glanced at the folder on the desk. 'No,' she admitted. 'Perhaps he just couldn't swim?'

'I don't believe it. Look, let me explain it my way,' I begged.

'I'd love to hear your theory,' said Pereira, sarcastic again. 'I'd be interested also to know at what point before this morning you were planning to confide it to me.'

'Before this morning, I couldn't have. It was only this morning and last night that I got it sorted out in my own head.' I paused but she said nothing. The wasp made a sad, small fizzing noise.

'Dancers are like actors and there are always more of them than there are dancing jobs,' I began. 'I should have asked myself at once what was so special about this one that Mickey Allerton sent me after her. But I didn't. Mickey was holding my dog as surety against my carrying out his little commission, right? I didn't do it for the money. I want you to know that. I didn't like the job. But I did want my dog!'

Pereira nodded. The wasp was silent now, crawling slowing around the perimeter of the window-pane.

'So I came here. I contacted Lisa and arranged to meet her. How do you think I felt when I got there and found Ivo floating in the river? I didn't want to get mixed up with murder. Who would?'

'You thought it was murder? You had some reason for that?' she asked.

'Oh, come on. How could it be an accident? Ivo? You said yourself just now what a big strapping bloke he was. He just tripped and fell in the river? Someone mugged him? Come off it.'

'Accidents happen. People don't automatically think of murder,' she objected.

'Where I come from, if an accident like that happens to someone like Ivo, they do,' I countered.

'But you attempted, you told me, to drag him ashore. That was how you fell in yourself, so you said. You thought he might be alive.'

'Trying to grab him wasn't the brightest idea,' I agreed. 'But I wanted to do the good citizen bit. I'd have thought twice about touching the body if I had known at once who it was. When I saw his face, bobbing in the water next to mine, it was horrible,' I reminded her. 'I still think about it.'

Pereira made a sympathetic murmur but it sounded perfunctory.

'So,' I went on, 'you know what happened next. I saw Lisa arrive. I didn't know it then, but it was her second arrival on the scene. I signalled her to scram, because I knew Allerton wouldn't want her involved.

'Later when I told her the dead man was Ivo she freaked out or made like she did. I've studied acting and believe me, she's good. She said he must have come to Oxford searching for her with the idea that if he returned her to Allerton, he'd be in Allerton's good books. Jasna, another Croatian and a dancer at the club, looked likely to lose her job. Ivo, according to Lisa, wanted to help her. I learned later, not from Lisa, that Ivo was also worried about his own job. At the time Lisa's explanation made good sense to me and when I talked to Vera she seemed to back it up.'

Pereira spoke at this point. 'My impression so far is that you have an extraordinarily active imagination, Fran. Even so, I've yet to hear a motive for Lisa Stallard killing the man, let alone how she is supposed to have done it. But I'm sure you've got one.'

'Hang on,' I said. 'I'm getting to that. Up to this point I'd believed everything Lisa, Allerton and Vera had told me. Why shouldn't I? But then I went to Lisa's flat in London to fetch her passport. The moment I set foot in the place I realised the relationship between Lisa and Allerton was a lot more than just that of a dancer and guy who'd been employing her. You should see that place! You should see the clothes in the dressing room—'

I paused at the memory of Julie and the carving knife. 'Then Julie Allerton turned up and I learned that Mickey had walked out on a twenty-four-year marriage because of Lisa.

'I gave that a lot of thought. Allerton had had flings with girls who worked for him before. That he'd ditch his wife for this one and go through a messy divorce actually to marry Lisa, well, that makes things different, doesn't it? Either the man was totally infatuated, or suffering a mid-life crisis, or—'

I paused dramatically. This is partly because of my drama training and partly because I could see I now had Pereira hooked with my story and I wanted to prolong her suspense. She didn't say anything but she was waiting.

'Or,' I went on, 'Lisa had something Mickey wanted more than anything else in the world. When I looked round the flat, before Julie arrived, I found a bit of card in the waste bin in the bathroom. It was a scrap of packaging from a pregnancy testing kit. Julie told me she and Mickey had no children. They'd wanted kids, but none had come along. Julie said there was nothing wrong with her, so the suggestion was it was down to Mickey. Think about that, DS Pereira, will you? You've spoken to the London cops. They told you what sort of man Mickey Allerton is. He moves in a world in which being seen to be successful is everything. It's a man's world, full of tough guys. Yet this is a man with a secret he's kept from his macho mates. He believes he can't father a baby. Think what that must mean to him! Think how it's been eating at him during twenty-four years of childless marriage. Suddenly he finds out that his little girlfriend, Lisa, is pregnant. He's over the moon! He can father a kid, after all. He'll leave his wife. He'll marry Lisa. He'll take her and the infant Allerton off to live in Spain in his splendid villa and open a posh club for the discriminating punter. There's a marvellous future for all of them and when Lisa runs off – well, the poor guy doesn't know what's made her do it, but he does know he wants her back!'

'I see all that,' Pereira said. 'Or I see that it's feasible. That doesn't mean it happened. I return to my main question. Why should Lisa kill Ivo Simić when all she had to do was run off and leave him floundering in the river?'

'Because,' I said patiently, 'Mickey isn't the father of Lisa's kid. Ivo is.'

That stopped Pereira in her tracks. She blinked at me. 'I've got to give you credit, Fran. Active is hardly the word to describe your imagination. Lurid, is more like it, completely over the top.'

I interrupted her. 'Of course, Mickey doesn't know Lisa's been playing around with a doorman,' I went on quickly. 'It wouldn't occur to him the child isn't his because he believes no girl in her right mind would two-time Mickey Allerton. But Lisa never expected Mickey to react to the news of a baby the way he did. I don't believe she ever meant him to know she was pregnant. She'd have got herself a termination and he'd have been none the wiser. But Mickey had taken to turning up at the St John's Wood flat unexpectedly. I think he did that one day and he found the pregnancy testing kit. Mickey is the sort of man whose questions you answer. "Are you expecting a kid?" he asks Lisa and she has to admit she is. Mickey flings his arms round her crying out "Darling!" or there's a scene something like that.'

Pereira was opening and shutting her mouth and gazing at me in amazement.

I carried on undaunted. 'Next thing he's opening the champagne and discussing clinics. That's when she panicked and ran.

'Ivo doesn't know about the baby yet. But he follows Lisa to Oxford because he wants to help Jasna. He contacts Lisa and suggests they meet. Lisa is worried but can't see a way of getting out of it. She's already arranged to meet me the following morning, but Ivo is insistent, so she suggests he comes earlier to the same spot. Her big fear is that she doesn't know what he'll do if she won't go back to London with him. Ivo's not bright but he is vain and the way she dumped him for the big boss must have rankled with him. He's got scores to settle and doesn't think things through. He's dangerous.'

I paused here and waited to see if Pereira would raise any more objections to any of this. But I'd defeated her. She just gave a nod which I interpreted as a signal to continue.

'But Ivo has a weakness: he's scared of snakes. It's called ophidophobia,' I added, 'I looked it up on the Internet. Lisa knows all about this and it so happens that in the garden of the Stallards' house there's a grass snake, a sort of pet of Lisa's dad's. A grass snake is harmless but, as far as Ivo is concerned, if it's a snake that's enough to send him completely out of his skull. So Lisa pops the snake in a bag and sets off to meet Ivo. He won't touch her while she's holding a snake.'

Pereira stirred in her chair and spoke, sounding a lot less confident and sarcastic. 'Lisa has admitted this much.'

'She had to admit it,' I said. 'Ned blurted it out in front of me and Ganesh Patel.'

Pereira nodded. 'She also admits she may have jabbed it towards Simić to make him back off. She had no idea, when he fell in the river, she was leaving the man to drown.'

'She made sure he drowned,' I said. 'This is all about snakes, really. How do people trap a snake?'

'I don't know,' said Pereira slowly. 'They use forked sticks, don't they, to pin them down?'

'Exactly, and there just happened to be a convenient little item like that to hand, a long, thin forked branch which had fallen from one of the trees along the riverside path. I fell over the thing myself but I didn't then know what it meant or how important it was. Lisa saw Ivo threshing in the water and an opportunity to get him out of her life permanently. She dropped the snake and grabbed the branch. She reached out, held the forked end round his neck and pushed his head under. Like you said yourself, she's an athlete, a strong girl. Ivo was face-down in the water and didn't know what was happening. He was already in a panic at the sight of a snake, poor harmless old Arthur, that's the snake's name.'

Pereira's eyebrow twitched again.

'So he drowned,' I said. 'How long would it have taken? Only a few minutes, I'd have thought. You're the expert. You should know. Unfortunately, the snake slid off into the undergrowth while all this was going on and was lost. Paul Stallard has been missing his pet and Lisa wanted to find it, if she could. She loves her father and she knows what the pet meant to him. Also, she doesn't want anyone guessing what she did. She took Ned with her to hunt for it. She had to tell him how she came to lose the creature down there by the river, but Ned will do anything she asks.'

'I'm not an expert,' Pereira said. Her hand wandered to the folder on her desk; it hovered there a moment and then she removed it. 'I'll have a word with the pathologist. As it happens, there are unexplained scratch marks on the deceased's neck, to either side, below the ears. But that still doesn't mean your explanation is correct, Fran. It's not enough.'

'If you're lucky and go back to the scene you might find the forked branch. But it's probably not there now,' I added despondently.

'Is this the forked stick I saw you examining when I

came on you down by the river?' Pereira asked. 'Because, if so, that one is upstairs now in my office, wrapped in plastic.'

'What?' I gasped.

'Contrary to what you seem to think,' Pereira went on with an allowable touch of triumph in her voice, 'I am not totally unobservant and unable to work out anything for myself. I noticed how you examined the branch. After we parted company I went back and took a look at it myself. I couldn't see how it had anything to do with what had happened, I admit. But on the off chance I brought it back here and kept it. I haven't done anything with it and I was on the point of throwing it out. I had no excuse for sending it over to forensics but now I will.'

'But this is great!' I exclaimed. 'Perhaps they'll be able to get skin scrapings from it, either Ivo's from the forked end or Lisa's from the end she held it.'

Pereira shook her head. 'The public has a lot of faith in DNA these days. Don't get your hopes up, Fran. I'll send it off to forensics. But like I say, don't count on it. And before you leave here I'll have to ask you to give a sample for DNA testing for process of elimination. After all, you did handle the branch. I saw you do so myself.'

'Oh, wonderful,' I said, deflated. 'So, ten to one, the only DNA on it will be mine!'

Pereira gave a wry smile. 'I still don't see what gave you the idea Lisa might have been playing around with Ivo.'

'Oh, that,' I said. 'That really came into my head after talking to Cheryl, the woman who was looking after my dog and lost her. I suppose it's all about falling for unsuitable people. Allerton fell for Lisa like a ton of bricks. But you always want what you can't have. On the other hand, because something's being offered to you on a plate you don't necessarily take it. Take loyal old Ned here in Oxford. He and Lisa have obviously got some past history and Ned is still smitten, poor dope. So what would have attracted Lisa to Ned for a while? He's young, tall, well built, puts in lots of weight-training I'd guess. Then I realised I could be describing Ivo.

'As for Mickey Allerton,' I went on, remembering the scene at the club, 'if he ever had a physique it's just a memory now. I mean, he's looked after himself but he's no he-man. When I last saw him in person he was putting sugar substitute in his coffee and he told me he'd tried the Atkins Diet.'

'He'd do better to attend a gym,' said Pereira.

'He'd probably have a heart attack,' I said. 'You know, Lisa said something to me once which sort of explains things. She said that when you work "with people like that", it's a great mistake to "let them into your life". She was talking about Jasna at the time, but I think she meant everyone connected with the club. Lisa *is* devoted to her parents. But emotionally the Stallards are a needy pair. They urged her to leave home and make a dancing career but she only left them physically, if you like to think of it that way, never in her heart. She's always known how much she means to them and tried to return their devotion.

It hasn't left room for anyone else in her life, not emotionally.

'Sex without involvement is different. She enjoyed sex with someone like Ivo, who only wanted his vanity flattered, or in the old Oxford days with Ned who could be fobbed off with friendship. But the other thing Lisa likes, besides hunks, is money. Believe me, that girl could spend for Britain. You should have seen the clothes and shoes in her closet before Julie got at them all with a carving knife.

'She wanted a sugar daddy to pay for her expensive tastes and she found one in Allerton. But he wasn't content with that role. Unlike Ivo or Ned, he started to talk commitment, mutual commitment. She discovered she was becoming less his pampered mistress than his possession and, if they ever went to Spain, she'd virtually be his prisoner there. And there was still disgruntled old Ivo. He could prove difficult. No wonder she cut and ran.'

There was a long silence. The wasp huddled in a corner of a pane, just quivering its wings. Pereira spoke. 'It's a good story. But it will be a difficult one to prove. In the meantime, Fran, if I charge anyone, I ought to charge you with obstruction.'

'Great,' I muttered. 'Lisa walks away from murder. I'm done for obstruction.'

'No, not *yet*, anyway.' Pereira's voice and look warned me. 'I've been talking to Inspector Janice Morgan on your home patch in London. She's been telling me all about you.'

'Oh, right,' I mumbled. Was this good or bad?

'In the circumstances, I'll let any charge of obstruction lie on file. I won't be taking any action. That might change if you start playing detective in Oxford again. Consider yourself very lucky. When you've made your statement you can go back to London. I suggest you don't play detective there, either. Leave it to the professionals. It's not for amateurs.'

Not for amateurs? Would they have worked it out as I had done?

'I know she did it,' I said.

'We often believe we know who's responsible for a crime. Proving it is another matter.' She gave a smile which was almost wistful.

I looked up at the window. 'Do you mind if I let that wasp out before I go?' Why should Lisa be the only one to go free?

Unexpectedly, Pereira spoke again. 'Perhaps I shouldn't tell you this, but word has just come through that Paul Stallard collapsed after Lisa left with me to come here. He's in hospital, in intensive care. It's his heart. His chances don't look good. Jennifer Stallard is apparently in a dreadful state. So Lisa isn't avoiding all the fall-out from her behaviour.'

'She isn't the one in intensive care,' I snapped.

★   ★   ★

I signed my statement and came out of the police station into the afternoon sun. There she was, right there, walking across the car park towards the gate ahead of me.

I called, 'Lisa!'

She turned and waited for me to catch up with her. She didn't look pleased to see me.

'So,' I said. 'They've let you out.'

'Compassionate grounds,' she said coldly. 'My dad's in hospital. My mum needs me. I've made a statement, anyway.'

'I heard about your dad,' I admitted. 'I'm sorry for your parents.'

She scowled furiously at me. 'But for you, they wouldn't have found out anything about this! This wouldn't have happened!'

'Hey,' I said. 'Don't blame me. You should have told them the truth from the beginning. And your parents don't know the half of it, do they?'

'Get lost,' she advised me. 'I don't have to talk to you. I don't have to talk to anyone, not even the police any more, until my lawyer gets here.'

'What lawyer?' I asked.

'Mickey's sending him down from London. I just phoned.' She gave me a little smile of triumph. 'He said I shouldn't have made any statement but phoned for a lawyer first. Anyway, now he says sit tight with the statement I've made and wait for my legal adviser.'

'We're not talking about Filigrew, are we?' I gasped.

She looked surprised. 'Filigrew? That funny little man who does odd legal work for Mickey? No, of course not. Mickey's engaged a real top-notch man.'

She swung on her heel and walked off towards the gate.

Flabbergasted isn't too strong a word for how I felt. I stood where I was until I heard my name called and saw Ganesh signalling to me.

'What are you doing here?' I asked absently, my mind still with Lisa.

'I had to make a statement, too,' he said huffily, 'about what I saw down by the river and the fracas in Ned's flat.' He peered at me. 'You've got a black eye coming there.'

'Are you surprised? You didn't pull her off me!'

He looked offended. 'Was it my fault? I was stuck in a beanbag with a body-builder sitting on top of me.'

I grinned. 'You looked like an upturned tortoise, feet waving in the air, unable to right yourself.'

'Thank you. Who designed beanbags? Stupid things.' He pointed after Lisa. 'What about her?'

'Mickey's hired a good lawyer for her. That's not his baby, Ganesh. I'm sure of it. I think it's Ivo's.'

'Oh yes?' said Ganesh dourly. 'If it turns out you're right about that and Allerton finds out, it won't be a lawyer he'll be hiring to take care of Lisa, but a hit man.'

'How's he going to find out? Lisa and the lawyer will put up a cast-iron defence to any accusation of murder and the police will buy it. She's clever, Ganesh. I hate to admit it, but she's one very smart person.' I turned to look at him. 'That girl's a murderer, Ganesh. I know she is. But Mickey's wizard lawyer will get her off, Mickey will marry her and they'll go off and live in a luxury Spanish villa with a kidney-shaped pool.'

'How do you know the shape of the pool?' he asked, smiling down at me. He was growing his hair long again, much to his uncle's annoyance. Strands of it rippled in the warm summer air.

'Julie told me. Anyway, those places always have kidney-shaped pools. I've seen pictures. There's no justice, Ganesh.'

Ganesh took my arm. 'Come on,' he said. 'Let the local police sort it out. And don't worry about justice. That has a way of getting done. Let's go home.'

Chapter Thirteen

By the time we got back to London my wrist had swollen up like a balloon, so stiff I couldn't move it, and was very painful. At Ganesh's insistence we went directly from Paddington to the nearest A and E department.

They took my details and asked me how I'd come to hurt the wrist, also get the black eye which had developed nicely on the journey from Oxford, to the great interest of other train passengers and some signs of embarrassment on the part of Ganesh. A large stout lady sitting opposite us had kept glaring at him. As she came to leave the train she declared, on rising to her feet and fixing Ganesh with a gimlet eye, 'There is no action lower than that of a man who raises a hand to a woman!'

She then sailed majestically away leaving poor Ganesh with his mouth open and she'd gone before he could rally and explain he hadn't been responsible.

'Never mind, Gan,' I said to him. 'She probably wouldn't have believed you.'

This did not make things better and the remaining passengers had now caught on and we got even more curious, sympathetic (for me) and critical (for him) looks. It was mostly because of this, I fancy, that he'd insisted we go straight to A and E on arrival in London.

In reply to the nurse's question now about the cause of my injury, I told her I'd been in a fight, which was true. She didn't ask how or why or with whom. It was a pretty normal explanation for injury in their world. She just wrote it down.

'What about you?' the nurse then asked Ganesh.

'What about me?' returned Ganesh, nettled.

'Keep your hair on,' she said cheerfully. 'I only want to know if you were injured in the same fight.'

'Well, I wasn't,' said Ganesh.

'Don't be rude!' I muttered at him as the nurse scurried away with her clipboard.

'What did she mean, then? What's it got to do with me? I'm just here with you, as a friend, supporting you.'

'Yes, thank you, Gan.'

We sat for an hour after this before seeing anyone. During this time Ganesh sat with his arms folded, glowering at everyone else and muttering that if we lingered there much longer we'd catch some horrible disease. I pointed out that A and E didn't deal in diseases, but in accidents and unforeseen medical emergencies. How did I know, asked Ganesh, what diseases all those other people waiting might harbour?

I told him he was beginning to sound like his uncle. This didn't improve his mood and he sulked. I found a copy of the *Sun* newspaper which someone had left behind and read that, which didn't take long. Fortunately I was called at last and after examination sent along for X-ray. We then had to wait for the result. The wrist wasn't broken, thank goodness, only badly bruised. I was advised to rest it, as if I could do anything else with it. They gave me some painkillers.

All in all, it was quite late when we left the hospital. Ganesh was still in a sulk and mumbled at intervals all the way back to Camden. I gave up trying to listen: it all seemed to be on the same theme, i.e. how complicated I made his life and why couldn't I be like everyone else?

When we arrived he said loudly and distinctly, and fixing me with a stern gaze, that he had to go straight home to Hari to explain what had happened in Oxford. He thought it better I didn't go with him. If I walked in with a black eye and arm in a sling, Hari would probably pass out among the magazine racks and suffer a prolonged nervous breakdown after he came round. Moreover he, Ganesh, had had enough of people giving him funny looks and asking leading questions.

'First that fat woman on the train and then the nurse at A and E. All the other people in the waiting area were giving me odd looks, too, like I'd committed some crime.'

I told him he was being neurotic. But I wasn't anxious to have Hari lecturing me on the entirely foreseeable results of my rash behaviour and was happy enough to go on to my place alone.

Sadly, alone was what I found myself when I got there. No sign of Bonnie and enquiries among my fellow tenants and neighbours failed to turn up any hopeful news. The flat had an empty, abandoned feel to it. Dust had settled on all the surfaces and the jar of marmalade on which I'd breakfasted only that morning hadn't been returned to the fridge and had managed to grow a coat of grey mould already. I threw it in the bin. Then I put Bonnie's dog bowl in a cupboard out of sight. Not because I feared she wasn't now ever coming back; I refused even to consider that. But the sight of the unused dog bowl was more painful than the throbbing wrist.

Over the days that followed several people told me they thought they'd sighted Bonnie in a variety of locations. I went immediately to every one but didn't find her or anyone there who'd seen a dog like her. Erwin's musician friends were especially keen to help but their sightings of her were, I suspected, often influenced by banned or semi-banned substances which made it difficult to be sure what they had actually seen. One of them brought me a very small dog with very little hair which he said he'd found in the street. It was a nice little thing but it wasn't Bonnie and I told him to take it back where he'd found it or to the RSPCA.

'You sure this ain't your dog?' he asked, uncomprehending, picking it up in one hand and staring at it thoughtfully. The little dog stared back with bulging eyes.

'Yes, I'm really sure. My dog is a bit bigger than that one.'

'Bigger, right!' he said, put the mini-dog in his jacket pocket and departed.

Two days later he was back with a bewildered Doberman on a length of string. I explained that was too big and begged him to return it immediately to the backyard of the drug dealer from whom he'd probably abducted it. I watched them leave. The Doberman seemed to have taken a fancy to him and returning it might not have proved so easy.

Next I was asked to return to Oxford for the formal opening of the inquest on Ivo. Lisa was there, accompanied by a chap in a City suit with an expensive briefcase. This would be the lawyer Allerton had hired to watch over her interests. Pereira told the court that the deceased had been identified by a cousin (I assumed this to be Jasna but she wasn't there in person). He was Ivo Simić, who had been working as a doorkeeper at a club in London. I was asked to explain how and where I'd found the body. The inquest was then adjourned. The coroner said he understood the police were awaiting forensic reports and making some further inquiries.

At this I caught a fleeting expression of alarm on Lisa's face, but the smart lawyer whispered in her ear and she relaxed. My heart sank. Whatever questions came out of the further inquiries, the pair of them were pretty sure they had answers.

When the inquest was resumed, not long afterwards, there were more people there. Lisa appeared escorted not only by the lawyer but by her mother, who looked pale and drawn and wore black. Hovering protectively over the pair of them was Mickey Allerton himself, sporting a black tie. I deduced from this that Paul had probably passed away and Mickey had taken up the role of man of the family. I was sorry if this was the case. I'd liked Paul and sympathised with his situation. Nor did I like Mickey making himself prominent as the family's protector. It reinforced my belief that this inquest was unlikely to turn out as I might wish.

I stole a look at Lisa. She was also very pale and wore a dark trouser suit, the jacket bulging a little over her stomach. She had tied her hair back with a black ribbon. But she took the stand to give her account in a composed manner. She left London, she explained, after a dispute with her employer. This had all proved to be due to a misunderstanding but at the time she had been upset and returned home to Oxford. Simić had followed her and made contact. She knew him to be a violent and unpredictable man. She went to meet him as arranged because she did not want him to come to her family home. Her father was in poor health. He had since passed away.

There was a short break during which she sipped a glass of water, was asked if she wished to sit down, declined the offer, sniffed into a nice clean handkerchief, and carried on. She had also arranged to meet Francesca Varady, a private detective sent by her employer and she asked Simić to come to the same place, but earlier, as this was convenient for her. She took with her to the meeting a grass snake which lived in the garden of the family house because she knew that Simić was afraid of snakes. She carried it in a cloth bag. She had handled the snake before and wasn't afraid of it or of being bitten. Or the smell, she added.

'The smell?' asked the coroner, interested. He had appeared impressed by Lisa's lack of fear of snakes. He probably didn't suffer as Ivo had done from ophidophobia. But most people were nervous around snakes, I supposed.

'They can discharge a smelly substance as a defence,' she explained. 'But Arthur knew me.'

'Arthur, Miss Stallard?'

A blush and prettily contrived confusion on the part of the witness. 'We called him that. He was a sort of pet.'

By now, I thought sourly, she had added the coroner to her list of pets. But then, she looked such a nice girl, standing there. Pretty, apparently frank, well-spoken, bereaved and to top it all in what the Victorians liked to call an interesting condition.

I stole a glance at Jennifer Stallard. She looked twice as tense and nervous as her daughter on the witness stand. She leaned forward slightly and watched Lisa's face with a desperate intensity. Her thin white hands were twisting a handkerchief into an unrecognisable rag. She's lost her husband, I thought. Now she sees the possibility of losing her daughter, too, although in a different way. Has she guessed? Has she got some inkling of what Lisa really did down by the river that morning?

Lisa was speaking again. She explained that Simić had panicked on seeing the snake. He had stumbled backwards and fallen in the river.

'And when Simić fell into the river, what did you do next?' asked the coroner in a kindly way.

'I panicked too,' she said with a catch in her voice. 'But I thought he'd be all right. I mean, I was sure he could swim. Anyway, I didn't think the river was very deep. But I knew he'd be angry and I'd dropped the grass snake. It slid away, so there was nothing to stop him attacking me.'

'So you simply left the scene?' the coroner asked her.

She hesitated. 'He was near the bank and I thought he would climb out.' Her voice began to break. She stifled a sob. 'I didn't think he'd drown! I wouldn't leave anyone to drown!' Tears began to trickle down her cheeks and an usher offered more water but she gestured the glass aside. The tears burst out uncontrollably. I was more than startled. I was shocked. I had assumed she'd been acting her distress but this was all too real. I saw Jennifer begin to rise to her feet and Mickey Allerton put a hand on her arm. Jennifer sank back, her face a picture of utter misery.

Did my mother, I wondered, after she'd left us all, ever spend a night of misery like that, thinking about me? Had she loved me like that? I could never know now. For years Jennifer had been a prisoner in that house in Summertown with her invalid husband. No thought of her own freedom or of fulfilment, but comforting herself that Lisa, at least, had every opportunity and was making the most of it. And this was how it had ended, in a coroner's court, cool and dim in marked contrast to the outside heat, already building up although this was still quite early in the morning. Here she sat and listened to all her dreams fall apart.

I looked across the room to Pereira but her face was expressionless.

Lisa was helped back to her seat where Jennifer put her arm round her shoulders.

Mickey was then presented to the court as Mr Michael Allerton, a businessman and club owner. He said he wished it to be known that although he had employed Ivo Simić, he had not sent the man to Oxford in pursuit of Miss Stallard. He had in fact been on the point of sacking Simić due to Simić's unsatisfactory behaviour during his time in his employment. He, Allerton, had asked Miss Francesca Varady, a private detective, to go to Oxford and talk to Miss Stallard on his behalf. Miss Varady had done so. As a result, the matter under dispute between himself and Miss Stallard had been resolved to the satisfaction of both parties.

I must say, Allerton looked pretty satisfied when he said this.

'Ah, yes,' said the coroner, shuffling his papers, 'we heard from Miss Varady the – ah – private detective at the previous inquest.' Private detectives, in his view, were obviously to be categorised together with snakes.

A pathologist's statement was then read to the court, stating that death had been from drowning.

What had been the result of the further forensic tests? Pereira was asked when she took the stand next.

'Inconclusive,' she said briefly.

'So you have nothing further to add, Sergeant Pereira?'

'No, sir.'

The coroner summed up with the air of a headmaster doing his best to be fair. This whole sorry affair had arisen from a dispute at her place of work between Lisa Stallard and her employer, Michael Allerton, a dispute the coroner understood had now been resolved. At the time of the tragedy, however, Lisa Stallard had left London in haste and in some mental confusion. The deceased, Ivo Simić, had followed her to Oxford and made contact, requesting a meeting. The coroner accepted that Lisa Stallard had been afraid that Simić had come to Oxford to force her to return to London with him. The court had heard from Mr Allerton, Simić's employer, that this had not been so. Mr Allerton had in fact sent Miss Francesca Varady to make contact with Miss Stallard and as a result the matter under dispute had later been settled in a peaceful manner. But at the time Simić contacted her, Mr Allerton and Miss

Stallard were not on speaking terms. Being with some justification afraid of Simić . . .

Here the coroner rustled papers and observed that police records showed Simić had a conviction for affray and another for assault and could therefore be assumed to have been a dangerous man. So, being afraid of Simić but aware Simić suffered a phobia regarding snakes, she had taken a grass snake from her family's garden. Mrs Jennifer Stallard, who on medical advice was not being asked to give her evidence in person, had given the court a written statement that the snake had lived in her garden and been a pet of her late husband's. The court was sorry to hear of Mr Stallard's recent demise and the coroner would not prolong his summing-up unduly, causing more distress. However, Lisa Stallard took the snake as insurance, shall we say?

He peered at us over his spectacles as if this was the moment when one of us, had any of us an objection, should jump up and say so. Rather like a priest conducting a marriage ceremony. *If any one has just cause* . . . I had just cause but no evidence. The usher would probably eject me from the court if I made a fuss, Allerton would be seriously displeased and Pereira would tell me I was out of order and what the hell did I think I was doing? I sat on my hands. If ever justice was done for Ivo Simić, it wouldn't be here.

The coroner took up his thread. Yes, an insurance against an assault on the part of Simić. Unfortunately, Simić's reaction on seeing the snake had been so violent as to involve his stumbling back and losing his footing, falling in the river. While Miss Stallard should really have remained and made sure that he had climbed out, knowing him to be young and fit and seeing that he was conscious and moving in the water, she can be forgiven for believing he was well able to climb out unaided. Her explanation for leaving the scene was – ah – unfortunate but understandable.

Accidental death.

We all left the court. Lisa, her mother, Allerton and the sharp-suited lawyer formed a tightly knit group. I was standing alone on the pavement watching them when I heard my name called and turned to find Pereira standing nearby.

'So, she got away with it,' I said. 'I knew she would.'

'There was no evidence to support your theory, Fran,' Pereira told me.

'What about the branch?' Despite Pereira's warnings, I'd fixed my hopes on that branch.

'It had been lying in the open for a while. Any DNA on it was too degraded. We couldn't make a match. Anyway, if you're right and one end of the branch had been in the river, the traces would've washed off – oh, we weren't even able to get a trace of yours, Fran. Perhaps that was just as well. Think about it.'

I stared at her in horror. 'You mean I might have ended up charged with killing Ivo?'

'You were the one who was discovered in the river with

the body,' she reminded me. 'You handled the branch. I think, Fran, you should go home and try and forget all about this.' She paused. 'As for the parentage of Lisa's baby which you questioned in your interview with me, that did not arise. It's a serious allegation, Fran, and I'd keep it to yourself, if I were you. You have no reason to believe you are right and unless Mr Allerton himself should get suspicious and ask for the relevant tests . . .'

'Don't worry,' I said. 'I'm not going to tell him. But I'll tell you this: I wouldn't want to be there if he ever finds out! Lisa's going to have to worry about that for the rest of her life!'

I turned away and left her. I don't know quite where I intended going, probably straight to the station and back to London; then I saw Jennifer Stallard had moved away from the others and was standing alone in the shadow of the building. Mickey, Lisa and their lawyer had their heads together, not looking my way.

I hesitated but common courtesy dictated I expressed my condolences to the widow. I went over to her, cleared my throat and said tentatively, 'Jennifer? You remember me? Fran.'

She turned her head and smiled, a slow sad smile which didn't reach her eyes. 'Yes, dear, of course I do.'

'I'm very sorry,' I said, 'about your husband.'

'Thank you.' Her gaze drifted away from me towards the group of three conferring together.

I said awkwardly, 'He'll look after her.'

'Mr Allerton? Oh yes, you know Lisa's fiancé,' she said.

Fiancé? Mickey was making sure things were going to be done according to his rules from now on. I peered across at the consulting group of three again and could just make out a sizeable stone on Lisa's ring finger.

'He employed me,' I said bleakly, 'to come to Oxford, as you heard back there in court. I'm sorry about that, too. I didn't do it by choice or for the money. There was another reason.'

She seemed not to have heard me. 'I did hope,' she said, 'that one day Lisa and Ned might make a match of it. I suppose I knew it was unlikely but we've known Ned for years and he and Lisa were such good friends.'

'Yes,' I mumbled. 'I suppose Allerton isn't quite what you had in mind for a son-in-law.'

She hunched her shoulders. 'I hoped she'd choose sensibly. I was worried when I knew she'd taken up with a married man but now that his divorce is going through and they are to be married . . . well, I have to accept it.'

I blinked. 'Hang on,' I said. 'You knew she'd taken up with Allerton? You knew before all this?'

Now she turned back to me and her smile was both warmer and more rueful. 'It doesn't do to check up on your adult children. They don't like it. Lisa never knew but I did check up on her. I knew all along what kind of work she did at that club. I knew that man – Mr Allerton – had put her in a flat. I knew, when you came to our door, that you'd probably come from him. But I couldn't do anything, say anything. I didn't want Paul to find out. If Lisa had found out that I'd, well, snooped, she'd have been so angry. Even worse, she'd have been so upset. She didn't want us to know. It would have hurt her terribly to find out we did know, or at least I knew. I couldn't tell my husband. He had a rather unreal view of Lisa.' Jennifer's mouth twitched. 'Men like to believe their daughters are always Daddy's little girl. They don't like the idea of them growing up. Funnily, when I did admit to Lisa, after Paul died, that I'd always known, she was relieved. We both cried. I told her I understood and that everything would be all right now. And it will be.'

She spoke these last words with a kind of serenity.

I stood there frozen to the spot and unable to breathe a word. Eventually I managed to croak, 'It was you! You picked up that branch and pushed Ivo's head under the water! Lisa knows you did it.'

She sighed. 'I had to tell her after the police came to the house and it looked for a while as if they might accuse Lisa of causing his death. I told her not to worry. I had done it but I'd tell the police and Lisa would be in the clear. Lisa said I mustn't breathe a word. Mr Allerton would get her a lawyer if she asked and it would be all right.'

Jennifer frowned and nodded towards the lawyer a little distance away. Allerton was shaking him warmly by the hand, a really happy little scene.

'Certainly he seemed a very competent man when he turned up. He told us that the coroner's verdict would almost certainly be accidental death. We were a little worried, Lisa and I, when the police spoke of further forensic tests. But Lisa said we were to keep our nerve and keep our mouths shut. We did keep our nerve and our silence but I can tell you, because I want you to know, that Lisa didn't kill him and I know you won't say anything to anyone. Mr Allerton pays you too, doesn't he?'

I wanted to burst out that, whatever Allerton paid me for, it wasn't to keep quiet about murder. But she was right. I would keep quiet. This unfortunate woman's life had been devoted to an ailing querulous husband. Her one joy was her daughter. Jennifer now had a chance of a good life of her own, Mickey would see to that, and a grandchild to look forward to. I could destroy all that with a word in Pereira's ear. It was a word I could never drop.

'What did you do?' I whispered. 'Follow Lisa?'

'That morning? Yes. Paul was asleep. He'd had a very bad night and eventually took some sleeping pills which knocked him out. I got up early and went down to the kitchen to make a cup of tea. I heard movement and looked into the hall. Lisa was sneaking out. I knew something was up. I was worried about her. I knew Paul wouldn't waken until nearly lunchtime. So I hurried after Lisa and tracked her to Christ Church Meadow. I couldn't imagine what she wanted there. Then I saw her meet that awful man. I could see from her body language how scared she was and from his how threatening he was. He was a strange-looking man, very tall and strong with blond hair, good-looking, I suppose, yet somehow, I don't know how to describe it, there was something wrong about him. They began to argue and I was about to run out and let them see I was there. I was so frightened for my daughter. But then I saw her delve into a cloth bag she had with her and she brought out a snake. I'm sure it was the one from our garden, the grass snake my husband always called Arthur. She held it out towards the man and the result was remarkable, extraordinary. He became a gibbering wreck. I couldn't believe my eyes. He waved his arms around and his eyes bulged. He was truly terrified. He staggered back away from her and he fell in the river with a tremendous splash, water going everywhere. Lisa ran away and I came out from my hiding place. He was threshing about and making for the bank. So, so I picked up the branch lying nearby and pushed him back in. I held his head under.'

She stared at me, her eyes wide and dark with memory. 'I did it for my daughter,' she said. 'I thought he'd come to take her back to London and she didn't want to go. I thought, if she didn't go with him, he'd do something to her, attack her, perhaps scar her face . . . one reads about such things.'

She had done it for Lisa. Lisa, who after all that had happened had been on the point of escaping both Ivo and Mickey Allerton for ever, had been forced to turn back to Allerton to ask for his help. He, in return, had made clear his price.

'Mummy!' Lisa's voice came across the intervening space, a worried note in it.

Jennifer broke off her narrative and gave herself a little shake as if awakening from a bad dream. 'Excuse me,' she said. 'I must go. It was nice to see you again, dear.'

I watched her rejoin them. Allerton bent over her solicitously. He would be a most attentive son-in-law.

Someone else had been watching the scene. I almost walked into him as I turned to leave and he stepped in front of me.

'That's him, then,' he said. 'That's Allerton. He looks like a thug.'

'Hello, Ned,' I exclaimed. 'I didn't see you in court. What are you doing here?'

I meant, why was he putting himself through all this agony? His unhappiness seeped out of him.

He stared at me morosely. 'I stood at the back and slipped out before you all turned round and saw me. I know I've been an idiot but that doesn't mean I want everyone pointing me out. This is all your fault, you know. She'd have got away from him but for you.'

'Rubbish!' I said. 'Of course it's not my fault and don't go imagining Mickey Allerton is so easy to escape. Look, Ned, things don't have to be anyone's fault. It's just life. Lisa made a choice when she went after Allerton. She got more than she bargained for but she should have thought about that.' I took pity on him because he looked so stricken. 'Come on, Allerton will look after her and Jennifer.'

'It's about money, isn't it?' he said as if he'd just discovered a new law of nature.

'The apple's dropped, has it?' I apologised immediately. 'Sorry, Ned.'

He flushed and burst out, 'She wasn't like that before she went to London. Lisa was different when I knew her here in Oxford. She was gentle, sweet-natured and all she wanted to do was dance. She'd never have got herself involved with a man like that!' He threw out a quivering hand to point to where Allerton had stood.

'Sure,' I said wearily. Let him keep his image of her. 'But you can't undo what's happened, Ned.'

He just grunted at me and strode off. I told myself he'd get over it. Not quickly, and not easily, but eventually.

I went to see Beryl before I left, partly to tell her the result of the inquest but mainly to say goodbye properly. I liked her. She seemed to be expecting me and led me downstairs to her sanctum where Spencer leapt about in his demented manner. Seeing him almost made me regret coming. There would be no dog to greet me when I got home. I hadn't thought I could feel the loss of an animal so keenly.

Beryl urged tea and biscuits on me and asked how it had gone.

'From Allerton's viewpoint, pretty well,' I said. 'The

verdict was accidental death.' I explained about Lisa and the grass snake and Ivo's ophidophobia. I couldn't tell her about Jennifer. That was something I couldn't ever tell anyone, not even Ganesh.

'Well, I never,' said Beryl comfortably when I came to the end of my narrative. 'I'm glad things have turned out all right for Mickey.'

'When I first came here,' I said, 'you knew exactly why I'd come, didn't you? You knew about Lisa and her relationship with Mickey and all the rest of it?'

Beryl tucked a stray wisp of red hair behind an oversized pearl earring. 'Of course I knew about her, Fran dear. Mickey got in touch with me straightaway, the minute she ran off and left him. He was in such a state you'd hardly believe it, babbling down the phone. I could hardly believe it was Mickey. We're old friends. He had to talk to someone so he poured it all out to me. He reckoned she'd come to Oxford because one of the other girls had told him her parents lived here. He wanted me to find her and talk her into going back to him.

'I told him straight off I was the wrong person for the job, a washed up ex-dancer with a false leg, old enough to be her mum.' Beryl chuckled throatily. 'What you need,' I said to Mickey, 'is someone of her own age and type, someone dreaming of being in the entertainment business, like her.'

I don't know if Beryl saw me wince at that. If she did, she ignored it and went on, ' "You look round and find the right girl," I told him. Seems like he listened to my advice and he did.' Beryl nodded at me approvingly.

'One thing's been bothering me,' I said. 'Mickey could've forced her to come back if he'd threatened to get in touch with her parents. She was desperate to keep them from knowing what she'd been up to in London. He must have had a shrewd idea that was the case.'

Beryl looked past me into the middle distance. 'He wouldn't have done that to her, not feeling the way he does about her.' She hunched her shoulders. 'He must be getting on, Mickey. We're none of us as young as we were. But age doesn't matter.'

'You're not going to tell me, I hope,' I said, trying to keep the incredulity from my voice, 'that he's *in love*. He wants to own her, but that's not the same thing.'

'What's the matter? Love is only for the young?' Beryl's gaze returned to me, surprisingly sharp. 'Twenty, forty, fifty, you can make a fool of yourself over someone at any age. Only don't tell Mickey I said so!'

'It's not my intention to tell him anything!' I retorted.

She gave me another sharp look but she didn't ask what in particular I meant by the remark. Some information it's easier not to have.

I went home, but forgetting about everything that had happened wasn't easy. I just couldn't get over it all. It wasn't Mickey's love-lorn heart that bothered me. It was that other, far more frightening, love of which Jennifer had given me a terrifying glimpse. Mother love. I'd many times wondered about the nature of any love my defaulting mother might have had for me. I'd deplored its fickleness and so often wished it had been stronger. But was the alternative this? Jennifer loved her daughter with a strength that had led her to commit a dreadful crime. The knowledge of that had given Lisa a burden of responsibility she would carry all her life.

I hoped it was now all over with but a week later a ring at my flat bell announced a visitor. I wasn't overjoyed to see Filigrew on the doorstep clutching a well-worn document satchel to his less-than-manly chest. I wasn't that surprised, either. Mickey was tidying up the loose ends and I was about to be bought off.

'Hello, Mervyn,' I said without enthusiasm.

My instinct was to tell Filigrew to go away. But he'd argue and I wasn't going to have a slanging match with him on the doorstep with any passer-by chancing to overhear, so I was obliged to invite him into the flat.

His lack of enthusiasm was equal to mine. He sidled in, his manner suggesting he was entering a den of lions, and stood by the door of the room, ready for flight. He looked much as he'd done in Oxford, pale and tidy with a drab suit and a puce tie. I didn't invite him to sit down and he didn't appear to expect it. We both wanted to get this over with.

'I have come from Mr Allerton,' he said stiffly.

'I don't want anything more to do with Mickey Allerton,' I said promptly. 'Tell him so.'

He ignored my outburst. 'Mr Allerton is satisfied with your work on his behalf. Also, he is sorry to hear about your dog being lost.'

At this my jaw dropped and I said nothing.

'So,' said Filigrew, laying down the document satchel and unbuckling it, 'I am asked to give you this.' He drew out a plump plain brown envelope and held it out to me.

'I don't want it,' I said.

Filigrew gave me a weary look. 'It was agreed. Mr Allerton would pay you the balance of what he owed you, depending on results. Miss Stallard has returned to London and Mr Allerton considers you did very well.'

'Is she back in St John's Wood?' I asked, diverted.

'No,' said Filigrew unwillingly. 'I believe she is living at another address.'

So Julie had at least been successful in claiming the flat. Not that it made much difference. Lisa was now installed in a similar one elsewhere.

'I still don't want that,' I said, indicating the envelope.

Filigrew sighed and put it down on the table by the document satchel. 'Whether you want it or not is quite irrelevant,' he told me. 'Mr Allerton wishes you to have it. I am instructed to give it to you and I have done so.' He rebuckled his ancient satchel and tucked it under his arm. 'You will find he has included an additional sum as compensation for the dog. I think that concludes our business. Goodbye.'

When he had left I picked up the envelope and prised back one corner of the seal. It was stuffed with notes. I didn't know how much it contained and I didn't care. I didn't want it. I particularly didn't want money in compensation for Bonnie. How could he do that? Just think he could pay me off like that? It was entirely his fault Bonnie wasn't here with me. Allerton had got what he wanted and felt generous. He didn't have a clue how I felt. How could he imagine money would take Bonnie's place? But a man like that believes money solves any problem. Knowing Lisa would only have confirmed him in that belief.

I sat for a while on my sofa, drinking coffee, contemplating the envelope and wondering what to do with it. I was so angry he'd added money for Bonnie I felt like burning the whole thing. I couldn't return it to Mickey and I couldn't keep it. Not that I hadn't earned it! Even leaving Bonnie's loss out of it (although that mattered to me more than anything), I'd got a black eye from his girlfriend Lisa and a bruised arm from her chum Ned. Fortunately both injuries had subsided by now. I had the use of the arm again and the area around the eye showed only a faint mauve tinge. The woman on the train would be pleased.

Battered women! I thought, sitting up so suddenly I nearly spilled the coffee. How could I have forgotten St

Agatha's Refuge? I had even gone there a couple of times during my search for a missing person in a previous case. Ideal! I thought. It was local too. I got a pen and wrote on the envelope: 'To the Secretary, St Agatha's Refuge for Women.' I waited until it was dark and trotted round to the refuge. There were lights showing at upper windows and I could hear a very small baby crying. The front door showed signs of recent violent assault and the window to the left of the door was boarded up temporarily. This sort of damage was standard at St Agatha's. I pushed the envelope through the letter box and heard it fall to the parquet floor on the other side with a satisfying thud. A weight lifted from my chest.

'Good!' I said aloud. 'That's settled with you, Mr Allerton!'

I set off back home through the lamplit streets. I passed the Rose pub which was agleam with lights and noisy with laughter. It had a new landlord but he had kept up the previous landlord's habit of engaging live acts to entertain customers. They must have had a comedian on stage tonight and one who was being reasonably successful to judge by the guffaws. He was probably one who had realised that sophisticated humour didn't go down well with the patrons of the Rose. They just liked the blue jokes.

As I passed through the gap where there had once been a gate into the forecourt of the house where I lived, I heard a rustle in the dead privet hedge to my left. It was alive when I moved in. I did that hedge to death, though not intentionally. Inspired by one of those TV gardening programmes, I pruned it, whereupon it died. I didn't pay much attention to the faint sound because small creatures still took up temporary residence in the tangle of dead twigs. But as I fumbled for my door key I heard it again. It was followed by a faint whimper.

I froze and turned. In the shadows under the hedge something moved and crawled out, limping towards me into the yellow glow of the street lamp. It was a small bedraggled white dog with black patches.

The vet who checked Bonnie over said that although very hungry and grubby and suffering sore pads on all four paws, she was unhurt. I explained how she came to be lost and she came up with a theory.

'People find dogs which are lost or simply wandering about on their own. Although the animals are in good condition and well cared for, they still assume they are abandoned,' she said. 'Instead of taking them to the nearest animal shelter, they take a fancy to the animal and decide to adopt it. They take it home and home may be miles away. They keep the animal indoors or restrained for a while until it gets used to its new home and so it's some time before the dog escapes. Sometimes, of course, they don't escape. They just settle down happily with the new owner. Others slip away and try to find their way home. We don't know how animals do find their way home over long distances but they do, and I think this is what Bonnie has done. The condition of her paws suggests she's walked a long way.' She scratched Bonnie's ears. 'Unfortunately, she can't tell us. But I think whoever had her looked after her all right. You may find she clings to you for a while, follows you round the house and doesn't like to be parted, wants to sleep on your bed, that sort of thing.'

'She did that before,' I said. 'She used to belong to a homeless person.'

I carried Bonnie home but I told her she ought not to get too used to travelling like that. Once her paws were better she would have to start walking again. 'Just remember that!' I said. She stretched up and licked my chin with a look in her brown eyes which clearly said, 'But I like being carried.' 'Tough!' I told her.

I felt as though Bonnie's return was the last in a series of events which had gone wrong from the start but now had finally come right with her reappearance. But in fact it still wasn't quite all over.

A week after that I was wandering up the Strand early in the evening when a taxi drew up ahead of me, just by the entrance to the Savoy. And who got out? Mickey Allerton and Lisa. They didn't see me. I stepped into a convenient doorway and watched as he paid off the cab and they both went into Simpson's-in-the-Strand restaurant. Nothing but the best for Lisa, I thought sourly. But I got a good look at both of them. Mickey looked well pleased with himself. Lisa was beautifully dressed in clothing cut to disguise the bump. All the clothes vandalised by Julie must have been replaced. But it was her face which struck me most. She looked completely blank, features frozen into complete nothingness. As I watched, Mickey took her elbow and propelled her forward into the building. She went with zombie-like obedience and indifference. Mickey had indeed got what he wanted; and he didn't mean to let her slip from his grip again – ever.

I went to see Susie Duke. She's in the detection business and she's known Allerton a lot longer than I have. I couldn't tell her what Jennifer had done and could no longer accuse Lisa of murder, but a chat with Susie might help me sort out what I felt about the whole unsatisfactory affair.

I found Susie taping up her toes and heels with strips of adhesive tape cut from a long roll of the stuff.

'What have you been doing?' I asked.

'Running!' she grumbled. 'They ought to put me in for the Olympic Games. I was doing a check on this feller. He's been claiming compensation for an accident at work which has left him unable to do any sport, or so he says. His employer doesn't believe it. He heard the injured feller had been seen out jogging, right? So the employer hired me to snoop round and see if I could catch him at it. I staked out his house with my little camera and waited.'

'And he spotted you and chased you,' I said.

'Yes and no. He spotted me and set his perishing dog on me. Ruddy great thing with flapping ears and a long red tongue, legs like a pony.'

'Did you outrun it?' I asked, impressed.

'It nearly caught me. I jumped in a taxi and then it chased the taxi. Look at 'em!' she ordered, sticking out what now looked like a Chinese concubine's bound feet for my inspection.

I sympathised and told her about my adventures in Oxford.

'Always steer clear of cases like that,' said Susie immediately. 'Too many personal angles.'

'Like I had a choice!' I snorted.

Susie pulled a pair of cotton socks carefully over the bandages, then leaned back and tapped the roll of adhesive tape against her top teeth. Traces of fuchsia lip gloss began to appear on it. 'There are things about this you can't tell me, right?'

'I really can't, Susie. The coroner's verdict was "accidental death". Let's leave it like that. But whatever really happened, Lisa was responsible for Ivo being in that river. Every time Allerton looks at her now, he's got to think about that and, maybe, just wonder a little.'

'Not enough to let it worry him,' said Susie, gesturing at me with the mauve-stained roll of tape. 'If your friend Beryl is right, then Mickey's in love with the girl. You never want to believe anything nasty about someone you love, do you? You sort of suppress it even when the evidence is jumping up in your face. Look at my late husband, Rennie. He wasn't perfect.'

'No,' I said tactlessly. Rennie Duke had been a shifty little double-crosser, in my view.

'But he had his good points,' Susie retorted. 'And I loved the little squirt, see? So I overlooked the bad ones.'

'Susie,' I said. 'However you interpret it, what kind of life is Lisa going to have with Allerton?'

'I don't know why you should think she'll be so miserable,' said Susie briskly. 'I wish I could find a bloke who'd buy me designer wear and carry me off to live in the sun in a luxury villa. Blimey, Fran, what do you want from life?'

'Freedom!' I said promptly.

'To do what, starve? Or earn a crust being chased by a hound with teeth like a croc?' Susie laced her trainers and stood up, experimentally taking the weight on the damaged digits. 'You thought again about coming to work with me in the Agency?'

'You've got to be joking!' I told her. 'Anyway, I've given up taking an interest in other people's business. It's too complicated.'

'You haven't given up. You've got bitten by the detection bug, like me. There must be a dozen different safer ways I could earn a living. I know this time you didn't choose to take on the case, it was forced on you. But just wait, next time something will come along and you won't be able to keep away from it.'

'It's what worries Ganesh,' I said.

* * *

I didn't tell Ganesh what Susie had said but I did tell him about seeing Allerton and Lisa in the Strand.

'It's not that I feel sorry for her,' I said. 'She got herself into that situation, like I told poor Ned. She'll have to put up with it. But she'll be a bird in a gilded cage.'

We were taking one of our favourite walks along the Regent's Park canal beneath the shade of the overhanging trees. Bonnie, her paws no longer sore, pattered along ahead of us. A tourist barge with sightseers on it chugged past cutting a V-shaped ripple on the green surface of the water. I could hear an animal at the zoo bellowing in the distance. We had a can of Dr Pepper apiece which Ganesh had brought from the shop together with a couple of Mars bars. Hari was still so pleased that Bonnie had come back that he'd agreed to us having these items without the usual lament that he was never going to make any money if we ate all the stock for free. Ganesh made no reply to my observation. He'd been silent during the whole walk.

'But funnily enough,' I went on, undeterred by the lack of response, 'I do feel a bit sorry for Mickey. I never thought I would, not for that man. But she'll find a way to wriggle out of his control eventually. She's pretty resourceful, I reckon. He'll take her out to Spain and she'll run off with a flamenco dancer. Anyway, I still think that's not his baby and when it's born . . .'

'I do wish,' said Ganesh breaking his silence at last,

'you'd shut up about Lisa's baby. It's nothing to do with you, and I'm fed up with hearing about babies.'

'Ah,' I said. 'I'm looking forward to seeing Usha's. Are they glad it's a boy?'

'The whole family has gone baby-crazy,' grumbled Ganesh. 'My mum, my dad, my aunts . . . all they talk about is Usha's baby and babies in general. You'd think no one ever gave birth before. Jay is going around being the proud father. All right, it's a nice baby and I don't mind being an uncle.' He paused. 'But I'm not going to be an uncle like Hari is to me. I'm going to be a modern one.'

'Good,' I said.

'The worst of it,' added Ganesh in deepening gloom, 'is that they keep looking at me and saying it's about time I settled down.'

'Oh,' I said. 'I see.'

'No, you don't,' he retorted. 'Anyway, I've told them I'm considering going to evening classes and making a new career. I can't be thinking about settling down until I've done so.'

'What will you study at evening classes?' I asked.

'I don't know! I haven't decided. Nor have I persuaded Hari that he'll have to give me time off to study. He's being a bit difficult at the moment so it's not a good time to ask him. He's got rid of that horrible rocket at last. It kept breaking down. But he's annoyed about it and grumpy. However, when I find the right study course, I will sign up and Hari will have to agree.' Ganesh's gaze became distant and dreamy. 'With any luck,' he said, 'I can spin it out indefinitely.'

'Right,' I said. 'Why did the rocket keep breaking down?'

'How should I know?' he said.

'You'd never make an actor, Ganesh,' I told him. 'Your voice changes when you're being economical with the truth.'

'That,' said Ganesh loftily, 'is because I am an honest man.'

'An honest man with a guilty conscience.'

He stopped and turned to me. 'You talk to me about conscience? You've got a nerve.'

'Why? What have I done?' I demanded.

'What haven't you done? One of these days,' said Ganesh, 'I'll write it all down and make a book out of all the things you've dragged me into, and it'll turn out to be in three volumes like those Victorian novels.'

'OK, Watson,' I said.

A Restless Evil

Ann Granger

It sends a shiver down Detective Superintendent Alan Markby's spine when he hears that a rambler has stumbled on human bones in Stovey Woods in the heart of the Cotswolds. Twenty-two years ago, he had a rare failure in the hunt for a brutal serial rapist preying on local women. After the fifth rape, the attacker went to ground, never to be heard of again. Now, with a new investigation prompted by the grisly remains, the trail could be warm once more. But almost at once Markby is confronted with another body and a thoroughly up-to-date murder. Could the two be connected? It seems that some of the village residents would be just as happy to let sleeping dogs lie and secrets – both old and new – stay hidden . . .

The critics love Ann Granger's mystery novels:

'Characterisation, as ever with Granger, is sharp and astringent' *The Times*

'You'll soon be addicted' *Woman & Home*

'Ann Granger has brought the traditional English village crime story up to date, in setting, sophistication and every other aspect of fiction writing . . . sheer, unadulterated bliss' *Birmingham Post*

'A good feel for understated humour, a nice ear for dialogue' *The Times*

0 7472 6804 5

headline

Now you can buy any of these other bestselling
books by **Ann Granger** from your bookshop
or *direct from her publisher*.

FREE P&P AND UK DELIVERY
(Overseas and Ireland £3.50 per book)

Mitchell and Markby crime novels

That Way Murder Lies	£6.99
A Restless Evil	£6.99
Shades of Murder	£6.99
Beneath these Stones	£6.99
Call the Dead Again	£6.99
A Word After Dying	£6.99
A Touch of Mortality	£6.99
Candle for a Corpse	£6.99
Flowers for his Funeral	£6.99

Fran Varady crime novels

Watching Out	£6.99
Risking it All	£5.99
Running Scared	£6.99
Keeping Bad Company	£6.99
Asking for Trouble	£6.99

TO ORDER SIMPLY CALL THIS NUMBER

01235 400 414

or visit our website: www.madaboutbooks.com

Prices and availability subject to change without notice.